HELL HATH NO FURY

When Rosemarie Hirte, a respectable spinster and
insurance broker known for her moderation and
cool, falls unexpectedly for the handsome Rainer
Engstern, she knows that, at fifty-two, this could
be her last chance for happiness . . .

Where once there was order, chaos now reigns,
and Rosemarie finds herself in the grip of an obsession that shakes her ordered world to its foundations: soon she is phoning Engstern just to hear
his voice, finding excuses to walk by his house,
spying on him from his garden. But Rosemarie
doesn't like what she sees, for she is not the only
woman who wants this charismatic man, and how
can she possibly compete with a woman half her
age, not to mention an unpredictable wife?

Terrified that the outside world will undermine
the relationship, Rosemarie spins an intricate and
deadly web into which she lures and then destroys
all those who come too close to the object of her
dangerous love. It seems she will stop at nothing
to make Engstern hers, but how long can she con-
tinue before she comes face to face with her own
downfall . . . ?

Hell Hath No Fury is a gripping tale of *amour fou*,
deadly passions and murder from an author who
has been hailed as the next Patricia Highsmith.

HELL HATH NO FURY

Ingrid Noll

Translated from the German by
IAN MITCHELL

HarperCollins*Publishers*

Collins Crime
An imprint of HarperCollins*Publishers*
77–85 Fulham Palace Road, London W6 8JB

First published in Great Britain
in 1996 by Collins Crime

1 3 5 7 9 10 8 6 4 2

First published in Germany with the title
Der Hahn Ist Tot
by Diogenes Verlag AG Zürich in 1991

© Ingrid Noll 1991

The Author asserts the moral right to be
identified as the author of this work

A catalogue record for this book is
available from the British Library

ISBN 0 00 232574 8

Set in Meridien and Bodoni

Photoset by Rowland Phototypesetting Ltd
Bury St Edmunds, Suffolk

Printed in Great Britain by
Caledonian International Book Manufacturing Ltd, Glasgow

Indian Summer

September gold,
The wine is new.
My heart so cold,
To stone it grew –
That heart of gold.

October red,
Hunting the hare,
Love now is dead,
Lips in despair –
All crimson fled.

November grey,
The dead asleep.
My hair now grey,
With blue I keep
Harsh time at bay.

1

Among my teachers in school, there were two spinster ladies who claimed their fiancés had been killed in the war. Whenever a woman is, like me, not married, nor widowed or divorced, has no partner or boyfriend – far less any children – and cannot even come up with any short-term relationships, then she is still tagged with some disparaging label, just as she was in those days. But an old maid like my teachers I am not. And then there are also some people who look upon my status positively: married colleagues often regard my independence, my trips abroad, my professional career with envy and credit me with all sorts of romantic holiday escapades, to which I respond only with a meaningful smile.

I'm making good money, and I take good care of myself. At fifty-two, I look better than I did in my youth. My God, when I look at photographs of myself in those days! A good twenty pounds overweight, unflattering spectacles, those clodhopping lace-up shoes and that embroidery-trimmed dress. I was one of those 'good sports', the type of women that end up looking more and more like their own horses. Why did no one ever tell me there were other ways! Make-up was something I always scorned, yet without ever managing to achieve the 'natural' look. I was a mass of complexes. Today, I am slim and sophisticated, my clothes, my perfume and, above all, my shoes are expensive. And what good has it done me?

In my embroidery-trimmed days I was studying law. Why that, of all things? Perhaps because I had no particular talent for foreign languages, or, to be honest, for anything else either. I thought, rather naively, I would find a niche in that neutral field of study. For many years I went around with Hartmut. We met in the very first semester. Flaming passion it was not; we would study together until well into the night, and finally it would be too late to go home. So a steady relationship developed, and I suppose I was convinced that, in the end, it would all boil down to marriage, with two children and a joint legal practice. Shortly before the finals, when my mind was full of nothing but article this and subsection that, Hartmut informed me, in writing, that he was shortly to be married. That brought me down with a bump – in the exams, too. Hartmut passed and, shortly after, he became a father. I would occasionally see him walking in our park, with wife and pram.

I was in a bad way at that time. I put on weight dramatically, then lost it again, and refused to resit the examinations at any price. It was then that my mother passed away; my father had long since been dead. I have no brothers or sisters; I was very lonely.

During vacations I had often worked for a legal insurance firm. They offered me a post in a specialized department; it was nothing exciting and it was poorly paid. Nevertheless, I accepted, since after all I had to stand on my own two feet, even though I did have a modest inheritance from my mother. That's the way things were for me twenty-seven years ago.

I stayed in Berlin for another eight years. I made some headway in my career in insurance; I was extremely busy, I had the ambition of a 'nearly'-academic and, besides, I had hardly any other distractions. At least professional success made me feel good, and so I began to come out of myself outwardly, too: I became more self-assured, took good care of my figure, went regularly to the hairdresser's and the beautician's and bought myself expensive and very English-style clothes. In my last years in Berlin, I caught the eye of one of the bosses and got a promotion.

After a gap of five years, I had my second romantic affair. Maybe I was even a little bit in love, but the main thing for me was being appreciated. This man found me intelligent, chic, nice – even pretty – and I really blossomed out. The fact that he was married didn't matter at all to me. When, after a couple of years, everyone down to the most junior office-boy knew of our affair, his wife became the last to hear about it. The whole thing was more or less on the wane already when the terror campaign cut loose. I would be startled in the middle of the night by the phone ringing, anonymous threatening letters would be lying in my letterbox, there would be wads of chewing gum stuck to my car, and once she had even squeezed a tube of all-purpose adhesive into the car locks. It was obvious only she could have done all this. But since he never stayed the night with me, I couldn't understand how she could be phoning me from home at four in the morning without his finding out. I discovered only later that he already had a new lady-friend, and greatly enjoyed spending the night at her place. When his wife found herself alone in bed yet again, she wanted to be able to disturb him at least with a ringing phone. Of course, she assumed he was with me.

After that, I fired off numerous applications simultaneously to insurance companies in all sorts of towns and cities, but it took a whole year before I clicked. I didn't give a hoot where I landed, I just wanted to get away and to make a fresh start.

When I was in my mid-thirties, I moved to Mannheim. I knew neither the city nor a single soul in it. Six months later, however, it struck me that my old schoolfriend Beate must be living somewhere in the area, in a small town on the Bergstrasse, north of Heidelberg. When I had moved to Berlin after our final school exams, we had lost touch with each other, and in all that time I had seen her only once, at a class reunion.

In our young days in Kassel, Beate had lived at the end of my street. Whether we would otherwise have become friends, I can't tell. On my way to school, I had to pass her house. I would stop and whistle. I was always most punctual, very unlike Beate. Sometimes I almost got the impression it was my whistle that wakened her. I always had a long wait before she finally emerged from her front door, and often I was late for school just because of her. But I never went alone, almost

9

compulsively I waited outside her house. Beate had a best friend and a second best, then came several 'good' friends, and I was one of them. I, on the other hand, probably had only two or three of the latter sort, and absolutely no bosom friends at all.

Beate had married an architect, but that was about all I knew of what had become of her. When I phoned her, she immediately invited me to a party she was having in a few days. So I went along and was met with a picture of domestic bliss: three sweet children, a good-looking, charming husband, a wonderful house, a radiant Beate, who had cooked a superb meal for her many pleasant guests. Everything was straight from a picture book. Deep down I was consumed with hostility towards so much sunshine. I drove home in a foul mood, burning with envy. Despite all that, though, I reciprocated Beate's invitation, and if she was shopping in Mannheim, she would occasionally drop in after the shops closed. Not very often, though.

This fairly casual relationship changed abruptly when, ten years later, Beate's ideal world fell apart. The sweet children became difficult and rebellious, failed exams and had to repeat a year, smoked hash, shoplifted, stayed out all night. The charming husband had an affair with a much younger colleague. Just as in the case of my Hartmut drama all those years ago, this woman ended up pregnant, he got a divorce and set up a new family. Beate went into a depression and for weeks on end she tearfully bent my ear both on the phone and at first hand. Somehow she felt I would understand, and suddenly I had the comforting feeling of being able to give help and consolation. It was only from that time on that we became really close friends.

In any case Beate's cry-baby phase didn't last too long; that just wasn't in her nature. Nor did she remain embittered and withdrawn, but fought back and worked hard. Of course, she had to move out of the house when the children moved away to study. It was sold. From her ex-husband, Beate got a three-bedroom flat as well as an appropriate maintenance settlement. But she wanted to earn money by her own efforts and at forty-four started, for the first time in her life, working for a salary. Of course, she had not been altogether idle during those preceding years, for it had taken a deal of hard work and organizational ability to cope with running the large house, doing the books and looking after an overworked husband; in the last of those tasks, she had not, of course, succeeded. Now Beate worked half-days as a secretary in the adult education centre, on a temporary basis at first. Two years later, she packed it all in and devoted herself completely to her new vocation: Beate threw herself into one new course after another – she could attend them free. She began with pottery and silk-screen printing, then moved on to belly-dancing and transcendental meditation, learned Italian and joined other women in discussions about their position in society.

Apart from Beate, I hardly ever had any visitors. Anyway, my flat was too small to accommodate a lot of people. Beate sometimes called unannounced, to which I had no objection. A second exception was an older colleague, Frau Römer. She was on the verge of retirement and had been working in our firm since the year dot. Frau Römer knew everything and everybody and enjoyed all sorts of privileges: she had a comfortable office to herself, which her work did not actually justify, and more than that, she was allowed to bring her old dog to work with her. When, years before, her daugther married and moved away, Frau Römer, for the first and only time in her life, nearly threw a fit, because the dog, which the daughter had looked after up until then, could not be left on its own all day. She kicked up a fuss, claiming that she would have to do away with the dog since she didn't have a car and lived too far away to be able to walk home at lunch-time and take the dog out. In the end, she was in such a state that all the people at work took it in turns to complain to the boss and pester the life out of him about Frau Römer's dog. She was allowed to bring him in with her for a trial period; he was old and fat and lazy, and just lay under her desk and never made a sound. The boss, however, had urgently

11

impressed upon everyone that this was, and had to remain, a one-off case.

Frau Römer had another peculiarity: an illegitimate daughter. Among her generation, one lapse with such consequences was a catastrophe, and she had once told me that she had been disowned outright by her father as a result. Only after his death had her mother dared to re-establish contact with her. As for the father of her daughter, Frau Römer never mentioned him; at office parties, when the mood had relaxed, if anyone asked about him, she would just say that it was a long story, but not one she wanted to go into. Nor did she ever say anything to me about it, although as time passed we grew fairly close, almost to the point of becoming firm friends. This came about because one day she had another problem with her dog. I suggested quite spontaneously that she could leave her old darling with me now and again. To tell the truth, I am no animal lover – in fact, I'm afraid of dogs – but after all I knew this old boy well enough from the office, and I reckoned I could manage to survive a weekend with him. Frau Römer was overjoyed. So it was that, every four weeks, she went off without her dog, and I had the fat spaniel under my bed. As time went on, we even developed an amicable relationship, and I sometimes caught myself coming out with a nauseating kind of baby-talk to him.

Somehow I admired Frau Römer for having had her illegitimate child all those years ago. In my youth, before the era of the pill, I had always lived in fear of a possible pregnancy, but nowadays, when I'm past having children, I regret that. Yes, I'm almost sorry not to have at least gone through an abortion or a miscarriage like so many women, because even such a negative experience would have let me know what it was like to be pregnant for a few weeks, if nothing else. As a woman, that's completely missing in my life. And my affairs with men were not exactly satisfactory. The Hartmut episode had left a festering wound. The business with my boss in Berlin, too, had not been what you would call an edifying experience, in fact it was almost humiliating even to think back on it. Later on, I never had anything to do with colleagues, because I didn't want to expose myself to all that gossip and scandal. In the company, I am seen as very respectable, I am highly regarded, even trusted. On holiday, when I was younger, I would often strike up a friendship with a man, but the last fling of that sort was a good five years ago, and it left a bad taste anyway. Now I was probably too old for romance and just had to close that account showing a loss.

So, Frau Römer and Beate were my only visitors. My flat is small, tidy and, perhaps, a little impersonal. I'm not a creative person. Music, the theatre, painting and so on leave me completely cold, I'm afraid. Of course, I like reading, but I prefer non-fiction, a financial newspaper or a good whodunnit rather than so-called literature. At times, Beate wanted to take a hand in my life, finding my clothes, my furniture, my taste altogether much too dull. For all that, questions of taste play an extremely important part in my life, it's just that I am incapable of applying my highly individual concepts to myself.

At Beate's, of course, everything looks very different from my place – rather chaotic, in fact. All those bunches of dried flowers, those pop-style posters, the hand-crafted junk, they would drive me mad. For my part, I find Beate dresses far too young. I consider it more dignified to accept my age. But we are good friends nevertheless, I in my grey tweed skirt and ivory silk blouse, string of pearls and twin-set – the Grace Kelly Look, says Beate – and she with her crazy riding breeches and colourful waistcoats. My furniture: black and white, austere in the Japanese style and timeless, top quality; hers: always something different, the IKEA kind of stuff – all natural wood – then painted by herself in gold and purple. Beate also tries other ploys to convert me to her 'way of life'. She is quite happy to have me in tow, invites me to her parties, repeatedly attempts to recruit me in her beloved adult education courses. I promised her I would come along to the odd individual lecture.

In the end, after a long interval, we decided to go to a talk on the poetry of the wars of liberation against Napoleon. It started at 8 p.m., and I was at Beate's punctually at seven-thirty. From the stairs, I could hear the out-of-tune piano that one of her children had left behind. Beate opened the door. 'Heidi, Heidi, the Hills are your World,' resounded insistently. The youngest daughter, twenty years old, but, to my mind, thoroughly infantile, was home on summer vacation. Beate had a peculiar expression on her face. 'Guess what – I'm going to be a grandmother!'

I stepped in and saw the singing Leonore at the piano. I shot an inquiring glance at Beate. She nodded. 'Yes, Lessi's pregnant!'

Horrified, I couldn't help letting it slip: 'But surely it's still not too late to do something about it!'

Lessi spun round and, in unison with her mother, said, '*What* did you say?'

The two of them had absolutely no intention of terminating the pregnancy, in fact they seemed delighted. For all that, Lessi's life was still a mess: no regular boyfriend, in the early stages of her training as a PE teacher, and still dripping wet behind the ears. I was irritated by the irresponsibility of it all, yet my indignation was tinged with a certain envy of these two little innocents.

'Don't be cross,' said Beate, 'but I only heard the news ten minutes ago, and I can't possibly go out now. Be a darling and go on your own, and then you can tell me all about it tomorrow.'

I got out of there fast, and I would as soon have driven straight back home. The fact was, I was only going to that literary waffle for Beate's sake anyway. If I had gone straight home, the fate of a few people would have taken a different course.

But I went along, even though my heart was not altogether in it. Now that I had planned the evening along these lines, it made no real odds one way or the other. The little room was well filled. When the speaker entered, there was an immediate burst of applause. He was a good-looking man, with a mop of grey-brown hair and deep blue eyes. Casually dressed, but carefully casual. Medium height, almost delicate. A handsome man; I forgot Beate and Lessi. When he began to speak, I forgot about everything around me and I can't even remember now what he said about the poets Ernst Moritz Arndt, Theodor Körner and Friedrich Rückert. His voice rang in my ears till I felt dizzy, my heart was hammering and I had butterflies in my stomach. It wasn't the celebrated love-at-first-sight, but at-first-sound. It was his warm voice that worked such an erotic magic on me that I floated right off into dreams and, an hour and a half later, drove home in a half-daze.

That's how suddenly I was smitten – me, an old biddy who had been convinced she was totally immune to handsome men and thrilling voices. 'There's no fool . . .'

The next day, I phoned Beate at lunch-time. But she wanted to talk of nothing but her pregnant daughter and I had to listen to that for a while, whether I liked it or not. Eventually, she did ask about the previous evening's lecture, and at last I managed to quiz her as to what she knew about the speaker.

'Oh, well, I know all the lecturers hereabouts, some better than others. But he's not local, he lectures here only about once a term. I really don't know anything about him at all.'

Naturally, I'm not one to rub my confused emotions right under the nose of even my best friend. I'd hate nothing more than to make a fool of myself. I chose my words really carefully in an attempt to squeeze a little more out of Beate.

'I could ask around,' she offered at last. 'Somebody's bound to know him. He's supposed to have written a book as well.'

The next day was Saturday. I went into a bookshop in Mannheim, not my regular one, and asked about the author Rainer Engstern. The assistant riffled through her bulky catalogue. At last she revealed that, yes, there was a writer called Rainer Witold Engstern, who had produced a short monograph on painting in the fourteenth century, and did I want to order the little volume. Of course I did and yes, I would be able to pick it up on the following Tuesday.

In the meantime, it seemed to me as if I were rejuvenated, if not downright adolescent. Only at that age had I been prone to going off into such fantasies and having such unrealistic desires. What on earth was happening to me?

I spent the entire weekend pottering about, smiling, humming to myself and standing in front of the mirror. Maybe I really did do myself up rather too old? I decided to buy something stunning, something along the lines of a frothy summer dress with a full skirt that had a swing to it. Actually, I had always stuck to straight skirts, severe suits and trouser suits, maybe I should go for something romantically frivolous? Should I ditch this hairdo, this urchin cut I had had for thirty years now? But what for? I didn't even know this man yet, far less did he know me. He was sure to be married, to have children, and to move in altogether different circles from mine. But this feeling of madness, of being in love, did have something to be said for it, for I had always been firmly convinced I was past experiencing it.

I went to collect the book I had ordered. A man of many talents, I thought: his talk had been on Romantic literature, but now, in this book, it was all about the real world in fourteenth-century painting. Was this versatility – or a tendency to dilettantism? On the back flap there was a brief biography of the author, with a photo. What a wonderful man, I kept thinking. He was three years younger than I, married, a teacher, lived in the Heidelberg area. He had studied German language and literature, art history and French.

I read the monograph twice through. The publisher wasn't one I knew, the print-run small. I found the text clever, without being academic, as far as I was able to judge. As I said already, I'm not very interested in art, but these illustrations of slippers, candlesticks, fabrics and buildings would really appeal to anyone, while the explanations of the cultural background made interesting reading. Undoubtedly he must be an excellent teacher!

Frau Römer brought me down to earth with a thump. She had been for a precautionary check-up and had to go into hospital the following week – suspected breast cancer. She was composed and put on a brave face. There was pleading in her eyes, and I knew it was to do with her dog. Of course, it would have been very selfish of me not to have offered right away to look after her beloved pet while she was in

16

hospital. I went so far as to lie and insist that I was looking forward to having him, since he would keep me company through the lonely hours. With hindsight, I can see now that things might have turned out differently if I hadn't been minding Frau Römer's spaniel.

Usually when I come home from the office, I really have no motivation for leaving the house again. I have a bath, put on a housecoat, maybe do some washing or ironing, make myself a sandwich and stretch out in front of the television. Not very exciting, but I'm sure most people do the same. The dog was none too pleased, though. Fair enough, he too wanted to get home to be fed and watered – he had spent the whole day in the office as well – but then he no doubt felt that, by customary right, he should be taken for a walk. Whenever he was with me over the weekend, I would take him into the park regularly around midday; in the evenings, I couldn't be bothered. Now, I had a crazy idea. I thumbed through the telephone directory. Where did my Rainer Witold Engstern live? Or should I just call him Witold? My first flick through produced nothing, but at last I struck oil. R. Engstern, Ladenburg – got him! Good grief, with no rush-hour traffic, I could drive there in fifteen minutes. I even dug out a street-plan of Ladenburg and found his street too, a little way outside the old town. The dog was giving me questioning looks. I felt young, thirsting for adventure. I still had a jogging outfit from my last stay at the spa in Bad Sassbach, although I never wore it now. So, on with that, dog on its lead, back down the stairs, into the car and off we go!

With heart thumping, I saw the twin spires of the St Gallus Church in Ladenburg rising up ahead. I turned off into Weinheimer Strasse and then parked in Trajan-Strasse; this wasn't too close to his house, but a good three blocks further on. I got out, let the spaniel snuffle around at the kerb and set off walking my dog, all very casual. The area where Witold lived was certainly very nice, country-style houses, medium-sized and fortunately not so tartily renovated as in the old town. In the street itself, there were some newer houses and almost at the end was number 29, with wild vines growing

17

up the walls. Obviously I couldn't just stop and inspect the premises. It was still daylight; I crossed to the other side of the street where I had a good clear view of the detached house. No lights on, it looked quite deserted, but there was a car at the door. My foolish heart was still hammering, as if I was about to accomplish some daredevil feat. I went the short distance back along to the end of the street and turned around again. On the opposite side – his side! – I started my way back and had another look at the house from a different angle. Foxglove and hollyhocks in the front garden, at the back a rather overgrown orchard. The neighbouring plot had not been built on. I let the dog off the leash and allowed him to root around this patch of stinging-nettles and golden rod for a bit. That gave me the chance to stand still for a while.

Soon, though, the dog had had enough of this dawdling, so we went on our way.

I was still pretty worked-up. We had to cross the next street but one. Because this was such a quiet area, bathed in end-of-the-day tranquillity, I wasn't really paying attention. A bicycle bell startled me out of my daydreaming.

I caught my breath. Witold! I had almost walked into his bike. He braked, looked at me and smiled. I smiled back, totally bemused and with that roaring in my ears again. He probably said something like, 'Watch out!' and then he was gone again. He had looked at me! Smiled at me! I was as blissfully happy as a little child. I drove home singing, hugged the dog, kissed him, took myself off to bed and didn't sleep a wink. All night long Witold was there looking at me, sitting on his bike, casual in his jeans and red sweater, smiling.

The next evening, I did the same trip at the same time, but in more flattering clothes. The upstairs windows in the house were open now and I could faintly hear a radio. All right, I could be patient; I could try again each day to catch a glance and a smile. Maybe the dog would stray into his garden, and I would have to retrieve him, Witold would be standing there with his secateurs, by a fragrant rosebush, he would look into my eyes, smile, maybe even pass the time of day. New, happy possibilities kept flooding into my mind.

Another day later. I had promised Frau Römer I would visit her in hospital. By this time I had heard that they had removed her right breast, which distressed me deeply. I packed up punctually at the office. By now I was working in Frau Römer's room because the dog was accustomed to his place under the desk there, by permission of the boss. When he had moved in, years before, always keeping as quiet as a mouse, the boss had come in one day to ask affably how the animal was getting on. In those days, the dog answered to Mickey, or something similarly banal. When he caught sight of the boss standing in front of the desk, he started howling in a velvety tone.

'Well now,' said the boss in surprise, 'you've got a very refined baritone voice, haven't you? Are you the animal world's answer to Fischer-Dieskau?' From then on, Mickey was known only as Dieskau.

I drove with Dieskau straight from the office to the hospital, stopping to buy flowers on the way. I left the dog in the car and went up the polished hospital stairs to Frau Römer. There she lay, with a draining-tube sticking out from under her nightdress, but otherwise looking pretty well her normal self. Things weren't too bad, she reckoned.

'You know, I'm over sixty already, and at that age how you are isn't so much a matter of the physical side any more. If this operation has really got rid of the cancer, I'll never so much as mention it again.'

Her first concern was with Dieskau, and she was delighted when I told her about our marvellous evening outings, without, of course, mentioning where we went.

That day, everything ran later than usual. I didn't get home until seven, but I still had to have a bath and something to eat, and then I spent ages standing in front of my wardrobe. What should I wear this time? On no account the jogging suit, which was mousy-grey and boring. A suit? No, not that either, for that would make me look like a very prim office worker. Finally, I put on white slacks, a dark-blue sweater and flat shoes. The daylight was already fading, and this time I came across Witold in the street parallel to his, but without

19

his bike. He hurried past me without a glance in my direction, but with a preoccupied expression on his face; obviously he was heading back into the little town. The car was standing outside his house, the windows were closed, no light anywhere. I went back to my car with Dieskau. We had hardly settled down when I abruptly got out again and left the dog on his own. He never objected to this, having adopted the car as a second bed.

I went into the old town centre on foot. The streets were wet, it must have been raining recently. Just as well that I was wearing comfortable shoes, as the cobblestones were hardly ideal for high heels. Witold must be somewhere around here, maybe in a pub. Normally, I would never go into pubs on my own in the evenings, and only rarely with friends. I was very unsure of myself. It was easy to look around the first bar, the low, open windows afforded a clear view from outside, but I couldn't see him.

I entered a second one and glanced around. 'Come to take your old man off home, Mother?' a drunk inquired. I left at once and couldn't bring myself to set foot in the next one. Finally, I looked around for a better-class establishment, sat down in a corner and ordered a white wine and soda. Of course he wasn't here either. I paid and strolled across the marketplace, had a look at the fountain, with its statue of the Virgin Mary on a tall column. All around, the remains of an old town wall; outside a school – was it his one? – I read: *About 90 AD, Roman soldiers erected a stone fort in the vicinity of the Celtic settlement of Lopodunum.*

Maybe Witold had gone to the cinema? I had a look at what was showing and wondered whether to go in for the late screening. Then I looked at some more shop windows and just drifted around. In an old half-timbered building, a wedding reception was in full swing. A washing-line full of baby things hung in an arch above the doorway.

When darkness fell, I went back to Witold's house. A light was on in the ground floor now. There was no one to be seen in the street, the whole district seemed virtually deserted, but then, it was summer, and the holiday period at that. I slipped

20

across the neighbouring plot with its cherry and walnut trees, till I came to Witold's garden. It wasn't difficult to lift up the dilapidated wire fence and to slip underneath without any great gymnastic effort. All the same, the white slacks were hardly the right choice: for one thing, they got dirty, and for another, they might show up in the dark.

The leaves of the walnut trees stood out black against the dark sky. I reckoned I was well hidden behind a sturdy apple tree. My pulse was racing. I felt like a burglar, like someone else altogether, who had nothing whatsoever in common with the very prim and proper insurance clerkess.

The house opened broadside on to the garden at the back. The front, on the other hand, seemed rather closed off, probably the entrance hall, toilet and kitchen were on that side. A large glass sliding door afforded a view into a well-lit living-room. A desk had been set right next to the glass front, a figure was seated at it, probably Witold. I groped my way very carefully, very slowly, forward. Damp twigs brushed across my face, a snail's shell crunched under my feet. Fortunately, the fruit trees around me were thick and bushy, so the beam of light did not reach me. Now I could clearly make out the object of my desire. He was working at the desk. School exercise books? No, it was the school holidays after all. Maybe a new book, a lecture for the adult education centre, a letter. Every now and then he would pause and gaze out into the darkened garden – straight into my face, or so it seemed to me. But he certainly couldn't see me.

I was unable to tear myself away from this picture. I'm a female Peeping Tom! flashed through my mind. Witold was dressed in corduroy trousers, cheap black Hong Kong-made espadrilles, trodden down at the heels, a green knitted cardigan with a button missing and holes at the elbows. I cannot abide such sloppiness myself. Missing buttons are sewn on at once, torn sweaters go straight into the Red Cross bag. His wife was obviously not so fussy. Come to that, where on earth was she? The whole living-room was in a state of some disorder, with a woollen rug lying where it had slipped off the sofa, a dried-up azalea on the windowsill, overflowing

21

ashtrays, piles of newspapers. Either the lady of the house was a slovenly bitch or she was away or ill, or maybe her own job was just too much for her. I hoped she was nowhere around.

Witold wrote and wrote. From time to time he took off his half-moon glasses, smoked the occasional cigarette, rose and paced up and down. Once, the telephone rang. He talked, his face agitated, angry even, then he suddenly crashed the receiver down on its rest and at once lit another cigarette. After that, he didn't resume his writing but prowled around the room like a caged tiger. Then he phoned someone, talked for a long time, was silent, then spoke at length again and stopped abruptly. When he left the room, I crept out of the labyrinth of trees, nearly tripping over a fallen branch as I did so. There was a storm coming up. I finally set off for home; it was late, and I was thoroughly confused.

I lost weight during those days, although it was a long time since I had actually needed to, I slept badly, had dark rings and, so it seemed to me anyway, a lot more lines under my eyes. I was tortured by hot flushes, something I had been spared up till then. In the office, I sat unable to concentrate on my work, stopped putting in overtime and had difficulty setting my thoughts down on paper. This did not escape the boss's notice. He was kind enough to put it down to my probably having been deeply affected by Frau Römer's illness.

'You're an excellent psychologist,' I said as affably as I could manage, and he smiled, taking it as a compliment.

At the weekend, I went shopping with Beate. She was supposed to advise me. It all got a bit fraught, though. It ended up with her having bought two shimmering blouses from C & A, a baby-jacket for the impending grandchild, a trouser suit in the sales and weird pointed shoes with curled-up toes. I had acquired an expensive summer dress in a violet floral pattern, which I kept on. That was the one item on which we had been able to reach agreement.

Out in the street, we met two men – well, Beate knew absolutely everybody. Apparently her husband had once built a house for them. One of them was a graphic artist, the other a buyer for a department store. We went for a coffee, and Beate flirted brazenly with both of them. My overall impression was that she was not exactly living a cloistered existence since her divorce, but she never talked to me about it, no doubt out of a sense of tact. In my beautiful dress, my cheeks flushed by the coffee and with the unfamiliar, tensed-up feeling in my gut, I suddenly discovered myself drawing some attention too, with my knowing smiles, cooing laughter and the constant fluttering of my eyelashes. Good grief, why hadn't I cottoned on to this thirty years sooner!

When the men had gone, Beate said, 'They're a fantastically nice pair. They've been living together for years. You can always have a super chat with them. By the way, I heard something about that Rainer Engstern recently.'

I felt like yelling, 'Why didn't you tell me right away!' And then the sudden fear: was he maybe gay, since Beate had mentioned him in this context? I would never have been able to slot these smooth-talking men into the right category, I had no experience in that direction.

'Well, wait till I tell you,' Beate began. 'Lessi has a friend, Eva, and she's friendly with one of Engstern's sons.'

'And what's he like?' I asked at once.

'Dunno, probably a nice lad. He's in the middle of his community service.'

'No, no, I'm talking about the father!'

'Yes, well, he's a schoolteacher in Ladenburg.' (That much I've managed to find out for myself, I thought.) 'The pupils call him "Engstirn", Old Narrow-Mind, but he's quite popular, so Lessi says. She used to go to that school, you see.'

'And the mother?'

'Ah, yes' – Beate became quite conspiratorial – 'there's something not quite right there. She's supposed to have been away for quite some time now.'

I didn't dare ask anything else, but inside, I was jumping with joy. There's something not quite right! Absolutely perfect. So my Witold was perhaps there for the taking.

Back home, I was once again gnawed by doubt. Supposing

he really was available, always assuming, of course, we actually got to know each other in the first place. I was spending more time in front of the mirror now than I had done in all of the last twenty years. I examined myself critically. Maybe I should have my face lifted, even though I've always despised that sort of thing? He was forty-nine and incredibly good-looking – men of that age, so people keep saying, don't necessarily prefer women of my age.

In the evenings, I now had a fixed routine: in the twilight, I would set out with Dieskau to try to meet my dream-man. In the darkness, I would creep around in his garden – without the dog, of course, and only in dark slacks; like a burglar, I had adopted a kind of working outfit. In addition, I would occasionally dial his number, not, I might add, from my own phone (there had been so much talk of phone-tapping, I was too scared), but from a phone-box. I would hear him give his name, sometimes brightly, sometimes sounding weary, and then hang up again at once, knowing that he was at home, maybe sitting at his desk. A second time, I almost collided with his bicycle, this time quite intentionally. He smiled again, just like the first time, and said, in his breath-stopping voice, 'Good evening. Still lost in thought, eh?'

I returned the smile, but was unable to come back with anything clever or quick-witted.

After two weeks in hospital, Frau Römer was discharged, and I brought her Dieskau back to her. I was half pleased, half sad, not to have a companion any more. But what was to stop me going out in the evenings for a walk even without a dog? And Frau Römer had something else bothering her: she was to go off to recuperate at a spa soon, and so the problem with the dog arose again. Her sister was allergic to animal hairs, her daughter was in the States for a year. Well, of course I immediately assured her I would be only too happy to look after the dog for a further four weeks.

That first evening without Dieskau, I didn't go out again. In any case, there was a whole lot of unfinished business that I had neglected during the last two weeks. My little flat was looking quite scruffy, my laundry basket was filled to over-flowing and I urgently needed to do something with my hair and to let a facial mask do its soothing work. But I felt like some addict who has to exert every last bit of willpower to keep herself from succumbing to her craving. For an old boiler, I was well fired up.

The next day, though, I drove off again, minus canine company. Dusk was setting in as I passed Witold's house. A second car stood outside. Visitors! I was petrified by the thought that Beate's daughter, Lessi, who after all had been here already with her girlfriend, could by some mischance be around and might see me. But that would have been a very big coincidence; in any case, the car didn't look the kind that young people would drive, much too sober. I walked around Laden-burg until it had got completely dark. I knew my way about pretty well by this time. Under cover of darkness, I started my second round. As on the previous occasion, I crept around in the orchard, getting dirt in my eyes and taking the loud thumping of my heart to be a sign of rejuvenation. Yes, there was indeed a visitor there. Obviously not the son, but a woman. The big glass door was open, and I could make out scraps of conversation. Could that be his wife? Bent double, in fact almost on all fours, I crept a little bit nearer. The stranger must have been in her early forties, but she looked a mess. She was skinny, with black hair and a face that was interesting but by no means beautiful. Over a melon-green blouse she wore an ostentatious piece of oriental jewellery. She smoked incessantly, and Witold, too, seemed to have lit up a fair few cigarettes himself. I can't stand that fug. If I had been his wife, he would have packed in that habit long ago. An empty wine bottle was rolling about on the floor, and at one point the woman gave it a hefty kick; another opened bottle stood on the table, with two half-full glasses beside it.

Witold wasn't saying much, and then always very quietly, with the result that I couldn't make him out at all. But the woman was shouting in a high-pitched, almost hysterically shrill voice. All of a sudden I realized what was wrong with her. Obviously, she was an alcoholic. Not that she was exactly drunk, but all through my youth I had witnessed at first hand the decline of an aunt who was hooked on drink, and now it was as if she had risen again from the dead.

So in fact this probably was his wife. As far as I could make out, she was hurling bitter recriminations at him, blaming him for the breakdown of their relationship. At one point I could also hear Witold clearly.

'Hilke, this was your last chance, you should never have broken off! Now it's starting all over again!'

Aha! Hilke had been unable to go through with a drying-out course, she had absconded. And in the hall behind could be seen two travelling bags, still not unpacked. I felt very sorry for Witold. The poor dear soul didn't deserve such a wife. She had let the house go to the dogs, hadn't looked after her husband and children! The reasons for Witold's unhappiness were dawning on me.

Although it was high summer, I was shivering under the damp apple trees. I crept another metre closer. An apple fell to the ground, snapping twigs as it dropped. For a second or two, Witold and Hilke seemed to listen to the noise, but then they went back to their talking, smoking, drinking. Up till then, I had witnessed scenes like this only in films. The two of them let it all pour out, accusing each other, tearing each other to pieces, hating each other from the depths of their being. She called him 'Rainer'; fine, but for me, he was 'Witold'.

For a long time now I had been eavesdropping, trying not to let my clattering heart make so much noise that the pair in the living-room might hear it ticking like a bomb. Witold, as was his wont, sometimes went pacing right across the room and once he threw his lighted cigarette end through the open French window into the garden; it landed right next to me and I was almost afraid its glow might intensify and reveal my presence. The cigarette went out, and I decided it was time to go. Despite the great excitement, I was dead tired, and anyway it was very late.

Just as I was turning to go, Hilke let out a sudden yell: 'In that case, I'm going to do away with us both!' and drew a

26

revolver from her jacket pocket. In terror, I fell painfully on my right knee. For God's sake, had she gone mad? I wanted to rush forward and throw myself in front of Witold. But he had already taken two long strides towards her and now he simply took the thing from her grasp. She put up no resistance.

Well, I couldn't go home now. After maybe five minutes' silence, with the two of them just staring at each other in disgust, it all started up again. Witold was sitting on the sofa, the revolver in his hand. Where she had got it in the first place seemed to be of no further interest to him. The past was dredged up again, other men, other women, mother-in-law and sons, money, even this vine-clad house. Most of it meant nothing to me. But suddenly Hilke said, in an icy, cutting tone, 'If I hadn't slept with him, your shit would never have been published.'

Witold went white as a sheet.

He raised the revolver and fired at her. The detonation jerked me to my feet and I ran out into the glare of the light on the terrace. Hilke keeled over, blood seeping from her green blouse.

Witold was at her side at once, shouting to her, then he ran to the phone, stopped, picked up the phone book, thumbed through it before realizing he had no spectacles handy, cursed, looked back at his bleeding wife and then seemed to lose his head completely.

I stepped into the room. He didn't seem in the least surprised.

'Quick, call a doctor,' he said. Deathly white, he staggered into a chair. I lit a cigarette for him and pressed his glass into his hand.

'I'll take care of everything,' I said as levelly as I could manage. He stared at me vacantly, as if he were swimming under a thick glass bell, and didn't touch either his cigarette or his drink. In shock, I thought. Then I took a look at his wife. Her skin was pallid, no breathing to be heard. As if in close-up, I could now see her jewellery of coral, silver and mother-of-pearl, not against a background of green, but standing out against her darkly glistening, blood-soaked blouse.

'Your wife is dead,' I said. He let out a loud moan.

'The police,' he gasped, gesturing with his glass in the direction of the phone. I went over to the instrument. No, you can't do that, the thought flashed through my mind, he'll be convicted, now, just when we're really getting to know each other. He'll get years for this!

'You've got to make it look different,' I said. 'You'll get life for murder. It's got to look like manslaughter.'

He gaped at me helplessly again and suddenly threw up.

'Have you any spirits in the house?' I demanded, for I had read umpteen times that a crime committed in a drunken stupor can't be regarded as planned and premeditated. He felt his way towards the cabinet, groped for an opened bottle of whisky and held it out to me.

'Now listen carefully,' I said, trying to sound convincing. 'Drink this, the whole bottle. When you fall down and pass out, I'll wait ten minutes and then call the police. When they question you, you'll tell them you can't remember a thing.'

Witold wanted to argue; despite his state of shock, he seemed to think there was something about this plan that wasn't logical or wasn't quite right. Several times he said, 'But,' before at last putting the bottle to his lips. Somehow the idea of quick oblivion on the floor and being out of circulation for hours did strike him as being one of the best solutions after all. He drank and drank, retching from time to time, and I was really afraid he was going to bring the whole lot up again.

In five minutes, during which time we simply sat staring at each other, he had finished off the whisky. I laid my hand on his. 'It's going to be all right,' I said, maternally. All at once he grinned like some mentally retarded child and felt the urgent need to lay himself down on the carpet.

So, what now? Right, the police, I thought. Then, behind me, I heard a groan. The blood froze in my veins. I whirled round. Hilke was moving, whimpering – she was alive. That couldn't be, Witold had to be free of her for good. I picked up the revolver where it lay right in front of me on the coffee-table, went to the French window, aimed at her heart – and hit her in the head. She slumped in a heap. Witold let out a moan, but hadn't been able to grasp what was happening.

It was clear to me at once that I had made a mistake. Firing a second shot after the first had failed didn't look at all like unpremeditated manslaughter. So now it had to be made to look like self-defence; well, in any case, Hilke had been the first to threaten to shoot. I had to fire a shot in Witold's direction from where she had been sitting.

However, I was now verging on hysteria myself, and suddenly all I could sense was the panic urge to run away. But it had to be done. I went over to Hilke's chair and fired a shot at the carpet close to Witold's leg. Witold let out a yell, which became a moan, and then I noticed that his leg was bleeding. I must have hit him, or at least grazed him. I pushed up his trouser-leg, but thank God, it was a mere scratch, I didn't have to give it a second thought.

Had anyone heard the shots? Luckily, Witold's house stood some way apart from the others, next to it was the vacant lot, and the neighbours were away on holiday. But all of them? I had to get away as fast as I could. I left the house by the French window and crept back through the apple trees. Stop! I told myself suddenly. Fingerprints! What had I actually touched? I went back inside. Of course, the gun, the glass, Witold himself. I stuffed the revolver and the glass in my handbag, I just hadn't the strength to wipe them clean now. I left almost at a run. Had anybody seen me? At last I reached my car, got in and drove off, shaking all over. I had an uneasy feeling that I had done everything absolutely wrong. Then it occurred to me that I had to call the police. After all, I had promised Witold, hadn't I?

I stopped at a phone-box I had got to know well of late. Fortunately, the emergency number was clearly printed on the front of the directory, for at this moment I couldn't have remembered my own one. I heard myself saying, in a voice I barely recognized, 'I've just heard shots . . .' They stopped me at once, wanting my name and address first. I ignored this and simply yelled, 'Get there right away!' and gave Witold's address then hung up. I climbed hastily into my car and drove off home. Back at my own place I dissolved in a fit of tears that seemed to go on for ever.

My teeth were chattering. I was absolutely exhausted, and yet wide awake, my mind crystal clear. I couldn't imagine myself sitting in the office in a few hours, working away, and yet that was what I had to do, for I was never off ill and had to avoid attracting any kind of attention. I ran a hot bath and steeped myself in it to thaw out and cut down the chattering of my teeth. Hardly had I settled in the warm water when the horrible thought struck me that the police might not have understood the address properly and Witold might lose blood faster and faster and end up dying – his lifeblood seeping away because of me, without his having looked at me, smiled at me, ever again. I had to make sure, had to ring his number. But I still had this obsession about tapped lines. So, out into the street again, find a phone-box and call from there! But if anyone in the neighbourhood were to see me now, in the middle of the night, in a phone-box, that would be bound to arouse suspicion. Still, I couldn't just let Witold bleed to death!

With a struggle, I heaved myself out of the bath, half dried myself and picked up my neighbour's key. She was away on holiday, and I went in every day to water her plants. I went across the landing, let myself in, went to the phone and dialled Witold's number. 'Hello, who is that?' a strange man's voice asked. I hung up; everything was all right, Witold was being patched up and put to bed. With some degree of relief, I shut up my neighbour's flat and got back into the warm bath.

But then it suddenly occurred to me: what if someone had noticed a light going on next door, and her supposed to be away? That too would be sure to arouse suspicion! And if the phone is tapped, it'll certainly attract attention if a call is made from a woman's flat when in fact she is in Italy.

And then, oh my God Almighty! In my handbag there was a glass that didn't belong to me – not to mention the murder weapon. I could no longer relax in the bath. So, it was out again, dry off a second time and get into my dressing gown.

I wrapped the glass in a towel and banged it a couple of times on the kitchen table. I put the broken fragments into the wastebin, which I would empty in the morning. Should I get rid of the revolver the same way? That would really be very careless, though. I would have to find a cleverer means of disposing of it.

At long last, though, I thought things over and concluded that I was in no immediate danger. Nobody could connect me with this affair, nobody in Ladenburg knew me. Witold had no idea who I was; he had seen me, or might remember seeing me, only three times. On two of those occasions he had looked at me without the slightest interest, and the third time he was in shock. Anyway, he really would not be able to remember everything; he hadn't been properly aware of the two shots I fired.

So what were the police to think of the whole business? Had I made other mistakes, left something lying around? No, I don't smoke, so I couldn't leave cigarette ends lying as evidence at the scene of the crime, nor do I go about dropping monogrammed handkerchiefs. Then a thought burned into my brain: my footmarks in the damp garden, and finally even on the carpet. I had been wearing training shoes, the better to creep around in. Normally I never wear such a thing – they were, like the mousy-grey jogging suit, a relic of my time at the spa. They'll have to go! I thought. I picked them up at once and stuffed them into the half-full bag for the Red Cross. It would be collected next week. As for the revolver, I put it in a suitcase in the lumber-room and resolved to think up a better hiding place for it the next day.

2

What do you do when you haven't slept a wink and you look like something the cat dragged in, yet you still have to turn up bright and cheerful at the office? I washed my hair, put on my most flattering outfit, spent a great deal of time on my make-up till it was flawless. Fortunately, Frau Römer would be on sick-leave for a while yet, so for the time being, even though Dieskau wasn't there, I was able to go on using her room, where I was less exposed to the inquisitive stares of my colleagues. But it was still early on when the boss came in. 'Well now, just look at you today. It's obvious right away that you're really blossoming out now that Frau Römer is getting better. I'm sure Dieskau and the daily hospital visits must have been a great burden on you. But today you're looking the very picture of health!'

'You never miss a thing, do you?' I responded as jauntily as I could, for all that I could feel I was sweating from every pore. If I had spent the night with my teeth chattering, I was more than making up for it now with hot flushes.

'Nothing gets past my eagle eye here,' the boss assured me, 'but I'm sure you have a bit more time now and you can take care of this damages claim.' With almost paternal generosity, he laid a file on my desk. Then he left me on my own. On my way to the office, I had bought a copy of the *Rhein-Neckar-Zeitung*, but so far I hadn't had the chance to open the paper. Luckily there was still not a word in it about the events of the previous night.

When I walked into the canteen at lunch-time, two young typists stopped in mid-gossip, looked at me and went into suppressed giggles. They had been talking about me, that much was obvious. On the whole, I was on friendly terms with most of the staff in our company – as one colleague to another, but nothing too close. The trainees and younger secretarial staff were a little afraid of me, because I never let them get away with any sloppiness in their work. If something was not correct, they had to do it again. They might thank me for it in the end, for if you don't get into the habit of working in a disciplined way early enough, there are bound to be problems later on. You know what they say about teaching an old dog new tricks. No doubt there were some who thought me far too strict and ran me down behind my back.

I realized now, too, that they had been talking about my clothes. It certainly hadn't escaped the notice of these young things that I had recently been going for a more youthful look. Probably I would have to tone it down a little in future, because folk are so quick to jump to conclusions. I've never been one to indulge in scandal, and I've even cut younger colleagues off short whenever they started to tell me about 'who was doing what with whom'. All the same, I was always kept informed on important matters by the trusty Frau Römer; since she was a kindly, older person, I was happy to let her bring me up to date every now and then.

Had I been slipping in my martinet's role lately? Was love shining from my eyes and giving me away? Beate had recently come out with some saucy remark: she had a good nose for sniffing out feminine emotions.

Somehow I got through that day. On the way home, I got myself a mild sedative from the chemist's and then I went early to bed. But sleep was again impossible. I kept seeing gory pictures: Hilke's green blouse, gradually turning black, the wounded Witold. I had killed that woman! Witold was no murderer. There was the horrendous possibility – which had not occurred to me before – that she might not even have been killed by my shot.

The next day, several newspapers, including the Ladenburg local one which appeared only once a week, carried a report:

In circumstances that are still under investigation, the body of 43-year-old housewife Hilke E. was discovered by police shortly after one o'clock yesterday morning. Her husband lay unconscious on the floor, with a gunshot wound in his leg. So far, he is still unfit to be interviewed. Both the dead woman and the injured man had been drinking heavily. The murder weapon is still missing.

Footprints were discovered both in the garden and on the carpet, which point to the presence of a third person. The couple's elder son is at present on a holiday trip through Turkey and cannot be contacted; his younger brother is doing his community service in a Heidelberg hospital, where he was on night duty at the time in question. Police are looking for a man of unusually slim build, who takes size 41 in shoes, and who was seen outside in the street that evening.

In addition, the police are asking an unidentified woman caller to contact the Ladenburg investigating authorities without delay.

That evening, Beate rang me.

'Have you seen the *Mannheimer Morgen*?' she asked.

I knew at once what was coming and tried to sound as noncommittal as I could: 'Yes, why?'

Beate was always delighted to be able to let me in on some scandal. 'Did you read the bit about "Murder in Teacher's House"?'

'Could be,' I muttered. 'Didn't give it a second thought, really.'

'Just think,' Beate babbled on, 'that's that Rainer Engstern's house, the man you were recently asking me about. His wife has been shot, and he's been wounded. I was told she had a drink problem. Listen, maybe he killed her and then sort of shot himself in the leg, to divert suspicion.'

'D'you think so?' I asked.

'Well, actually, I found him rather sweet when I heard him

last year at my adult education centre. But you can never tell a murderer from outward appearances.'

I would have loved to defend Witold, but of course I wasn't that stupid.

'Wasn't there something about some other person as well?' I inquired.

'That's right,' replied Beate. 'Maybe it was just some boring old ordinary robbery after all, and the police haven't found out what's been stolen yet. Well, anyway, there was lots of talk about this Rainer Engstern today. He's supposed to have had some kind of an affair with a schoolgirl. But everyone reckons that's the kind of thing people are only too quick to say about a handsome man who's also a teacher.'

I felt it was all going well so far. They were looking for a slimly built man; for once, I was quite pleased I had such big feet. Witold was not officially under suspicion, not yet. His wife had indeed been suffering from alcohol addiction, I had been right in that. Obviously then, their marriage had been on the rocks. And if Witold did have a girlfriend, she would have been bound to turn up at some time or other during the period when I was keeping watch on the place. But he was always sitting alone at his desk, working away in complete solitude. So I could entertain some hopes, even though I had no real plans as to how things would go on from here. But just how was I to come face to face with him in the immediate future? I'd have to depend on chance to help me there.

First off, I needed information; I bought a local paper every day. One short piece about the murder case: the police were following up various lines of inquiry.

Was Witold in custody? I called several times from a phone-box in Mannheim. Mostly there was no reply, twice his son answered. 'Maximilian Engstern,' he said, in a tone of voice that was very like his father's.

Maybe Beate knew something. I decided to go and see her at the weekend. What I really needed was somebody like her who could prattle on incessantly, a talent that I lacked completely.

'Yes, do come,' said Beate. 'Lessi's here too. We're thinking of going to the cinema.'

On the one hand, I couldn't abide Lessi, that pregnant adolescent, but on the other, she was the only one who, perhaps through her friend, who was after all friendly with Witold's son Max, knew anything about what had become of him.

At first, all Lessi could talk about was her blissful condition, which still had a good eight months to run. Nor could I give a damn about the choice of name for the poor unfortunate embryo! Nevertheless, I made an effort to be nice to Lessi and take part in this bubble-brained conversation. My suggestions did not, however, even merit discussion; Lessi was set on some Arabic or Ancient Roman name.

It was Beate who suddenly brought up the Engstern family. 'If it's a boy, you could call him Witold!'

'Oh God! After such an awful business? You're kidding!' yelped Lessi in disgust. 'How on earth can you come up with such a repulsive idea, Mother!'

'Well, he isn't *really* the murderer,' reckoned Beate. 'Or is he? What's the latest word?'

Lessi recounted how she had spoken to her friend Eva on the telephone only yesterday, and Max Engstern was at the end of his tether. The funeral was tomorrow, since the body had had to be detained in the police mortuary for quite a long time. And they had at last managed to contact the brother in Turkey by putting out SOS calls on the radio. He was due home today.

'And what about their father?' I asked.

Lessi thought he had been kept in hospital for two days, where he was continually interrogated by the police, but he was back home now. He was not allowed to go away anywhere; besides, he was in a state of total depression.

And did the police know who had murdered his wife, I wanted to know.

Apparently, Engstern couldn't remember a thing; he wasn't directly under suspicion, but there was some talk of a psychiatrist's report.

'So they do suspect him after all,' I put in.

Lessi gave a shrug. 'To be quite honest, I couldn't care less about the old guy. It's Max I'm sorry for, and his brother, although I hardly know Christoph. Your mother, murdered! Can you imagine what that's like?'

I pointed out that the same mother had been an alcoholic.

'So?' Beate asked.

And the Lessi brat turned on me: 'A mother's still a mother,' so I let the subject drop.

It wasn't easy, but for four whole weeks I didn't go near Ladenburg, even though I was saddled with Dieskau again and had to take him for his evening walks. He was getting something of a raw deal now; I was no longer taking him off in the car, but just once round the block for a quick sniff at the plane trees. Maybe Witold was being watched and his phone tapped, maybe some neighbour would recognize me, and my car and the dog might have stuck in someone's memory.

I decided to let my hair grow. For many years I had favoured a very short urchin-bob, which in fact I suited very well. Obviously, with this man's haircut and in my trainers and dark slacks I had been taken, in the twilight, for a man. Probably I had been spotted by some elderly person with poor eyesight – it had been the holiday season and almost all the younger people had been away with their children. With my hair longer and in a dress and dainty shoes, no one would recognize me as that slim man in trainers, and besides, I would appear before Witold as a charming, very feminine creature. I was already convinced that my austere appearance was not altogether to his taste. Everything in his house looked totally different from mine, more disorganized, more imaginative, more colourful, more vivid. But was it not just some blind chance in my past that made me the orderly person I am?

Beate, for example, had always had things much easier. She had grown up in a large family, where, yes, there had been occasional rows, but in general, cheerfulness reigned. From very early on she had been worldly wise and streets ahead of me. All I had was an overly pious mother who, once a year on my birthday, allowed me to invite three of my friends to the house. In my class – an all-girls one, by the way – there were a few others of my sort, that is, diligent and well-behaved, rather unattractive and not very popular. But most of them went to dancing class, talked about boys and had a boyfriend. Even if they didn't come from a well-off home, they at least had mothers who could enthuse over a pretty dress or could even make one themselves. The others – self-confident, fun-loving, in love. That's the way it began, and that's the way it went on, and the injustice of it has remained until this day.

Ten years after our final exams I attended a class reunion. Pictures were passed round, almost all of them of weddings, babies and small children, no other topic existed. I and a few other leftovers sat on the fringes like fossils. Never again did I go to a class reunion. I hate these contented mothers with their child wonders, hate these self-satisfied wives. But I've never actually taken a stand against them.

Now, for the first time in my life, I wanted something quite determinedly for myself, wanted it with all my heart and soul: I wanted Witold. To get him, I was willing to do everything in my power, I wanted to set my whole mind to the task, and to get him I would have put my career and my money on the line.

After I had let it grow for a few weeks, I didn't like my hair at all. When Beate phoned me, I decided to ask her advice. But she interrupted me:

'We'll talk about hair in a minute. Before that, though, I've got a couple of pieces of news for you. First, Lessi's not having a baby at all!'

I learned that, four weeks previously, Lessi had come up with a vaguely positive result on a pregnancy-testing kit from the chemist's, but had never gone to the doctor. That didn't stop her from telling the whole world about her pregnancy. A few days ago, Beate had gone with her to a gynaecologist, who, after an ultra-sonic scan, had told her otherwise. Today, she had had her period.

'To be quite honest,' Beate said, 'I'm really very relieved. I would have had to give up my job at the adult education centre to bring up Lessi's child. I mean, how was she to go on studying without a man around to take his turn at baby-sitting?'

So, Beate's joy at becoming a grandmother had been nothing but a big act, I thought bitterly.

'And what's the second bit of news?' I demanded with a thrill of excitement at the thought that it might be about Witold.

'Just imagine – I've met this lovely man,' Beate told me, and went on to describe the merits of a commercial traveller ten years her junior.

Although I suspected that Beate kept open house and a bed to match, I couldn't help asking sarcastically, 'So this is the ultimate happiness?'

Beate wouldn't be put off. 'Oh, listen,' she said, 'I don't know of any fifty-year-old woman who has found complete happiness just like that. Anyway, happiness only comes in small doses or it's short-lived. I'll not deny there's a downside, too: he's married with a young family. But they live in the Munich area and he goes home only at weekends.'

Well now, that really was a pretty small dose of happiness. I couldn't believe that Beate had got herself involved in something like this.

'What's the latest on the murder case?' I asked.

'I would never have thought you could get so interested in murder.' Now it was Beate's turn to get slightly bitchy. But she did go on to tell me that Witold's sons had stayed the last few weeks with their father, although they in fact had had their own places in Heidelberg for some time now. However, they were about to leave for Mexico with their girlfriends; it was, after all, the university long vacation. They had even considered taking their poor father with them. But that wasn't on.

'Why not?' I asked.

'Well, for a start, he can't, because school is starting again soon and he has to teach; secondly, he's not allowed to, since he must stay where the police can reach him. And thirdly, he doesn't want to. As far as Lessi knows, a friend has offered

39

him the use of his holiday cottage in the Odenwald; he'd like to hide himself away there once the boys have gone. Understandably enough, he's not keen on hanging around alone in the house in Ladenburg, being pestered by reporters and sympathetic neighbours.'

Of course, we hadn't said a word about my hair yet, but there had been much more interesting things to talk about. I was convinced I could soon locate this cottage in the Odenwald.

Once the new school term had begun, I rang up the office of the grammar school in Ladenburg. I claimed I was Inspector Krüger's secretary, since I had by chance picked up his name in the paper; Krüger was investigating the Engstern case. But did the police have such a thing as secretaries? When I had had to make a statement as a witness to a road accident some time before, I had come across only men, and my statement was typed out, personally and very laboriously, by a young policeman. Yet it occurred to me that in all the crime series on television there's often a sour-faced female whose job it is to make the coffee for the squad of detectives.

So I told the school secretary that she didn't have to drag Herr Engstern out of a lesson just for this call, but perhaps she could give me a bit of information herself.

'Herr Engstern is on sick-leave, so you couldn't talk to him here anyway,' came the reply. I explained that he had recently given me his new address over the telephone, but unfortunately I had mislaid the slip of paper I noted it on. My boss would be furious if he found out. She fully appreciated the need to avoid a boss's rage, and seemed to be riffling through some files.

'Yes, here it is,' she said brightly, 'put in the file by the headmaster himself. Right, he can be reached at Dr Schröder's in Bickelbach in the Odenwald, and the street is called Holzweg.'

I thanked her politely. That had worked a treat. If Witold himself had come to the phone, I would have been too excited to say anything and would have hung up. That would have struck him as suspicious, to say the least.

I discovered the tiny hamlet of Bickelbach on the map. Should I drive out there this evening, or wait until the weekend? At last I had somewhere to go, my evenings had a purpose again.

Of course, I couldn't hold out till the weekend. I drove out in the early evening, taking Dieskau with me. In Bickelbach, I parked the car in a side-street and set off on foot in search of the Holzweg. I didn't want to ask anyone the way, and in any case I didn't meet a soul; the whole place seemed pretty deserted. Holzweg turned out to be at the far end of the village and led up a hillside. There were several farmhouses that had obviously been renovated and converted by city dwellers. Gardens full of cabbages, antirrhinums, carrots, parsley and phlox, a delight to the eye of a townie like me. While I didn't have a house number to go by, I did know Witold's car. By now I had been walking for a good half-hour with the dog. The Holzweg dragged on, winding its way up the slope. There it was – on a patch of grass stood Witold's car. I became quite fluttery with anxiety. No, I didn't want to knock on his door today, I had to spy out the lie of the land first. But it wasn't such a simple matter here; the little house, a converted barn, was surrounded by an open field. I could be spotted from all sides. I strode past like someone out for a brisk stroll. Apart from the car, there was no trace of Witold. Where the Holzweg finally led into the woods, I did an about turn and headed back to my car; now I was in the know.

In the three days between then and the Saturday I worked out one plan after another, carefully considering what I was going to wear, whether the dog was to come with me, and so forth. At last, the time for action had come. That morning, I went to the hairdresser's and had a perm. With this rather tousled head of blow-dried curls I looked a new woman.

And so, on the Saturday, charming and young, excited and apprehensive, I climbed the four well-worn stone steps and simply rang his bell. It was some little time before Witold opened the door.

'Yes?' he asked gruffly.

'Don't you remember me?' I asked back.

His brow furrowed, suddenly something dawned on him.

'Come, come in,' he stammered, and now it was his turn to be agitated. He wasn't absolutely sure whether I was the unknown woman who had been present at the death of his Hilke.

I stepped inside, he gestured towards one of the four chairs standing round a circular oak table. He automatically lit a cigarette before holding out the packet to me. I shook my head.

'Just who are you, anyway?' was the first thing he wanted to know.

I was cautious and assured him that that was of no importance for the moment, but I'd tell him later on. Witold drew on his cigarette, went to fetch an ashtray and as he did so, he peered out of the grubby window; he wanted to see whether I was alone and what kind of car I had. But my car was parked down at the end of the Holzweg, and I had left Dieskau at home. I reckoned that a dog usually attracted more attention than a person, and I knew from experience that people are more likely to talk to you when you are walking a dog.

At last, Witold said, 'I've racked my brains a thousand times about how it all happened that night. How did you come to be there so suddenly?'

Yes, that was a sore point. Now I had to bring Dieskau into the story after all. I told him – although it didn't sound very convincing – that I had had a headache, so I had gone for an extra walk with the dog. On the open ground next to his garden, I had let him off the lead, when suddenly he disappeared. In my search for the dog, I had ended up in Witold's garden, where I heard the shot. That was when I had rushed in.

While I was talking, Witold watched me with close concentration, smoking nervously, unable to keep either his arms or legs still, and suddenly sneaking a quick glance down at my feet, trying to assess my shoe-size.

When I had finished, he began again, in some irritation.

'All right, fine, that might well be the way it was, although I can't recall having seen a dog. But after that, I can't understand anything at all. On the one hand, you obviously wanted to help me, but on the other, you very nearly killed me!'

'No,' I assured him, 'there's no way I meant to hit you; it was only supposed to look as if you had been shot at. Afterwards I checked to make sure you weren't dangerously wounded, and I didn't think it was all that serious.'

Witold bridled at that. 'Not all that serious?' he exclaimed. 'You're a fine one! The shot missed an artery by a whisker, I could have bled to death!'

He rolled up his trouser-leg, and I could see a small red scar on the outside of his calf, the bullet-hole I had seen at the time. But now he showed me the inner side of his leg, and that was something else again: the exit point of the bullet had left a deep crater.

Witold looked at me grimly – no sign of his charming smile there. 'I just don't understand you! You must have fired at my wife, too, but why? On the one hand you helped me, but on the other, probably *you* killed my wife and I only winged her.'

I thought for a moment. Then I asked him to tell me what the police knew and what he had told them in his statement.

'At first I really couldn't remember anything,' Witold began, 'but I don't think they accepted that. I told them my wife had broken off a drying-out course and had turned up unexpectedly. She was already under the influence when she arrived, and then we both had some more to drink. I don't normally drink much and I'm not used to large amounts, certainly not of whisky. I told them I had felt sick and had lain down on the carpet. Then I heard a bang, felt a burning pain in my leg and passed out. Now, the police probably don't believe me, but then again I couldn't have inflicted that wound on myself; the distance the shot was fired from was far too great. And anyway, I couldn't have walked about with that bleeding wound without leaving a trail of bloodstains. They searched everywhere for the murder weapon, but it was nowhere to be found –' He stopped short, and then, 'You must have it!' he shouted, getting quite worked-up.

I nodded. 'I took it away because it had your fingerprints on it.'

'I'm absolutely baffled by all this,' Witold exclaimed again. 'It doesn't make any sense! Why didn't you simply call the police?'

I smiled at him. 'I wanted to help you!'

'It's extremely questionable whether you did help me. The police are desperately looking for someone in trainers, whose footprints were left quite distinctly in the garden and on the light-coloured carpet. So they're probably assuming that some person unknown appeared from the garden, fired the shots and took the gun away with them. But what I can't get into my head is why you fired another shot at my wife! Wasn't she already dead, then? Only the shot to the head is supposed to have been fatal, but I honestly don't know where I hit her.'

I eyed Witold carefully. Should I tell him he hit her in the head? But he really ought to know that for himself, for after he had fired only her blouse was bloodstained. Probably, though, he had only seen her fall; or was he trying to put me on the spot, to find out whether I was lying, or whether I was simply crazy?

He went on: 'What reason could you have for doing such a thing? It just doesn't make sense.' (That was the umpteenth time he had said that.) 'I expected all the time that you would go to the police. When you didn't, I assumed that it was you who killed my wife.'

I told him I had panicked completely when I accidentally shot him. In a kind of state of shock I had also shot his wife, although I had no more idea than he did whether I had hit her in the head. And then I had fled and quite understandably not gone to the police.

'The best thing,' said Witold, 'would be for us to call the police now, together, and get the whole thing over and done with. It'll all come out some time anyway.'

I protested vigorously.

'Do you know what will happen then? That'll be the end

44

of your sitting here in the fresh Odenwald air, looking out on the fields and the forest. Instead you'll be locked up, staring at a barred window, waiting for your trial. And what's more, not a soul can connect me with this business, and the footprints could be anybody's. What sort of a motive am I supposed to have had, anyway? Besides – even if they did believe you – if I were to turn round and tell them about the shot you fired, you're right in it! Incidentally, are you being watched here?'

Witold mumbled sullenly to himself, 'At first they shadowed every move I made, probably opened my mail and bugged my phone as well – I didn't bother answering it. They came for me and questioned me practically every day.' He took a deep breath and looked at me accusingly. Then he continued, 'I suppose they thought at the beginning that my wife had been the first to fire, then I shot at her. But the angle of fire didn't fit. After I had been hit in the leg, I couldn't walk. The idea that we had taken turns to shove the gun into each other's hand didn't strike them as all that convincing, either. As I said, I couldn't have hidden it without leaving a trail of blood. But, against that, if I had hit her first, she was too badly wounded to have been able to fire. So it must have been a third person who did the shooting.'

'Who did they suspect?' I interrupted.

'Maybe they thought the one in trainers had been in cahoots with me, a paid killer. They checked my bank account and found that, two days before, I had withdrawn three thousand marks. But, for one thing, that money was still about, in full, and for another, four of my colleagues were able to confirm that I was intending to go off on holiday with them and had taken the money out for that.'

Witold nervously gathered up the cigarette ash and put it in the bin. 'Well anyway, about four weeks later, they eased off a bit and even allowed me to stay here for a while. But I've got to phone in every two days ... By the way, did anybody follow you here?'

'No, absolutely not. The road was very quiet the whole

way. But whether your neighbour saw me, I really don't know.'

My God, it suddenly flashed through my head, here I am, sitting face to face with the man of my dreams, and we're talking about murder and mayhem instead of love, and he's staring at me in utter mistrust. Somehow I had to give him at least a hint that I was on his side.

So, I lied. 'To tell you the truth, it was by sheer chance that I got mixed up in this whole business, but when I saw you, I recognized you at once from a photograph. I had read your little book on painting some time ago, and I was absolutely fascinated by it. Your picture on the sleeve had left a deep impression on me, and maybe because your book seemed to me so very clever and appealed to me so much, that was what caused this spontaneous reaction of wanting to help.' And I gave him my most beguiling smile. For just a fraction of a second, he smiled back.

'Well, well, so you've read my book . . .' I had uttered the magic formula, for his tense, hostile expression altered, and he once again became that lovable, attractive man with the erotic voice who, all those weeks ago, had changed my life at a stroke.

'I don't have all that many readers,' he went on. 'And you really liked it?'

In my eagerness to persuade him of this, I went enthusiastically into details about the beautiful slippers and carpets. I was being utterly devious, but after all, the end justifies the means.

But his amiability did not last long. 'How am I to know you're not some criminal lunatic?' he said, but with just the lightest undertone of irony, because now that I had passed myself off as an avid reader he could no longer seriously believe I was mad. 'It could all end now with you drawing your pistol from your holster and bumping me off.'

'Why would I do that?' I asked sorrowfully, and gave him a long, loving look. It seemed to be filtering in at last that I was not harbouring any homicidal intentions towards him, even if he had certainly not yet cottoned on to the fact that I was in love with him.

I decided to apply the magic words again. 'Some time after I had read your marvellous book, I went to a lecture you gave on the poetry of the 1815 Wars of Liberation. That was a wonderful evening. You taught me so many interesting things about that time that I drove home positively enriched.' (True enough, I was enriched by new surges of feeling, but I couldn't remember a word of the awful Romantic war literature.) He looked at me pensively, his face became pleasant again, completely casting off that morose expression. You're very vain, I thought, and that's how I'm going to get you.

'I'm pleased to hear that,' he said with sincerity. 'Shall I make us some coffee?'

I nodded, delighted. Not for years had any man made coffee for me. While he was putting the water on to boil, Witold remarked, 'It would have been ideal if you had stolen something, turned out some drawers and ransacked cupboards . . .' But again I could detect a friendly, mocking undertone, which I was quite happy to let pass.

'Yes,' I said, 'then the police would have had a motive for the shooting, a robbery or something of the sort. But then I had planned and thought everything through just as little as you. Both of us acted more or less as if something had snapped: you fired the shot in the heat of the moment, just as I did what I did in order to help you out.'

We sat there together, drinking coffee; a certain closeness was developing in that simply furnished room. Witold was thawing out a little, even coming out with the odd hint of humour. He joked about our complicity and about this conspiratorial meeting. But then he suggested that it would probably be best if we were never seen together and kept any contact to a minimum.

'They've been frantically sniffing around to see if I had a girlfriend and therefore a motive for killing my wife. But thank heavens the last affair I had was many years ago. But if I'm seen around with you, then that would be handing it to the police on a plate.'

Sadly, I had to admit he was right. On the one hand, I was delighted to hear that there was no girlfriend lying in wait for him, but on the other, I wanted to be his lover. But, naturally, I could hardly come straight out with that just then.

Witold asked me again about my name and address. I promised I would reveal my identity at our next secret meeting. And then I suggested we should meet the Sunday after next in Heidelberg, right in the middle of the main street, outside the Kaufhof department store, for example; that way we could be swallowed up in the throng of tourists. Witold wasn't keen on that.

'I keep running into acquaintances in Heidelberg,' he said, although he did seem to be in favour of the idea of another meeting. No doubt he felt an urgent need to talk about the stress of recent times, and there was no one else he could do that with. Finally, we arranged to meet in a car park in the Odenwald, where the danger of our being recognized was obviously very slight.

Two hours later, I was driving home. On that early evening, the gentle hills dotted here and there with the odd apple tree, the outline of the wooded slopes, the birds lazily wheeling in the sky, and the late sunlight, seemed to me so utterly beautiful that I felt as if I had just come out after years in prison and could now have a life once again. Like a complete idiot, I started singing at the top of my voice. I'm not usually one for singing, and certainly not the sort of soppy stuff that was coming out now. I was happy and full of hope, because it was no longer such an improbable idea that this man could become fond of me. In a week's time, I would be seeing him again.

3

On the Monday, after the office closed, I drove out with Dieskau to Beate's. I was in such a good mood that I didn't want to be stuck in the house on my own and, quite out of character, succumbed to a sudden need for company.

Beate goggled at me.

'You look totally different with that head of curls, so fresh and breezy! Not bad!'

She surveyed me from all sides.

'Listen, Jürgen will be here any minute.' (That was her new boyfriend, the business rep.) 'He was with his family over the weekend, as you know. We're going out for a meal, maybe you'd like to come too?' And, at the word 'you', she turned and bowed politely towards Dieskau. In the past, I would have immediately said no, not wanting to feel I was playing gooseberry. But in my exhilaration, I went along. Jürgen was originally from the Rhineland and was a great one for telling jokes, new and second-hand. He obviously needed an audience, and as such, I was welcome. He was no bad lot, about whom I would have had to warn Beate, but an honest sort, and he was quite straight with her. During the week, he wanted a bit of fun and company at the table and in bed; that seemed to be fine by Beate. She laughed heartily at his jokes, and ended up by infecting me, too. Only Dieskau was fed up. Though he had been discreetly slipped a mutton bone under the table, he didn't like men and wasn't used to them. He persisted in slavering and barking threateningly under the table, so that in the end I withdrew with him and left the pair of them alone. I envied Beate her relaxed way of treating men; I just couldn't be like that. My relationship with Witold had to be different from that, not so superficial; but bright and cheerful all the same.

A week later, on a sunny Sunday morning, I was waiting, with an excited Dieskau on his lead, for Witold. The forest car park was quite deserted. There wasn't a car to be heard, even in the distance. I hadn't been waiting long before I began to feel downhearted, my high spirits were ebbing. Maybe he wasn't going to show up after all! I was snatched from these gloomy reflections by his voice. From behind, I heard, 'Good morning, o mysterious stranger!'

Witold had come on his bicycle and was a little out of breath since he had taken a forest path rather than the main road.

I beamed at him. But he seemed to be busy trying to memorize my car registration number. When he saw that I had noticed, he gave me a slight grin.

'Today's the day, as you promised, when you lift your incognito. So, what's your name? After all, I've got to know what I'm to call you.'

'Rosemarie,' I said, slightly embarrassed; it didn't suit me, and, like most women, I'd always been unhappy with my name. He didn't seem to think it was quite right either.

'And then?' he said.

'Luise,' I added.

He was amused. 'And after that?' he insisted.

'Thyra,' I said, very quietly.

Witold burst out laughing. I knew what was coming; he was a German teacher, after all.

'Thyra,' he repeated, with a hearty laugh. 'All I really wanted to know was your surname. But that's quite something,' and, of course, he went on to quote Theodor Fontane's version of the Norse saga.

'And the Jarls came to the Feast of Jul,
Gorm Grymme sits in the hall,
And at his side, on ivory stool,
Thyra Danebod, his queen of all.'

He was still laughing. 'I'm going to call you Frau Thyra, for I've never met anyone called that. No doubt people call you Rose or something of the sort, but that doesn't suit your unsentimental character. Joking apart, though, you must tell me what your full name is, and your address, otherwise I can't help feeling that, somehow, I'm being taken for a ride.'

I beamed at him again – it just seemed to happen automatically! – and then I told him all he wanted to know.

'Actually, I had a Danish grandmother. That's where the Thyra comes from. Call me that if you like, but without the "Frau". It's great not to be called Rosie for once.'

'Right, Thyra. I'm Rainer.'

'Ah, but if you're going to call me Thyra, I'm calling you Witold,' I told him.

'Where did you dig that up from?' he exclaimed, greatly tickled. 'Nobody ever calls me that, either. Oh yes, that's right – I used the name on my book because it sounds more intriguing. As a child, I was always thoroughly ashamed of that middle name.'

We carried on making all sorts of jokes about our new names, yet we still remained quite formal with each other. By this time we had been walking for a good half-hour, and Dieskau was in his element.

'I've been thinking a lot lately,' Witold began. 'Just what have you done with the gun?'

'I've hidden it safely at home; nobody would think of looking for it there. But I'm going to get rid of it very soon.'

Witold was a bit uneasy at that. What did I have in mind? I wanted to throw it into the Rhine, one dark and foggy night, and from a bridge.

'But you must do it right away,' he said anxiously. 'Tonight if possible, even without the fog! I thought it would have been gone long before now. My wife inherited it from an uncle, and who knows, it could be traced back. Anyway, where did you learn to shoot?'

I promised him I would dispose of the gun in the river that very night. 'I can't shoot, actually. But when I was young I had a boyfriend who went with his father to a shooting range every Sunday to practise. I often went along, and now and again I had a go. I know in theory how to handle a gun, but that was a long, long time ago, and even then I was anything but a crack-shot.'

'Talking of friends,' said Witold, 'is there a Gorm Grymme waiting at home for you, and maybe a Young Harald as well?'

I was flattered by his interest in my private life and was keen to assure him that no one was waiting for me.

'I've had a few big disappointments in my time,' I hinted. Witold gave me a long, searching look, but was too tactful to dig any deeper.

After a while, I asked, 'Was your marriage a happy one?'

For quite a time he said nothing.

'You know, very few people can answer that kind of question with a simple yes or no. Come autumn, we would have been married for twenty-three years. If our marriage had been hopelessly screwed up, I don't suppose it would have lasted that long.'

I was quite satisfied with that response. We wandered happily on, now and then calling each other by our new names and giving them an ironic twist, and laughing a lot. When we had to cross a stream, Witold reached out a hand to me and held mine a few seconds longer than necessary, just as our eyes often held each other's just that shade too long.

After walking for two hours my nice new shoes had raised several blisters. I was flushed and thirsty – even Dieskau was searching every hollow for water. At every bramble bush we passed, I stopped and picked a few berries. But, as a seasoned teacher, Witold had not only a timetable in mind but a trail-map in his pocket. We'd be stopping for a rest soon, he promised. He knew a pub in a little village and there we were able to sit in the garden at the back. All the other customers were stuck in the stuffy lounge. Witold organized a tray from somewhere and brought a jug of cider and two portions of pungent local cheese.

'I didn't even ask what you wanted,' he said, 'but you won't find anything here more delicious than this.' He was right.

The exhausted Dieskau refreshed himself at a fountain in

the garden. Meanwhile, after two glasses of cider, which I knocked back greedily, the world appeared to me in shades of gold and pink and I felt an overwhelming desire just to kiss my Witold. But I hadn't changed as much as all that; I couldn't pluck up the courage.

Witold, for his part, drank several glasses and talked a lot. All the while he stroked the dog at my feet, until it finally dawned on me that this was really meant for my legs. I gazed at him, my eyes positively aglow.

'A pity, really,' said Witold in high good-humour, 'that we two accomplices can't meet just normally. Or should we go on another expedition into the unknown next Sunday?'

I certainly had no objection to that, but during the hours of tedium in the office I had worked out a strategy of my own.

'We could always meet for the very first time – in front of witnesses, if you like! Then no police inspector could possibly think we had known each other before or that I have anything to do with the whole thing.'

Witold caught my drift right away. He thought for a while.

'In the next few weeks there are all sorts of wine festivals, village fairs and town celebrations coming up all along the Bergstrasse. We could meet quite by chance at one of these, at a long table with any number of people around.'

I was very taken with the idea. We worked everything out in detail. I was to be sitting with a friend (just as well I had Beate at least!) at a table in one of the many taverns in Weinheim that specialize in their own wines. We were to be there as early as possible, before the place became too crowded for us to spot each other. Witold would then amble past with a friend (the same Dr Schröder who had lent him his weekend house) and the two of them would sit down next to us at the long table, quite by chance. Then our friends would be witnesses to our first meeting. That Beate knew Witold by sight didn't matter; in fact, I thought, it would make everything that much easier.

The cider had gone to our heads a little, so we sat for a long time in the shady garden, listening to the splashing of the

53

little fountain and watching the wasps scrambling about in our wineglasses. Finally, though, it was time to go. At the car park, we parted like conspirators.

'Till Saturday, then.'

'Don't forget about the gun!'

I couldn't have asked for more from a beautiful Sunday in late August. I reckoned I had never known a better one and doubted whether I'd ever have another like it. How right that was to prove!

Back home, the first thing I did was to kick the dainty little slingbacks off my big feet. I couldn't help thinking of Hans Christian Andersen's Little Mermaid who, for the love of a man, had swapped her fish-tail for two shapely legs and had to suffer agony with every step, as if she was walking on a double-edged sword.

On the Monday, still euphoric, I phoned Beate from the office to sell her the idea of an outing to the wine festival. I had to be quick off the mark before she could end up making any other plans.

Beate was staggered. 'For years I've been trying to drag you along to God knows what, and I've hardly ever succeeded. And now, here you are in your dotage, wanting to go to the fair – and getting yourself a curly hairdo! Tell me something: you're not finally in love, are you?'

'Well, of course,' I quipped, 'now that I'm living with a male, my whole outlook on life is different.'

'What did you say?'

'You know. Dieskau is sharing bed and board with me.'

'Oh God,' Beate sighed. 'I know I've heard of people going for lots of walks for the love of a dog, but never of them tearing off to the hairdresser's for its sake.'

But she did agree to come with me on the Saturday.

'It's just as well you didn't want to go on Sunday, 'cos the three kids are all coming for a meal. It could be that they'll get here by Saturday, and if they do, it's all off.'

During the week, Beate was fully taken up with her job and her Jürgen, but at the weekends her three grown-up children descended on her like locusts with monotonous regularity, casting off dirty washing and eating her out of house and home. I was glad I had been spared such a plague.

The week flew past. I concentrated hard on my work at the insurance office, wrote a long letter to Frau Römer, took Dieskau for his daily walk in the park, and washed my curtains. On Friday, Witold rang me; he didn't have a phone in Bickelbach, so there was no way I could reach him. 'Well, Thyra, is everything set up? Is tomorrow still on?' he asked conspiratorially. 'My friend Ernst Schröder will certainly be coming along, he was tickled with the idea because he's a grass widower at the moment.'

On the Saturday afternoon, Beate and I were strolling, as arranged, through the old town centre of Weinheim around five o'clock. At six, I tried to steer her unobtrusively along a planned course towards the planned table. This proved to be no simple matter, however. Beate hung around, egging on the muscle-men testing their strength with the big hammer and trying to ring the bell.

We were by no means punctual: it was gone quarter past six when I managed to get Beate to sit down. By that time, there was hardly any room at our table – where was Witold to squeeze in? At half-past, I caught sight of him from a distance, weaving his way over, along with a bulky, bearded type, and apparently already slightly the worse for drink. I flushed with anticipation and fear and wasn't listening to a word of what Beate was telling me.

By now, the two men were at our table. 'Excuse me, would you mind moving up a little?' Witold, with a sly wink, asked the couple who were sitting opposite us.

'It's cramped enough here as it is,' said Beate. 'You'll get a table over there at the back, there's more room there, surely.'

But the couple were getting to their feet. The man said they were just leaving anyway and he would settle up at the bar. Without further ado, they parked themselves, Dr Schröder facing me, Witold opposite Beate.

'Oh,' Beate exclaimed, 'I know you! You're Rainer

Engstern, aren't you? You give a lecture every year in the adult education centre in Heppenheim.'

Witold confirmed that this was so.

'I'm Beate Sperber,' she said, 'and this is my friend, Rosie Hirte.'

Then Dr Schröder introduced himself, too.

'Rosemarie doesn't really suit you, though,' Witold said, bold as you like. 'Don't you have any other Christian name?'

'Thyra,' I breathed.

Beate pulled a face.

'Oh, come on, Rosie, you're kidding! You've never told me about that!'

I looked Witold boldly straight in the eye and said, 'Rainer doesn't suit you all that well, either!'

To cut a long story short, in a very few minutes, we were all on first-name – or rather, middle-name – terms. That was Beate's idea. When Ernst Schröder was asked, however, he said he didn't have a middle name, although Witold sometimes called him Hakim, because he had studied medicine at first, before he became a pharmacist. Beate's middle name was Edeltraud, but she strictly forbade its use.

Witold's friend Ernst, or El Hakim, told me at great length that his wife was in America, that his son had just had to repeat a year at school, and that he had got to know Witold at a Social Democratic Party meeting. He was nice and friendly, but all I really wanted was to talk to Witold, to look into his eyes and smile at him. Beate seemed to be on the best of terms with him right away. She always got right into her stride whenever men turned up that she took a shine to. At first, I listened with only half an ear as the two of them launched into a serious conversation about the syllabus for the adult education centre. Then they started gossiping and making fun of some oddball among the older teaching staff until, finally, I noticed them laughing until the tears were rolling down their faces. I was a bit put out at this; I wanted to be part of this refreshing hilarity. But I couldn't very well offend the amiable Schröder, so I had to answer him and be nice to him. The merrier Beate became by my side, the more my happy mood ebbed away.

In any case, as the consumption of alcohol at our long table increased, the talk got louder, so that by now I could hardly make out anything at all. All of a sudden, Beate turned to me. 'Have you got a headache or something? You've got such a glum face on.'

I assured her I was fine, but maybe we could go and sit somewhere else where the air was a bit fresher, somewhere away from here. I was hoping I would then manage to sit next to, or, for that matter, facing Witold. The others agreed. Witold even gave me a sly wink, which made me feel a whole lot better.

We ambled through the narrow streets, all lovingly decked out with coloured lanterns. Ernst Schröder made a beeline for the shooting gallery.

'Now we're going to win a fine flower for the fair ladies!'

I didn't like the shooting at all, for it stirred up unhappy memories for Witold and myself. Ernst Schröder kept on shooting until he actually did get hold of a horrendous purple plastic orchid, which he presented to me with a sweeping bow. Witold said he couldn't shoot and didn't want to.

But Beate gushed, 'I'll have a go for you!'

She was an excellent shot, but then Beate always did have a natural talent for anything involving dexterity. She won a red rose, and made a great fuss of pinning it on to Witold's shirt, doing rather too much fumbling about for my liking. Then she got a bit too cocky and demanded a go on the swing-boats.

'Count me out on that,' said the roly-poly Ernst. 'I get giddy just watching.'

I was none too keen, either, on giving the assembled mob the chance to peek up under my wide skirt. But I wasn't even asked. Beate had simply grabbed Witold by the hand, and, standing face to face and almost touching, the two of them swung themselves as high as they could go, laughing and shrieking with delight. I found the whole thing utterly tasteless.

At last they landed back on terra firma. Witold had gone a cheesy colour and wasn't laughing any more.

'You look as if you're just about to say hello again to your last meal; after all, you're not in your twenties now,' said Hakim sympathetically.

Beate took this as her cue to behave as if she really was still only twenty (for all that she was exactly three months older than I was); she went on and on about what a good head for heights she had and how a slater or a chimney-sweep would have been the ideal job for her.

Witold paid her no heed and made a dart for a bench.

'Come on,' said Ernst Schröder, 'stop buggering about. Are you feeling ill, or what? Anyone would think you've lost a pound and found sixpence.'

Witold gulped.

'There I am, standing up there, grunting like an ape, when I look down and see two pupils from the school in Ladenburg staring up at me.'

'So what?' exclaimed Beate, all unsuspecting. 'Teachers are human too!'

But Ernst put her right. 'Rainer's on sick-leave, and the pupils think he's confined to bed. So, being seen up there on the swing doesn't make the best of impressions, and they'll be able to bring this up every time they want to dodge off school.'

'Hang on,' Witold objected. 'Sure, I'm on sick-leave, but what was diagnosed was "a state of extreme mental exhaustion, with bouts of depression". The doctor gave strict orders against staying in bed brooding. I'm supposed to go for long walks, that's what he recommended.'

All the same, Witold was no longer in the mood and suddenly wanted to go home, pointing out that, because he knew he'd be drinking wine, he had come on his bike. I offered to drive him home, bike and all. But he was downright grumpy and said he didn't want to put me to any trouble. Ernst would drive him back home to Ladenburg, he said; he wanted to sleep in his own bed tonight.

And so we parted. I had brought Beate here, and now I

had to drive her home, too. As soon as we were in the car, she started: 'Rosie, you really did make quite a hit with that Ernst Schröder. Congratulations!'

I said nothing. It wasn't true, of course, Beate was just saying that so that I would return the compliment and congratulate her on her own success, but I really had no desire to do her any such favour. Most of all, I would have loved to dump her in a dark street somewhere, but I had to avoid giving her so much as a hint of my anger and disappointment. I had no claims of ownership over Witold, and besides, she was supposed to believe that we had all four just met for the first time.

Since I wasn't playing along, Beate now struck up a hymn of praise to herself. 'I wasn't bad tonight myself,' she started. I could have screamed.

'Engstern and I have a lot of shared acquaintances, and besides, our kids know each other. We had any number of things in common right away.'

I kept silent. At last, Beate stopped prattling on and we drove along the rest of the darkened Bergstrasse without a word.

Shortly before we reached her place, I inquired, fearing the worst, 'Are you going to be seeing him again?'

Beate laughed. 'You must be joking. That's a man with charisma, he's a bit out of my class. For an evening like that, fine. But any more than that, forget it. It would only bring me grief. You know, when a fascinating man like that suddenly gets his freedom, then you can bet he'll be looking for somebody new that's at least ten years younger. Believe me, I know what I'm talking about!'

I didn't much like the sound of that either.

'But your Jürgen's much younger,' I objected.

'Of course he is,' said Beate drily, 'but surely you can see for yourself the difference in quality.'

Now I had recovered my fondness for Beate, and my leave-taking was less frosty than I had intended.

The days after that Saturday seemed to drag. We hadn't arranged a date, I had no rendezvous to look forward to;

when would I see Witold again? I couldn't call him in Bickelbach, and I didn't want to write either, because that would
somehow take the lightness out of our relationship. Anyway,
I was afraid of the teacher's red pencil, for composition had
never been my strong suit.

Instead of the hoped-for call, it was one from Beate that
came.

'Hello, Rosie, have you got over your unaccustomed orgy
at the fair?' she asked mockingly. 'By the way, our two con-
quests came to see me the Sunday after.'

I tried to make some noncommittal remark, but dark
despair rose in my throat like a worm, and all I could come
out with was a growl.

'Is that Dieskau complaining?' Beate went on. 'I bet you
haven't been out with him today. Well, anyway, what I
wanted to tell you was that on Sunday, about six in the
evening, there was this ring at the door, and I was none too
thrilled by it because of course the children were here and
I had just got dinner ready. Well, there they were, Rainer
Engstern' – luckily, Beate said 'Rainer' and not 'Witold' – 'and
Ernst Schröder. They were on their way to the Odenwald,
since as you know Rainer had gone back to Ladenburg on
the Saturday. They thought it would be a nice idea to look in
here on the off-chance. I'm more or less on the way.'

I managed a 'Hmm'. Unfortunately I was not really somewhere along the way, that I had to admit. Beate went on with
her tale: 'The two of them didn't need much persuading to
join us for the meal. Quite by chance, I had done a leg of
lamb, with garlic and green beans, which proved a great treat
for those poor wifeless souls.'

I well knew what a good cook Beate was. It was obvious
that was her direct route to men's hearts. That had to be the
reason for Jürgen's devotion as well.

'And the children?' I inquired dully.

'Oh, they can be really charming sometimes. They got on
tremendously well with Rainer. Lessi already knew him
through Eva and his son Max. But Vivian and Richard, too,
had friends who have been in his class at one time or another.

He had a great laugh with the kids and seemed particularly interested in Vivian's art studies.'

How could I compete with all that? Certainly no leg of lamb, no three children to bring a breath of fresh air into the whole business. Beate went on, 'I find Ernst especially nice, but Rainer is just a smidgin better. Rosie, it's all thanks to you that I've got to know these smashing blokes; without you, I wouldn't even have been there.'

I was in tears, but she couldn't see them. What common language she used!

Beate was still gabbling on. 'By the way, Rainer's staying on only for this week in his retreat in the Odenwald. He wants to go back to his teaching again next Monday, although he could certainly get longer sick-leave. Well, he wants to get back to his own house, and he said he's got a few things to sort out.'

I managed little sleep through that dismal night. That the man should really be the one to make the running in any romance was something ingrained in me by my upbringing. But what if he didn't do that? And anyway, weren't those ideas that I had inherited from my nunnish mother long out of date? Beate took a much more enterprising approach to such things. Should I be like her and quite simply take the initiative, drive out and see him again? Or was that too pushy? I just hadn't a clue.

On the Friday evening, I couldn't stand it any more. A wasted weekend lay ahead of me unless I did something. On the off-chance, I gave the Ladenburg number a try. Witold answered at once, which caught me off-guard.

'It's Rosemarie Hirte,' I stammered out my usual way of announcing myself.

'Who? Don't know anybody of that name, you must have dialled the wrong number,' he said coolly.

'It's me,' I squeaked like some whining child.

'Oh, Thyra.' He suddenly laughed. 'Well, of course. Sorry I didn't latch on to you right away.'

He didn't use the familiar 'du', but the formal 'Sie'. What

61

on earth was I to come up with? I asked him how he was and whether he had been back long from Bickelbach.

'I just got back here this morning,' Witold explained eagerly. 'You see, I teach a top set in the sixth form, and it's just not on for me to be absent any longer. I know for a fact that the substitution arrangements are just not working at all, and, let's face it, my pupils must be suffering from the fact that I've been having these depressions.'

To tell the truth, I hadn't noticed any sign of depression when we met.

'So now you've got to prepare your lessons?' I asked hesitantly.

'Well, yes, that too. But the garden's in a sorry state, the slugs have devoured almost everything. As of Monday, a Yugoslav woman is coming in to clean for me; some friends recommended her. But before she can even make a start, I'll have to do a thorough clean-up and get to grips with the washing machine as well.'

At this point, Beate would come straight out and offer her help. I had to overcome my inhibitions first before I could say something like that. I kept it neutral, so as to avoid having to choose between 'du' and 'Sie'.

'For once, I've got nothing arranged for this weekend; I could come over and give a hand. After all, I do know how to wash and iron, I could make myself useful doing the menial jobs in the garden, and now and then I could make the coffee and get in some cakes.'

I was careful not to mention cooking.

'It's extremely kind of you to offer. But no one can really help with the tidying up; that's something one has to do oneself. I can do the washing on my own, too, and on Monday the Yugoslavian woman can do the ironing. In any case, I'm expecting somebody on Sunday, so I'm all booked up. Thanks very much, Thyra, it was an awfully kind thought. Maybe I can take you up on it some other time.'

I begged him to get in touch whenever I could be of help. After some trivial, friendly chit-chat, we said goodbye without having arranged any sort of meeting.

In a fit of rage, I hurled a sofa-cushion on the floor. Poor Dieskau took it personally, came creeping to heel and begged forgiveness, as if it was all his fault. I gave him a reassuring pat and poured out my heart to him. 'Oh, Dieskau, for once in my life I really want something! I don't care what it costs – I want that man! But it's so difficult. I just don't know how to go about this kind of thing.'

I cried my eyes out, and the dog laid his muzzle on my knee and looked at me with an expression of unutterable melancholy. When it came to empathizing, he was a marvel.

So who could be Witold's Sunday visitor? Could it by any chance be Beate?

Sunday passed in profound gloom. I imagined Beate, deft as ever, making everything at Witold's place snug and cosy, as if by magic, cooking for him, laughing with him. The two of them are well suited, it gradually dawned on me: art, litera-ture, music – Beate knew a lot about such things, whereas I knew nothing. They'd have fun the whole day long . . . And in the evening? Would they drink champagne and go to bed? The very idea drove me almost out of my mind, so in the late afternoon I called Beate's number.

It was Lessi who answered. 'My mother isn't here,' she informed me offhandedly.

Where had she gone, then? I inquired.

'Vivian and Richard left yesterday for a few days in London, so she didn't cook a family dinner, 'cos I obviously don't matter,' the infantile Leonore complained. 'At any rate, I don't know where she is, maybe she went to a concert.'

I hung up. The whole thing was hard to take, but it was quite obvious: Beate was by now in bed with Witold, for all that tomorrow she'd have Jürgen back again. Why did other women get everything and I got nothing? Should I take her to task on this?

At eleven in the evening, the phone rang. Beate said, 'Lessi told me you called. The silly ass! I told her exactly where I was going. As usual, she didn't even listen.'

'So where were you then?'

'In Frankfurt, had a look round a fantastic Kandinsky

exhibition and then I went and had a Turkish meal with a girlfriend. It was really nice.'

Was she just lying off the cuff? But why on earth should she? She had absolutely no reason for keeping anything about her relationship with Witold from me, for she could have no idea that he belonged to me. Maybe, though, she did have a bad conscience about two-timing Jürgen; but then again, there was no need for that where a married lover was concerned. Racked by doubts, I went to bed.

On one of the following evenings, I sneaked back into Witold's garden under the cover of darkness. It was already dark by nine o'clock, and I had taken precautions so that he wouldn't discover me – a burglar's black rig-out.

Just as on the night I had first observed him, he was sitting there at the desk, writing. I loved him so much, this handsome, clever man, working away in such solitude and with such concentration. For at least an hour I stood there in the night-dark garden, before beating a silent retreat. The fence was just as dilapidated as it had been then. Witold had not considered it necessary to repair it.

It was like an addiction. Now I was driving out to Ladenburg almost every day, although that was not without its dangers, and all the neighbours had returned from their holidays. Witold was always on his own. I would have so loved to walk in through the French windows or to have rung the doorbell. But we had arranged that he would get in touch with me.

One evening, I saw a second car outside his house. It was Beate's. So I had been right! I felt utterly sick.

I had done it all wrong, I should have phoned him, visited him, written to him – what would I have had to lose! Now Beate was snatching my prey from me, because I had waited too long.

I crept into the garden. There was no one in the living-room. I waited for ages. Kitchen or bedroom – that was the only question now. In the end, it was getting too cold for me, and, shivering and chilled to the bone, I drove home, exactly as I had done that evening when Witold's wife died.

After days of deep depression, I decided not to give up, but to fight. I phoned Witold and simply invited him over. He was sorry, but he couldn't make it at the weekend. I offered him other dates, and at last he promised to come on the Thursday.

Now I had to go for broke. I had four days. I drew up a list: somehow or other I had to manage to create, on that evening, a charming, really cosy atmosphere, I had to look breathtakingly young and beautiful, had to engage him in witty and stimulating conversation and, on top of all that, had to serve up a delicious, but apparently effortlessly prepared meal. But above all, everything had to give the impression that it hadn't been arranged especially for him, but that paradise was the normal, everyday state of things in my house. I rushed to the beautician's, bought myself a wine-red velvet skirt and a crepe-de-Chine blouse with a heraldic pattern. I got in some candles, champagne, a new tablecloth, perfume.

But during the long hours in the office, the thing that caused me most worry was the meal. I couldn't very well ask Beate for her advice, although she would have had some idiot-proof suggestion off pat. I decided to grill salmon steaks – that was quick and couldn't go wrong, even for me. And to go with them, green pasta, a butter and tarragon sauce, and a salad. I had a try at making the sauce two days beforehand, and it worked. My God, was I excited!

Thursday, shortly before eight, one last look in the mirror. Much too formal! I thought suddenly. I mean, it's all supposed to appear casual, natural. He'll turn up in a sweater, and I'll be left looking like some dolled-up country bumpkin. I ripped off blouse and skirt and stood there in my petticoat and a panic in front of the wardrobe. Beate would have had everything under control, no matter what. I climbed into a pair of slacks and immediately back out again, blouses, skirts, everything was strewn around the floor. No, it was quite simply too late, he'd be here in five minutes. I snatched my new finery up off the carpet and put it on again in a mad dash, a hot flush suffused my face under the powder, as sure as fate, my make-up would soon start running down on to the pale collar. All the rejected rags were flung into the wardrobe, the door was slammed on them, I rushed to the window to watch for his car. Once or twice I shot into the kitchen – everything was ready, but I couldn't very well grill the fish before he arrived.

Witold arrived punctually – well, as punctually as academics do, a quarter of an hour late. In his hand he held an impersonal bunch of carnations with some greenery. Surely he could have picked something more original from his own garden.

'I hope I'm not late. Is your charming friend coming too? Not exactly rosemary – for remembrance – I'm afraid . . .' And he handed me, rather stiffly, his five yellow carnations, keeping the crumpled paper in his other hand. For a posy like that a 'You really shouldn't have' from me would have been only too appropriate. I let that be, thanked him, but added mischievously that Beate had a boyfriend who kept her fully occupied during the week. Witold smiled at this. Either he already knew, or he didn't care, or, again, he was in complete command of himself.

I poured out the sherry, rushed into the kitchen and put on water for the pasta. As a matter of fact, I wasn't overdressed after all, I reckoned. Witold's outfit was neither one thing nor the other – open-necked shirt and no tie, but a pale light-weight jacket and designer jeans. We were both slightly ill at ease.

'So, is the gun at the bottom of Father Rhine?' he suddenly wanted to know.

No, it wasn't, but I replied, 'Well, of course, it has been for weeks now!'

The last thing I wanted was for him to get edgy. While I hadn't of course forgotten about the revolver, I hadn't yet carried out his instructions, heaven knows why not.

The meal actually turned out a success. Witold praised it with condescending politeness, yet he ate little and didn't drink much either. The magical mood of the time when we shared the country cheese and cider failed to materialize, and it was all a bit artificial.

I tried to turn on the charm, touched his arm once as I

spoke, the way I had seen other women do it, but I was all tensed up. After the meal, we sat in my admittedly un-cosy armchairs, and I suggested opening a bottle of champagne. Witold declined, on the grounds that he had already had wine with the meal and a sherry beforehand, and after all, he had to drive home. In any case, it was only Friday tomorrow and that was just about his heaviest day.

'I hope you'll forgive me, but that's why I can't stay all that long.'

'At the fair, we had dropped the formalities.' It just slipped out, and, much to my chagrin, in a rather hurt tone at that.

'That's right!' exclaimed Witold with forced joviality. 'I'm glad you reminded me! Well then, let's drink to that again.'

He raised his glass with the remains of the white wine which he had brought over from the table, and said, 'Here's to you, Thyra!'

Bold as brass, I leaned towards him. I felt a fleeting brush of his lips on my cheek. And that was that.

Witold chatted for another quarter of an hour, talking about his sons and about school; by half past ten, he was gone, not without having once more heaped praise on the 'exquisite and delicious repast', but without arranging another date and without allowing me the slightest possibility of getting any closer to him. As for seduction – forget it!

4

The boss came into my room and perched with one cheek on my desk, something I could not abide. You would have thought that by the age of fifty-five, he might have learnt some manners. Even Dieskau was giving out warning signals in his soft baritone. But the boss merely laughed at this.

'You know, Frau Hirte, recently you've been getting younger and younger, it's really amazing!'

I waited, wondering what special jobs he had in mind for me.

'By the way, when is Frau Römer due to come out of hospital?' he inquired.

'The day after tomorrow. I'm picking her up at the station and taking her home. Naturally, she'll want her Dieskau back right away.'

'I don't think,' mused the boss, 'that Frau Römer will ever work again, but that she'll retire and take her pension. After such a big operation, she's bound to get a two-year pension from the company, and after that she'll have reached retirement age anyway. I don't think she'll be back here. I wanted to ask whether you might like to take over this office.'

I was delighted, since it was the most private and isolated room of them all, where one could be left in peace, with a nice outlook on to a chestnut tree.

'And besides, you should take some leave, while there's still a chance of catching up on a suntan somewhere,' he went on. He meant well, but I wasn't really in the mood for a holiday.

All the same, the boss was showing some concern for me.

That same evening, I received a phone call. It was Hartmut, my former boyfriend from my time in Berlin. He sounded rather embarrassed as he suggested that, since he was travelling through and we hadn't seen each other for almost a quarter of a century, he wondered whether I would like to go out for a meal. I was flabbergasted. It was all so sudden, and in any case I was exhausted. In the end, curiosity got the better of me, even though I had vowed never to see the man again. Hartmut apologized politely for the fact that he couldn't come and pick me up, but he didn't have his car here in the west.

An hour later, I was sitting, in my velvet skirt and heraldic blouse, in a high-class restaurant, sizing up my one-time beau. I would never have recognized him. Even in those earlier days, Hartmut hadn't been particularly good-looking – he suffered from acne – but he had been tall and slim and had a very evenly proportioned face. While he was indeed still tall, there was no longer the slightest suggestion of undernourishment about his figure. The regular features were gross, red, sweaty and unpleasant. My God, what if I had married him! I thought in disgust. All in all, it was lucky for me that I had been spared that and now had the chance of loving a man like Witold.

Hartmut was very much taken with the way I looked; after all, he had only known me when I was a grey little mouse. No, really, how pretty, elegant and young I looked! Even before the meal, he had put away two beers, and was sweating more than ever. I had to tell him the story of my life, so I treated him to a flattering abridged version of it.

By the time it was his turn, the meal arrived. Interspersed with vigorous chewing, chomping and gulping, his report was one of great business successes, considerable wealth, a villa in Dahlem and a sizeable legal practice with three partners. I asked after his family. The two elder children were grown up and had left home. Relatively late in life, his wife had had a third, handicapped, child. His eyes begged for sympathy, and I assured him of how sorry I was to hear that. At this, he knocked back a glass of wine. Then, finally, he blurted out

69

how unhappy his marriage was – his wife loved only this difficult child and no one else. She flatly refused to give it up, and so he was totally neglected.

I suppose I would have preferred to hear that his wife was constantly unfaithful to him, but this was just as good in my book.

'Ah, Rosie,' he sighed, and then, sweating and wheezing, 'for a long time after, I often thought of you. That wasn't nice, the way I behaved then, but I've been punished for it. Maybe we should be friends again.'

He disgusted me. I wanted to go home. Hartmut, well on his way to being drunk, held my hand in an iron grip. In the end, he begged me to stay the night with him in the hotel.

I got to my feet, snatched my hand away and said it was high time I went.

Back home, I wondered whether I might perhaps have made a similar impression on Witold to the one Hartmut had just made on me, for he had recently taken his leave just as quickly, politely and coldly as I had done now.

Anyway, Hartmut phoned the next evening from his Berlin office and, with the kind of chivalry that went out with the fifties, apologized for having 'rather made an exhibition of himself'. For him, that made everything hunky-dory again.

'Well, till we meet again,' he grated down the phone. Could there be a greater difference between two men's voices, or between Hartmut and Witold?

After that, I was in two minds whether to pour my heart out to Beate.

In my imagination I pleaded with her: 'Can't you see, I've never been so completely knocked out by any man as by Engstern. You've been through it all already, boyfriends when you were young, marriage at the right age, children. Now you have an interesting job, a lover and a wide circle of friends. I don't have, never have had, anything of that sort. Let me have him for myself, Beate, please! I've never begged you for anything before, nor have I ever asked any favours from anyone else. I don't find it easy to say this, but have some pity on an old maid who's in love for the first time!'

Wouldn't that be enough to melt a heart of stone, never mind the sentimental Beate?

On the other hand, if she were to plead with me for the same thing, I would never give way. So I decided it was better to keep my mouth shut. When it came to something like this, she was no longer my one and only friend, but my rival, who had to be fought off. But I couldn't shake off the need to talk to her.

Frau Römer was back, Dieskau was gone, and now I felt more stupid than ever, talking out loud to myself instead of to him.

One afternoon, I drove out unannounced to Beate's. Maybe it was a weakness in my make-up that I had never had the ability to share my needs and desires with others. Had I, in my youth, ever told the now nauseating Hartmut that I loved him, ever talked to him about a future together? I had left it all to him and mutely taken it for granted that everything would turn out right. And in my relationship with my boss in Berlin I had behaved in exactly the same way. Now my mind was filled with thousands of banal instances where, because of my own timidity, my own cowardice, I had had a raw deal. Now I wanted to do things differently and try at least to stand up to Beate.

Outside her house stood Witold's car. I didn't even stop, but drove straight back home in total despair.

Should I be like my boss's wife that time, and write an anonymous letter, to Jürgen, for instance: 'Beate is two-timing you'? But if it came down to it, Beate would drop Jürgen like a shot, if she hadn't already done so. And as for Jürgen, he already had a wife anyway, and was hardly in any position to lay claim to Beate's loyalty. So what means were left at my disposal for cutting Beate out of the equation? What kind of threats might she take seriously? She wasn't so easily intimidated. Any anonymous letters, and she'd take them straight to the police.

My impotent rage at Beate mounted inexorably. I could have throttled her on the spot. Strangle her? And why not indeed?

From that moment on, I could think of nothing else.

Beate, my one and only friend! I'll not hurt you, Beate, won't torture you. You'll die quickly, there'll be no dithering, no shilly-shallying. I won't make any long speeches, like in some murder film, before I pull the trigger. That's it, a shot to the head, unconscious right away, cerebral haemorrhage and it's all over. What a good thing that I hadn't disposed of the gun. But of course I would need to work out how, where, when. I had to make sure there was no way I could be connected with the deed. In this case, there were of course ties of friendship binding the victim and myself, and I would be sure to be questioned. My motive, however, and this was a great stroke of luck, was something no one could even guess at.

I had to arrange a meeting with Beate, at some place where there was nobody about; no one must know that I had met up with her, and no one must see me. It wouldn't be all that simple. Supposing I phoned her to make a date; it was odds on that Beate, in her usual talkative way, would tell someone about it, her colleagues at the education centre, her children, friends, neighbours, or even Witold himself. Still, I had the great advantage that she trusted me implicitly and I could lure her anywhere. Also in my favour was the fact that I knew a lot about her habits, her office hours and even the courses she was taking now that the summer holidays were over.

Maybe I wouldn't succeed at the first attempt; then I'd just have to keep on trying. The main thing was that Beate should suspect nothing.

After some sleepless nights, I had an idea. Almost every Saturday morning, Beate went shopping first and then to the indoor swimming pool, where she spent a good hour. She had even dragged me along there once or twice in the past, but I didn't much fancy starting off my weekends with reddened eyes and skin stinking of chlorine. So, I could try to waylay Beate by her car in the swimming pool car park and go off with her somewhere. But my first attempt failed; her car wasn't in the car park. I drove along her street and saw Witold's car there again. Right, I told myself, there's no room for sentiment, it's no more than she deserves. Anyway,

I could afford to wait, firstly for my opportunity, and secondly for Witold's love.

The following week, I struck it lucky. By now, too, my plan had matured. I had brought along a basket full of picnic things and was going to persuade Beate to come on an outing, just on impulse.

I waited in my car. From some way off, I could watch the entrance to the swimming pool. When, around eleven, Beate finally appeared, I slipped out quickly and stationed myself in front of her Polo.

'Hello there, Rosie,' exclaimed Beate, visibly surprised. 'What brings you to these insalubrious parts?'

'Oh, I saw your car here, and I just had this brilliant idea.'

Beate stowed away her bath robe and rolled-up towel on the back seat.

'Do tell,' she said brightly.

'Well, to tell the truth, the idea occurred to me at home. You know, without the dog, I'm not getting out any more, and I'm missing that somehow. What do you say to a little jaunt? We'll go for a walk and have a picnic together. I've got everything we need here in my basket.'

'Honestly, Rosie, recently you just keep on amazing me! It used to be me who was the spontaneous one, not you, but as I get older I'm getting more and more set in my ways. Right, get in, I'll have to think for a moment.'

We both sat in her car. Beate glanced at the clock.

'Let's go to my place first,' she suggested. 'I'd like to stow my shopping away in the fridge, hang up my bath robe and dry my hair.'

That was exactly what I didn't want. When we got there, Lessi or some other member of her brood would be sure to open the door to us, and besides, half the town could have seen me on the way there, sitting next to Beate in her car.

'No, listen,' I argued, 'it wouldn't really be worth the while then. I haven't actually all that much time. Your hair dries perfectly in the sun anyhow, and if your car's standing in the shade, your vegetables won't spoil in the space of two hours. Or have you some deep-freeze stuff as well?'

Beate shook her head. She hesitated, had another look at the time.

'All right, two hours, but no longer. You're right, the vegetables won't spoil, and the meat probably won't either. Where's your car?'

I said it wasn't far away, but we might as well go in hers, since, after all, we were already in it.

'Fine. Where to?' Beate started the engine.

'Well, what about up into the woods,' I suggested, 'it's such a marvellous day. Who knows how long this will last. Indian summer, just the right weather for people our age.'

'I know somewhere lovely – yes, that's where we'll go,' said Beate. I didn't want to waste time arguing, but if it was some favourite haunt for visitors, it would be the end of my plans for that day.

The swimming pool lay at the edge of town, so we didn't have to drive through main streets choked with shoppers. That was just as I had planned.

Beate did nod to one woman on the way, but she seemed to be no more than some vague acquaintance. She drove up into the hills, to a parking place in the forest.

'Is your basket heavy?' she asked. 'If it is, I could drive on a bit up the foresters' path, even though it's not strictly allowed. Then we wouldn't have to lug it so far.'

This was ideal.

'Well, yes,' I admitted, 'I've brought a flask of coffee and a bottle of champagne.' (It was the one I had bought for Witold.) 'It's a fair weight.'

Beate laughed. 'On this bumpy track, the bubbly will get a good shaking up, and it's bound to be warm by now, too. But it was such a nice thought, Rosie-Posy!'

She drove slowly up the slope, turned off on to a footpath to park the car out of sight under a bushy pine at the edge of a glade.

'Let's go!' she cried. 'That's twenty minutes gone already. You must be a mind-reader: I'm so hungry and thirsty after my swim. To tell the truth, I didn't have any breakfast this morning. I've absolutely got to shed a few pounds. But you

74

and your yummy picnic are leading me right into temptation.'

Beate pointed to a tall lookout tower.

'We really must go up there. I was here recently with Jürgen, and there's a magical view out over the Rhine Plain.'

Was that such a good idea? Now I had the gun in my big handbag, hidden in a zipped pocket, I was almost hoping it wouldn't work, that there would be strollers in sight or a forester's jeep in earshot.

The view from the tower was magnificent. In the blue haze, I could see Mannheim sparkling in the distance, while Ladenburg must be somewhere to the south-west. I scanned the closer surroundings for signs of human company, but found none. There had been two cars in the car park.

'Out with that bubbly!' Beate commanded.

I spread a red checked kitchen cloth out on the sun-warmed paving of the tower platform. The condemned woman's last meal, I thought.

Beate examined everything with eager curiosity.

'Grilled chicken bits and a baguette, ham and melon, grapes and cheese! Rosie, you're a genius!'

She made a highly efficient job of opening the lukewarm, violently fizzing champagne. Beate found this gaffe of mine amusing. She knocked back two glasses in short order and then helped herself to some slices of melon and a chicken leg. I pretended to eat, too, but the dry chicken breast almost stuck in my throat. The time had come for me to take out the gun behind Beate's back and shoot down in cold blood my pleasure-loving friend – my only friend. I just couldn't do it.

'What are you gawping around so solemnly for, Rosie? Come on, drink up!' Beate challenged me, filling up my glass. I hadn't brought paper cups, but proper crystal glasses and china plates.

Beate downed her third glass. She perched herself on the broad parapet.

'Come over here, Rosie,' she said. 'It's a shame to sit down there on the floor and not see anything of this wonderful view. Whenever I'm up here, I want to change into a swallow and swoop down, all light and elegant, on to the plain.' She let her legs dangle out over the edge.

'Come on!'

She had her rather broad back to me, her hair, still damp, was shining. Under her shrunk T-shirt, the line of her bra stood out clearly.

'Oh, Beate, I'd rather stand here, I get vertigo.'

'Hah! Vertigo – I don't know the meaning of the word! Even when I was a child, I loved nothing more than to play on a swing and to climb on roofs and walls. Watch this!'

Just like the child she once was, she stood up on the parapet in front of me and laughed at me so cockily, the way she no doubt drove her mother to distraction in those days.

One hefty shove with both hands against her tanned legs, and Beate fell, with a piercing, high-pitched scream and with a champagne glass in one hand and a chicken leg in the other, down the side of the tower.

I looked all around, couldn't see a soul, although I did hear a power-saw not too far off. There also seemed to be a dog hunting around nearby, but nobody called it to heel, so perhaps it was out poaching on its own. In the distance, the motorway, the cars tiny specks; no one could properly make out the tower from there, far less myself. I set off down the stairs, my knees trembling, with the result that my descent of the many narrow steps was a slow business.

Beate was dead all right, there was no need to try her pulse or her breathing. Her wide eyes stared in glassy, shocked incredulity into emptiness; to all appearances, her skull was fractured, her spine and all her limbs broken. I couldn't look at her for long, I felt sick, and, as at Witold's place that time, my one overpowering urge was to get away as fast as I could.

But the thing now was not to lose my nerve. The wineglass had exploded into a thousand fragments; I could never clear them up – that would take hours. But I most certainly did have to get my basket with the picnic things out of here. Why the hell had I left it at the top of the tower!

It was a struggle climbing back up there. And how was I to get home now, with no car and carrying all that stuff? I hadn't been able to work everything out in advance, not down to every last detail. I emptied the champagne bottle, there wasn't much left in it. Holding it in my handkerchief in my left hand, I polished any possible fingerprints off with the kitchen cloth and removed the supermarket price ticket. The bottle could stay here. The coffee, too, I poured away, the liquids would be immediately soaked up by the soil of the forest. I left Beate's handbag with her identity papers, her bunch of keys and her purse lying in one corner of the tower. But I had to take everything else with me. I repacked the basket, spreading the cloth over the top, then searched carefully for any other clues, but found nothing. After the long spell of dry weather, there would certainly be no footprints.

I had little time to lose. It was the middle of the day, shortly after twelve, when most ramblers would be having a break, or so I hoped. It was a long way back to my car on foot, or should I simply take Beate's? No, if it was found here later, it might all be regarded as a case of suicide or an accident. But if there were no car parked hereabouts, at least one other person was bound to have been involved.

I looked into Beate's car, but there was nothing of mine lying about. Fingerprints? Well, they could be there quite legitimately, after all I had often been in it with her.

I didn't dare take the broad foresters' road down, but instead I crept through the thickets and undergrowth, and in doing so once lost my direction completely. Whatever else, downhill was the right way. It was just as well I had kept under cover, for very soon after, a fair-sized group of ramblers from the Odenwald Association passed me. I lay on the ground like some trapper and watched as countless red stockings and knee breeches paraded past me.

Fortunately, I had sturdy shoes on, but I cursed the basket and would have quite happily dumped it somewhere, but of course that was out of the question. How long had it actually taken us to drive up here? Not all that long, it seemed, but on foot it was quite a drag. Soon I had to emerge on to the main road, and what a sight I was! Pine needles and cobwebs in my hair, dishevelled and scratched. I stopped for a break and carefully picked myself clean of moss, twigs, burrs and needles.

I didn't come straight out on to the main road, but cut along parallel to it, through fields of maize and allotments. Again and again, I came across gardeners making the most of the sunny autumn day to harvest their apples and dig over their little plot of ground. A large family of Turks sat having a meal under a walnut tree, and they gave me a cheery wave. Would all these people recognize me again? I had no alibi for the time the crime was committed; but then, on all the countless weekends I had spent alone, stuck in my flat, there were hardly any witnesses to testify I had been at home. Or maybe there were? My car, out in the street? How much notice did my neighbours take of whether it was there or not? It took me about two and a half hours to get back to the town where Beate lived, at least twenty people had seen me along the way, although there was no one among them who knew me. Still, if my photograph were to be published in the papers, they might just remember me.

At last I had reached my car, and by half past three I was home. I couldn't rest until I had thoroughly washed my glass, the two plates and the Thermos flask and put them and the basket away, hidden the gun and got rid of all the remains of the food. Then I went under the shower and filled the washing machine with the clothes I'd been wearing, carefully mixing them with other things I had had ready for the wash.

Once all that was done, I felt some slight relief.

At nine in the evening, the phone rang, as I had more or less expected. I let it ring a few times. It was Lessi.

'Have you any idea where my mother might be?'

I said no, and asked why.

'Well, you see, Rosie' – Lessi's voice had the same intonation as her mother's – 'I was supposed to meet Beate. We were going to go to Richard's in Darmstadt and then on to the theatre. But she's not here, and her car's missing, too. That all strikes me as a bit strange somehow, because she had put the theatre date in her diary. Me, I forget things like that sometimes, but she's not one to mess up an arrangement.'

I was in no position to calm Lessi's fears, and could only assure her I had no idea where Beate was and that it would all sort itself out. That day, no one else phoned.

During the night, I was ill. I was running a temperature, was vomiting and had diarrhoea; I could neither sleep nor keep down the tranquillizers or the camomile tea I took them with. I roamed about between my bed and the toilet and the kitchen, simultaneously shivering with cold and sweating, and I knew full well that my whole system was about to buckle under the emotional strain.

On the Sunday, things were no better. I tried to tell myself I had a right to love and happiness and so just had to do what I had done. But that theory struck me as highly suspect. Beate! I mourned for Beate, I wept and longed for my one and only good friend; I could see her lying broken on the stony ground in the forest. I had done something I could never undo. In the case of Hilke Engstern, I had felt hardly the slightest pang of conscience, but I was almost going mad over Beate.

In addition, I was terribly afraid. At that moment, I was completely incapable of pulling myself together; if anyone was to call, someone who had even the slightest suspicion, my behaviour would immediately give them all the proof they needed.

On the Monday morning I was still no better; I phoned the office and told them I was ill. Gastroenteritis, I said. I was wished a quick recovery and told on no account to be up and about again too soon, and not to be in a hurry to get back to work; knowing my single-minded devotion to duty they felt they could not emphasize that too strongly.

Would it be right to ring Beate's number, just to ask casually after her? For one thing, that would show that I had fully expected her to be there, for another, it would let me know whether she had been discovered and whether inquiries had been set in motion. But I was incapable of phoning, of speaking, of crying, all I could do was go on letting my teeth chatter in between bouts of vomiting.

My office clothes are always tip-top. Even all the other

outfits that I wear outside my own four walls are neat and well looked after. But when I'm lying in my lonely bed, I don't need to give a thought to what anyone thinks. My nightdresses are, I admit, old, shabby and just plain comfortable, which, for me, means there is no reason to throw them in the Red Cross bag. Once, when I had to go on a health cure, I bought two new sets of pyjamas, which had lain in the cupboard ever since, waiting for a suitable occasion. It could be that I'd have to go into hospital some time, and then I'd fall back on them.

On that Monday, then, late in the afternoon, I slouched around, sick and feeble, on the sofa in my oldest floral nightdress with the brownish singe-marks from the iron, riffling through the television magazine. I kept reading the same bit, without taking in a single word. The doorbell was ringing!

Don't open it! was my first reaction. And then: not a soul on this earth must set eyes on me in the hideous state I'm in at the moment! But then it struck me that I had officially reported sick; it was just possible that the boss had picked up the urgent file on my desk, pushed it into the hands of a colleague and wanted answers to vital questions on it. But would she not have phoned first? Or was it the boss himself? Out of the question. After all, I was never absent – there was no cause for him either to check up on me on the first day I was off, nor to bring me flowers. So it must be the police.

I pulled on a mangy dressing gown and, with my forehead bathed in cold sweat and a foul smell on my breath, shuffled to the door. I pressed the button and opened it. There stood Witold before me – the front door had been unlocked downstairs.

'My God, Thyra, you look awful!' he exclaimed. 'I phoned your office and heard you were ill. Please forgive me for bursting in on you like this, especially when you're obviously in a bad way.'

I gestured towards the living-room and had a feeling that his visit bode nothing but ill.

He came in and glanced quickly round the room. 'Thyra,

sit down, you look feverish. Shall I go and make you some tea?'

How wonderful it would have been if I had somehow known he would come. Then I could have slipped into some lascivious silk pyjamas reminiscent of those old Greta Garbo films, would have had a bath and washed my sticky hair and spent at least ten minutes cleaning my teeth.

I slumped on to the sofa and looked at him through my bloodshot eyes. Witold remained solicitous.

'No doubt you're surprised at me just dropping in unannounced like this. I'm afraid I've some very sad news, something I didn't want to tell you over the phone.'

'What is it?' I tried to squeeze the words out, but they were probably completely inaudible.

'Your friend Beate has had an accident,' he said, in his best bedside manner.

I went even paler, was unable to utter a word, and I would have happily fainted, but, in spite of the blackness in front of my eyes, I just couldn't manage it.

Witold knelt by the sofa, felt my pulse, hurried into the bathroom and fetched a facecloth soaked in ice-cold water, which he mercilessly allowed to drip on to my brow. Just don't let me open my mouth, I thought, I was sick only a few moments ago.

'What an idiot I am,' Witold scolded himself. 'I shouldn't have told you when you're running such a temperature.' He rushed into the kitchen and brought a glass of water.

I sipped at it and hoped that he would back off a couple of yards, which he eventually did once some colour had returned to my cheeks.

No doubt he was waiting for me to start asking questions.

'Is she dead?' I breathed.

Witold nodded.

'Car accident?'

He shook his head. 'I'll tell you about it another time,' he said evasively.

'No, I want to hear everything now,' I said. After all, that was the way you were supposed to react.

81

'On Saturday, Lessi phoned me to ask if I knew where her mother was. She must have called you too, because she went right through Beate's address book. Then, on Sunday, all the children were at home as usual, and they wondered whether they should contact the police. In the event, that proved unnecessary, because detectives came to them with the terrible news. Beate had been found in the woods; she had fallen from a lookout tower.'

'How did it happen?'

Witold reached for a cigarette, caught the sickly look on my face and put it away again. He hesitated.

'They can't reconstruct the incident exactly. Beate had apparently been shopping on Saturday morning, and then she went swimming. In her car, which was parked near the tower, they found her bathing things and her weekend shopping. But why she had driven out there remains a mystery. An empty champagne bottle and some splinters from a glass were lying around, but these could have belonged to other people. The question now is whether Beate had arranged to meet somebody at the place or had already met them. I wanted to ask you, Thyra, did Beate suffer from bouts of depression?'

Anyone who knew Beate was well aware that that was just not true. I thought for a moment.

'Not that I know of,' I replied. 'But the menopause gives any woman a hard time.' Right away, I could have kicked myself for those last words, since Witold knew that Beate and I were the same age.

'The police are trying to find out at the moment whether perhaps Beate had heard some kind of bad news from somebody that day. The first person they're checking out is her boyfriend. Oh, I find this whole thing so awful, because it brings back memories of Hilke's death.'

I looked hard at Witold. Was he really distressed about Hilke's and Beate's deaths, or was he just sorry for himself? The business about Beate didn't seem to have affected him all that deeply, otherwise he would probably have taken refuge in isolation again, instead of coming here to break the news so sensationally to me.

'Is there anything else I can do for you?' he inquired. 'Do some shopping, make you some tea, play the Samaritan, bring you comfort?'

I took him at his word, although I knew he wasn't expecting me to.

'I haven't a drop of fruit juice left in the house, and with gastric flu you're supposed to drink a lot of liquid. Could you perhaps bring me a few bottles tomorrow?'

Witold abruptly backed down a little.

'With an illness like that, fruit juice isn't the right thing at all, you should drink lots of tea instead.'

With a sigh, I told him that tea actually made me want to throw up. From past experience I knew that cola was a good thing against vomiting.

Now he was smiling at me. It was enough to melt my heart.

'All right, then, I'll bring you juice and cola tomorrow. But I must go now, I want to give Beate's children some support. No, no, don't get up!' With a hand on my shoulder, he gently pushed me back into my pillows and left.

All of a sudden, I felt better, the terrible imaginings receded, and a picture of hope began to emerge: tomorrow he'll come back and smile at me again. It will all turn out right yet, I just have to remain strong and see it through.

After two sleepless nights, I dropped off into a long, exhausted slumber.

5

I awoke at eleven, and forced down large quantities of tea – which did me good – and a slice of toast. I would have to eat a little and often that day in order not to give off the sour smell that comes straight from an empty stomach. Then I had a bath, washed my hair and blow-dried it. Witold wouldn't be coming in the morning, since he had to be in school. But as to whether he would arrive immediately after lunch or not until later, I could only guess. From two in the afternoon, I was waiting, in my silken pyjamas; I put away my tea-cup, fetched it out again, cleaned my teeth once more. By six, I was extremely edgy. Then, at last, Witold phoned; he's going to cop out, I thought.

'Well now, Rosemarie Luise Thyra, a bit better today?' he asked.

'Not a lot,' I whispered.

'In that case, I'll look in briefly. I've been up to my ears all day, so it could be a little while yet.'

Again, I rushed to the mirror. Rosemarie, I decided, you're too thin. Men like bosoms, and where's yours?

All the same, I didn't look as repulsive as yesterday, so maybe I stood a chance of being looked on favourably.

At last, at eight, he arrived. While he was still coming up the stairs, he called out with forced heartiness, 'Meals on wheels!', and the fact that I was no longer a picture of utter misery didn't even seem to register. He carried a plastic bag into the kitchen and unpacked apple juice, cola and biscuits.

'And something for the soul in torment,' he said, digging a cassette tape out of his jacket pocket, 'some incredibly beautiful sad music. Brahms songs. When I was at such a low ebb, I played them all the time. My personal therapy is something like this: shed tears over a stranger's troubles when you're hardened by your own sorrows.'

I thanked him. I had already shed more than enough tears over my own misfortunes. That kind of music would very probably not appeal to me in the slightest, but Witold wasn't to know that, was he?

'Come on,' he said, 'don't hang around in the kitchen, lie down on the sofa. I'll stay with you for a few minutes.'

In my silk nightwear, I tried to assume as decorative a pose as possible, a bit like Tischbein's painting of Goethe in the Campagna.

'I looked awful yesterday, you must have been disgusted by the sight of me,' I murmured.

'Don't worry yourself, that's how everybody looks when they're in a bad way.' Witold really did seem to pay precious little attention to my appearance.

'You know, it's a bad blow for me too that Beate's dead,' he remarked out of the blue.

Did I have to listen to this? Yes, I did.

'Thyra, you're a dear soul. I have something to confess: I've fallen in love.'

I did my best to keep my composure. After all, I had more or less guessed it. But what was I supposed to say?

'I loved Beate, too,' I said quietly, and that was no lie.

'Oh yes, she was marvellous, that's true,' said Witold. 'That wonderful daughter had a wonderful mother.'

He had lost me. 'Who, Lessi?'

'Of course not! Lessi might be a nice enough girl, but I could never have fallen for her. No, it's Vivian I'm talking about!'

I gaped wide-eyed at him.

Witold laughed. 'Yes, Thyra, that's the way it is. I'm in love with Vivian. It was through you I got to know Beate, and then, at her place, her enchanting daughter.'

I stammered, 'But – but Vivian's still little more than a child!'

'Oh, come on, now.' Witold felt under attack and reacted

touchily. 'She's a fine-looking young woman of twenty-six, and, as for maturity, she's a match for many a woman of my age.'

I could no longer hold back the tears. Beate, I've killed you, and all for nothing.

Witold was looking at me in some consternation. 'Of course,' he said, 'here you are, completely worn out, and here am I, wittering on about being in love. I'm sure it must strike you as very bad taste for me to feel this way so soon after Hilke's death. And that's why I really didn't want anybody to find out about it, but you already know more about me than any of my friends, and so I wanted to let you in on it.'

Through my sobs, I asked, 'Did Beate know about this?'

'At first, Vivian didn't want to tell her, since she feared her mother wouldn't approve because I suppose I am just those few years older. Beate never was one for quizzing her children, but maybe she had guessed something was up, because whenever she was home on a visit, Vivian would borrow her mother's car to come and see me. Well, anyway, Vivian had told her mother everything just the day before the accident.'

It was horrible. But in the middle of all my blubbering, I was hit by a brilliant idea.

'Oh, Witold, didn't you realize that Beate was in love with you herself?'

At that, his jaw dropped.

'No, I can't believe that – never! Did she say anything to you?'

'Yes, she confided in me. She apparently thought that your visits were on her account.'

Witold gaped at me. His mind was working overtime.

'It must have hurt Beate deeply,' I pursued my line of thought relentlessly, 'when Vivian told her of your relationship.'

'Oh, my God!' Witold was horrified. 'You surely don't mean that Beate did away with herself because of me?'

I said nothing, merely shrugged. Witold was a real Narcissus, and had no trouble in believing that somebody could jump off a tower out of unrequited love for him.

'Thyra, I beg you,' he said, all worked-up and grabbing my hand, 'you must never, so long as you live, tell Vivian that! She is an extremely sensitive person, and she would feel responsible for her mother's death!'

'No, of course I won't say anything to her. But if the police question me, I can't keep it from them, can I? After all, it is a conceivable motive.'

Witold stared at my blue carpet, deep in thought.

'And to think I didn't even notice! And yet – when I think back, I can see I must have been blind! Of course, now I remember certain situations when she looked at me so strangely. Oh, what insensitive creatures we men can be!'

The phone rang. It was Vivian.

'Hello, Rosie,' she said, in her slightly arrogant way, 'if Rainer's still with you, I'd like a word with him.'

I passed the receiver to Witold. After the odd 'yes' and 'no', he finally said, 'Right then, tomorrow. Take care, and good night.'

He seemed to feel he owed me an explanation for the call. He had actually been intending to go over to see her, but there had been so many relatives there the whole time, Beate's father, her two sisters and two brothers. Then he had been going to take Vivian out in the evening for a bit of fresh air. But now the architect, Beate's ex-husband, was there; all three children were to sit down with him and compose the obituary notice.

'So, I can stay here a few minutes longer,' Witold concluded. 'By the way, before I forget, the funeral will be on Friday. You should be up and about again by then.' I would have preferred to be ill for longer, but, whether I liked it or not, I would have to attend the funeral.

All of a sudden, Witold inquired, 'Where were you on Saturday, anyway?'

I had worked out my answer long ago, although I hadn't expected him to put the question, but the police.

'Oh, that was when this stupid illness hit me. Early that morning I was already feeling poorly, so I struggled out to buy a few things to eat, but then I went straight back to bed. Why do you ask?'

'Oh, it doesn't matter. It just occurred to me how strange it is that two women have died in a relatively short space of time and we're somehow mixed up in both cases, you and I. It's amazing, the tricks coincidence can play.'

I nodded and lay back wearily. Witold took that as a sign for him to be going so that I could get some rest.

'I'll phone you tomorrow,' he promised, not without a certain warmth, and took his leave.

Before he came along, before I met him, I was always on top of the world. I pictured how our meetings would be, two spirits in perfect harmony, full of love and erotic tension. And then, when they were over, only disappointment and doubt remained. Was he really so special, anyway? Did I really want him so ardently for my lover?

It was a good thing that I hadn't used the gun. They wouldn't have taken long to work out that it was the same weapon as the one Hilke Engstern had been shot with. Witold would certainly have been able to put two and two together, for I had been the last to have it in my possession. On no account must I ever use it, I had to get rid of it at once. I sat brooding: still, if I were ever to be unmasked as a double murderess, then at least I'd have the chance to shoot myself.

These apocalyptic thoughts made me so miserable it did me good! Witold was in love with Vivian, and I had killed my best friend. What was the sense of it all? Softly, I told myself, 'Rosie, you might as well shoot yourself right now.'

At that, my eye fell on Witold's cassette of the Brahms songs. What had he said? 'For the sick at heart', or something like that. I put the tape in the player. Maybe there was even a hidden message in the music. Maybe they weren't even Brahms songs at all, but Witold had recorded his own voice – a message of love for me.

Then I heard the song of the maiden who went out to bind her own wedding garland of roses. No question of that where I was concerned!

'O'er the meadow wandered she,
No roses found, but rosemarie.'

Or was this in fact some secret message after all, for Rose-marie – that was me! Then came the ending:

'Into the garden then went she,
No roses plucked, but rosemarie.
"Take thou this, my true love, let it
Lie with you, 'neath the linden, my
Own wreath for my grave!"'

I turned the music off and cried my heart out. Witold, I'm no rose, I'm only rosemary, nor will I ever carry a garland of roses to the altar, but a wreath to the grave.

At some point during the night, I left the sofa, took off the silk pyjamas and pulled on the wretched floral thing, and took to my bed. The next morning, I went to the doctor and got a sick-note for the whole week. When I got back, a policeman was standing at my door, on the point of leaving. He wanted to know my name, and was relieved not to have to come back a second time. Horrified, I remembered the revolver in the suitcase.

On the way upstairs, he told me he had tried phoning me, first at home, then at the office, where he had heard that I was off ill and he would probably find me at my flat. I held out my sick-note from the doctor. He smiled: 'That's all right. Obviously, when you're ill, you have to go to the doctor's. Anyway, it'll only take five minutes, then I'll be on my way again.'

He was friendly, young, and, I reckoned, no high-ranker, this was no five-man homicide squad.

The policeman began, 'You are a friend of Frau Sperber, and we have to investigate the cause of her death. We consider the suicide angle to be extremely unlikely, but all the same we're asking her friends whether she ever expressed any thoughts in that direction.'

'And what do her other friends say?' I asked.

'They're all in complete agreement, they can't imagine it

for a moment, and she never showed any signs of depression.'

'No, I can't really believe it, either. All the same, I did hear that, on the previous day, Beate had had a talk with her daughter. Vivian told her she had become friendly with a man twice her age.'

'Yes, we already know that. Her daughter has told us herself. But her mother took it very calmly.'

I hummed and hawed a bit. 'You must promise me that you will treat anything else I have to say about that with complete confidence. So, not a word to the children, not on any account; I owe it to my friend.'

The young man looked at me with some curiosity. 'As far as possible, we'll keep your information confidential.'

'Beate told me recently that she herself had fallen in love with the same man.'

While the policeman found this interesting enough, he nevertheless suggested, 'In the case of a level-headed woman like your friend, that would hardly amount to grounds for suicide. And how are we to account for the fact that, on that Saturday, a mother of three children behaves perfectly normally, goes shopping, then swimming, and then suddenly climbs up a remote tower in the forest with the intention of throwing herself off it?'

I had to admit that was very puzzling.

'No, this was definitely no suicide,' he assured me. 'In any case, the postmortem has shown that, beforehand, she had been drinking alcohol – probably a sparkling wine – and had had something to eat as well. In fact, it looks as if she had had a rendezvous with a man – a champagne breakfast, that sort of thing.'

'Her boyfriend is always at home with his family in Munich at the weekends,' I objected.

'Yes, we know that. But he has no alibi, only his wife's statement. It's still possible that he met Frau Sperber at the tower and gave her some piece of very bad news – for instance, that it was all over between them. But again, everybody says that her attachment to this man wasn't a deep one and she would scarcely have been very hurt if he had wanted to drop her. And now, if you say that Frau Sperber was in love with her daughter's friend, that would confirm the theory.'

'And supposing she had been the one to suggest to her friend Jürgen that they should stop seeing each other?' I threw in a new version.

'Could be, but it would hardly be a reason for throwing her to her death. But as I said, we're investigating this Herr Jürgen Faltermann; we'd like to have rather more concrete support for his alibi. Has anything else occurred to you, maybe, that we haven't dealt with?'

I said no, and asked whether they would end up treating it as accidental death.

'To be honest,' the policeman said, 'I myself don't see it that way. What kind of person drives out into the woods, all on their own, and drinks champagne up a tower? People just don't do that sort of thing. I believe there was someone else with her, and they're not coming forward. If that individual had a clear conscience, they would get in touch with us. So whether it was murder, suicide or an accident is something we can't decide for the moment. But since you ask me for a straight answer, I'd put my money on murder.' And, so saying, he shook hands, put away his notes and took his leave.

Hardly had I changed out of my outdoor clothes and, as a precaution, not into any old rags but slacks and a sweater, when the doorbell rang. Witold? No, it was Frau Römer and Dieskau, who greeted me with great exuberance. Frau Römer was out of breath after climbing the stairs, but proud of the fact that she, the invalid, was able to visit me, who was even more sick. If I hadn't been feeling so rotten, I would have been pleased at this.

Frau Römer had also heard about my illness via the office and now she brought me a bunch of roses and a detective novel (how ironic, I thought) and best wishes from the boss, to whom she had spoken. She told me at length about her plans: some time in the near future, she was going off to see her daughter in America. I heard the whole story of her convalescence, about the women she had shared a room with in hospital, and all sorts of similar news. I found it difficult to concentrate.

'It's a long time since I felt as well as this,' pronounced Frau Römer, dicky heart, amputated breast and all. 'I feel pretty good, all things considered, I have time to myself and will probably never need to go back to the office again. I'm sure I still have a few good years ahead of me.'

I found this outlook, coming as it did after her being ill with cancer, astonishing. 'Frau Römer,' I said tearfully, 'you've had to put up with all sorts of things in your life, and yet you're still an optimist. I just don't know how you do it.'

She looked at me intently. 'Serious illness also gives you new momentum, in fact, so does any great difficulty that you overcome! Listen, Frau Hirte, the important thing is – never give up!' Almost pleadingly, she took my hand, as if she knew what was going on inside me.

'Yes, I mustn't give up,' I said out loud to myself once I was on my own again. All is not lost. First of all, they're not on my trail, there's still not the slightest ground for suspicion against me, far less a scrap of proof. Secondly, Witold may well be in love with Vivian just now, but will that last long?

Vivian! I first got to know her when she was eight years old. During puberty, she had been an extremely difficult child. She had taken the divorce very badly. She had idolized her father, and she sometimes took it out on Beate because he was no longer around. For a while, she dressed only in the kind of rags you wouldn't even have given to charity. She used to go about in a threadbare plush coat, looking like some teddy bear on the moult. Beate put up with that with good grace – me, I would have blown my top. Then she started smoking hash and drinking, and, when she was only sixteen, sometimes stayed out all night. A fine wife Witold had landed himself with there! But I had to admit that, nowadays, Vivian's appearance was quite striking. Hair of the deepest black, a clear skin and big eyes, although she daubed them lavishly with mascara. With flagrant disregard for good taste, she had, over the intervening period, remodelled the rags of her adolescence, so that now she could be taken for some

Juliette Greco clone. Vivian was far from finished with her studies, still attending, or at least making a pretence of attending, the College of Art in Frankfurt. On Sundays, she usually took the train to Darmstadt, to her brother Richard, and the two of them would then turn up at Beate's in his clapped-out scrapheap of a car. Lessi, studying in Heidelberg, on the other hand, was constantly at home, guaranteeing a perpetual state of disorder. I had never taken any particular interest in my friend's children, but whether I liked it or not, every time we met, I had to listen to Beate prattling on about her little darlings.

How could a man of Witold's standards fall in love with a gypsy like Vivian? As far as my information went, Vivian had, in the course of ten sexually active years, managed to get through countless lovers. Even the easy-going Beate was not prepared to see yet another unknown face at table at every family Sunday lunch, and had laid down that Vivian's latest had to be one and the same for at least three months before being dragged along. This demand had prompted her daughter to turn up only on the rarest of occasions for two whole years. But she seemed to have grown out of such extravagant behaviour, and the relationship between mother and daughter had settled down recently into something little short of affectionate.

At last, Witold did in fact phone. He seemed almost to be developing some kind of friendly feelings towards me, even if they still fell far short of love. After he had solicitously inquired after my well being, I told him that I had had a visit from a police officer. He wanted to hear every last detail, but I did keep from him the fact that the policeman believed it to have been murder.

'You know, Thyra,' Witold said, 'I've come round to thinking, too, that Beate was keen on me. But I really can't begin to imagine that she would go shopping and swimming first, and then take her own life. And besides, she would have left a note for the children. I can't imagine it being an impulsive action, where someone has gone to the trouble of buying

93

meat and cabbage and pasta beforehand. There was a carefully thought-out shopping list in her purse.

'But something else occurred to me: that time, when I got to know Beate at the wine festival, I went up on the swing-boats with her. She made a big thing out of never suffering from vertigo. It could well be that she overestimated her head for heights, prancing about on the parapet at the edge of the outlook tower, but she had just been drinking champagne and maybe lost her balance. What do you think?'

'Yes, that could well be it,' I assured him. As far as the prancing about was concerned, he was close to the truth. 'Beate always did grab every chance for limbering up and climbing on things, but let's face it, she wasn't seventeen any more.'

'Exactly,' Witold agreed. 'She was no spring chicken. She should have accepted the fact that she was getting older and stopped cavorting about like that.'

You just had to go and say that, I thought. I was peeved. After all, I was the same age as Beate, and he wasn't exactly miles behind, either.

Down the phone, I could hear him drawing on his cigarette.

'Thyra,' he started off again, 'could you picture that Jürgen Faltermann pushing her off? Beate's children don't think much of him and, if anything, they tended to avoid him.'

'I don't really know Herr Faltermann all that well,' I said, cautiously. 'I can't say I'd believe him capable of anything like that, but who knows what goes on in someone's mind . . .'

'Would you think me capable of murder?' asked Witold. 'Well, no, let's drop that one, shall we?'

I thought his telephone might still be tapped, and I was not at all keen on attention being attracted to me.

'Where are you phoning from?' I asked anxiously.

Witold was laughing now. 'My accomplice is a scaredy-cat. I'm not phoning from home, obviously. Well then, I'll see you at the funeral. 'Bye, Thyra.'

In the days that followed, I sometimes wondered whether I should now do away with Vivian. But I rejected the idea. For one thing, I never wanted to murder anyone else again, because I simply didn't have the nerve for it. For another, I promised the spirit of my dead friend, with which I had so often talked far into the night, never to lay a finger on her children. And how on earth would I go about it? I couldn't use the gun again. Vivian and I kept each other politely at arm's length (to be more precise, we disliked each other), so I could never have lured her anywhere.

Witold loved her, and she loved him, or so he claimed. But that was pure illusion. Vivian was fickle, and sooner or later she would have someone else and Witold would get hurt. And then who could comfort him better than I? After all, I knew a lot about him – he had admitted that himself – and he didn't want to say a word about this new affair to any of his friends yet.

So there were no grounds for despair. No one suspected me, and I had moved a fair bit closer to the object of all my endeavours.

6

The letter announcing Beate's death arrived. Her father and her children, brothers, sisters and friends mourned her passing; her ex-husband was not included in the list, even though he had in fact composed the announcement.

For the funeral, I ordered a small wreath of blue flowers (Beate's favourite colour): delphiniums, aconites, cornflowers, irises and a few blue-tinged marguerites. It looked like a wedding bouquet, I thought, rather than a funeral wreath.

As for myself, restraint was the keynote of my turnout; black it had to be, of course, lipstick and rouge I eschewed. My self-confidence had taken a knock; apprehensively and timidly, I tried to arrive at the cemetery neither too early nor too late.

The funeral was an enormous affair, something I had not expected. The cars were parked along both sides of the street, because there was not enough room for them in the car park.

On the way to the main gate, someone behind me called out my name. 'Hey, Rosie, hang on a minute!'

I am on first-name terms with very few people; in the office in Mannheim with no one at all, even if they do think I'm a bit odd because of it. But I have always determinedly resisted the use of first-names at the workplace. I have no relatives, and few friends with whom I am on such familiar terms. Beate, yes, I had known her since childhood, and even her children called me 'Rosie', but not her former husband, and then recently again, there was Hartmut from Berlin – I could hardly avoid it with him, whether I wanted to or not; Witold

– thank heavens! – and, more or less by chance, his friend, Dr Schröder, too. Other than those, no one, I thought. But from the black stream of mourners, a fleetingly familiar figure detached itself, repeating my name – Beate's last boyfriend, Jürgen Faltermann. As a matter of fact, on the one and only occasion we met, he had quite simply forced first-name familiarity upon me. I had thought at the time I would probably hardly ever see him again, and anyway, I didn't want to seem too prudish. And now he was standing next to me.

'Rosie, I've been meaning to phone you for days, but I'm afraid I had forgotten your surname.'

He was a good deal too familiar for my liking.

'Hirte,' I said with a weary coolness.

'Yes, right, that's it! Hirte. Anyway, it doesn't matter now. Can you spare a few minutes afterwards? I have to talk to you, it's important.'

'If you must,' I said rather rudely, but he merely answered, 'Right then, wait here at the main entrance.'

We all squeezed into the little chapel, and I found myself a seat in the background, while Jürgen settled himself in the middle.

Beate had left the church some time ago, along with her husband, I recalled. I wondered whether a minister would conduct the service in spite of that.

At the front sat Beate's father, an old and broken man, and next to him, Lessi. He was holding her hand. Then followed Richard, Vivian and Beate's brothers and sisters with their families, in the rows behind them sat more distant relatives, as well as Beate's former husband and an enormous gathering of friends and acquaintances, among whom I also spotted Witold. Next to him sat, by sheer coincidence – I recognized her from a photograph – the new Frau Sperber, Beate's successor, with her daughter, a half-sister of Beate's children.

The address was given by Beate's brother-in-law, a professor from Hamburg. He spoke ably and intelligently, outlining the story of her life and praising her qualities. But his cold and rather businesslike speech triggered off no emotions among his audience; they coughed, shuffled, occasionally blew their noses, whispered.

When he had finished, there was a brief pause. Then there was a noise at the door and a score of middle-aged men, all dressed alike, walked in. The aged father, who had been a lifelong member of a male-voice choir, had asked these fine upstanding gentlemen to come along. Apparently, a funeral service minus preacher and prayers had seemed to him too cold an affair, and now he had seen to it that exactly the right sort of atmosphere prevailed. The elderly songsters put their left hands behind their backs and one foot forward and sang, by heart, 'I Pray to the Power of Love', moving abruptly from forte to pianissimo and effortlessly back again. Although, as I have already stressed, I have little idea of music, I could recognize from the very first notes that what we had here was pure kitsch. Where the orator had failed, the singers succeeded at a stroke: the most unholy sobbing broke out, young and old alike could control themselves no longer, and the whole gathering finally united in a communion of lamentation. The artistes, who had anticipated this success, pulled out all the stops and made sure that the tearful flood did not dry up too soon.

I felt a surge of pride: I, and these troubadours of mourning, had managed to unite so many different people in one great emotion. But for me, this unforgettable ceremony would never have taken place.

My elation lasted until I met Jürgen Faltermann. I couldn't stand the man, which was not unconnected with him so brazenly addressing me as 'Rosie'.

'Let's go for a drink,' he said without further ado. 'I don't fancy being goggled at by the whole clan.' He sweats like Hartmut, I thought in disgust.

We sat in some cheap caff, a real Greasy Spoon, that reeked of frying fat. Jürgen ordered a beer, I had a mineral water; he ate a schnitzel with salad, I had a vol-au-vent.

Jürgen poured the beer down his throat. He took off his jacket and sat facing me in a musty-smelling black polo-necked pullover in some synthetic material.

'Let's get straight to the point,' he began, keeping an eagle eye on the door. But no other funeral guests seemed tempted to stray into this place. I looked at him questioningly.

'The filth haven't stopped pestering me with questions. And in fact, on the weekend it happened, I was being a good boy at home with the missus and the kids in Munich. I've a receipt from a motorway filling-station, dated the Sunday evening, but much good that's doing me. I can't prove that I left here as early as Friday afternoon. Not a solitary soul saw me in Munich on the Saturday, other than my wife. Young children don't count anyway. The car was in the garage all the time. The weather was fine, sure, but, like an idiot, all I did on Saturday was squat in the house doing my accounts.'

He snatched the plastic flower from the little vase on the table and dismembered it.

I was just about to ask what all this had to do with me, when the accusations came tumbling out: 'It must have been you that talked all that nonsense to the cops about Beate being in love with Vivian's bloke, that snooty teacher. How could you even think of putting about such a lie?'

I reddened and assured him it was no lie, nor had I 'put it about', but had mentioned it to no one but the police, who, for their part, had promised total confidentiality.

Jürgen ordered another beer.

'The police – confidentiality? Don't make me laugh! That's really the biggest load of rubbish I've ever heard. OK, Beate and I weren't some romantic loving couple, but we got on fine and were straight with each other. Of course, somebody like you' – what did he mean by that? – 'couldn't begin to understand.'

I felt insulted. Cuttingly, I informed him I would not be spoken to like that. I had known Beate since our schooldays and she had been a good friend for a long time.

'Friend – that's a good one,' sneered Jürgen. 'You don't go spreading untruths about a friend. Anyway, she didn't trust you, otherwise she'd have told you what she said to me long ago.'

'Which was?' I demanded, my heart pounding.

'Beate had known for ages that Vivian was going with the teacher, she wasn't dumb! It was obvious that Vivian had a new boyfriend here and not in Frankfurt, because all of a sudden she started coming to see her much more often and then she would borrow Beate's car and stay out half the night. And on top of that, once he had got to know Vivian, this joker – I can't remember his name for the moment – started dropping in regularly, for no reason at all and as if by chance, and every time he did, Vivian just happened to be there too. Mothers are nosey! Naturally, Beate took a peek out of the window whenever Vivian was being picked up and, for a change, didn't need the car. That was when she saw the teacher waiting at the corner of the street.'

I was having difficulty breathing. 'All right, so she knew about it,' I said. 'But why shouldn't it be true that she herself was still in love with him?'

'Good God, you're slow on the uptake! She had no time for half-baked wets. We talked about him often enough. But on the other hand she reckoned his friendship for Vivian was no bad thing either. She said something like, ''Most teachers have a bit of the paedophile about them, and Vivian has a father fixation, so they've got something solid to work on.'' You don't talk like that if you're keen on the man yourself.'

'It could have been a cover-up, though,' I objected, 'so that you wouldn't notice.'

Jürgen stared at me, shaking his head.

'Just what kind of a world do you old biddies live in?' he bawled, so loudly that other customers looked round and eyed me with interest.

'Sorry, Rosie, it wasn't meant personally.' (How else, then? I wondered.) 'But you obviously can't get it into your head that Beate and I were getting along fine without all that crap about ''relationships''.'

I made to leave, but he held on to me, sweating and full of beer, just like Harmut so recently. An ice-cold rage welled up in me.

'Herr Faltermann, let go of me! I have just been to the

funeral of my best friend, and I'm not in the mood for listening to such insults from you.'

'Aha, so now, all of a sudden, I'm Herr Faltermann. The fine lady no longer wishes to be on first-name terms with a commercial traveller. Beate was a different kind of person from you altogether, she wasn't one to be stuck-up and prejudiced. And as for that namby-pamby character, she was never in love with him in her life' – here, he thought for a moment – 'now that's something I'd sooner expect from you.'

I felt my face flushing fiery-red, and he could see it.

'Come on, no hard feelings, Rosie. I didn't mean to insult a lady. I just lost my head because the cops are getting on my wick. And it seems I have you to thank for that. They think I had arranged to meet Beate for a champagne breakfast, and when she gave me the news that she was in love with somebody else, I bumped her off. You see, they also know that I had been up that tower with Beate once before; I bet you told them that, too.'

'Can I go now?' I asked. I was feeling really quite ill again; I was probably having a relapse.

'In a minute,' said Jürgen. 'Don't get so uptight, I'm a straight sort of bloke and I speak my mind. A woman of your age, with no man and no children, probably fantasizes about other people's love-life. So just don't stick your nose in things that don't concern you. Beate would never have done herself in because she was unlucky in love, and no more would I have done anything to her if she had given me the brush-off. Is that clear, once and for all?'

I nodded, and at last he let go of me. I paid at the bar and was out of there like a shot.

Looking back on it, I thought – too late – of quite a few things that I could have said to him. When he started up with old maids' fantasies, I could have come back with the fact that Beate had been quite explicit about the quality difference between him and Witold.

How do you go about killing a big strong man (who can keep a grip on you with two fingers) when you don't have a gun at your disposal? Poison? And where are you to get the poison from? And how do you get it inside him? I'd have to get a new gun from somewhere. How do you get hold of such a thing? Find a professional, a hired killer! That was the answer. No, quite out of the question, they would want – if the TV thrillers were anything to go by – at least a hundred thousand marks, and where was I to get that kind of money? And anyway, how was I, the respectable Rosemarie Hirte of the legal insurance business, to go about finding myself a killer? Magnanimously, I spared his life.

Apart from anything else, that creep had robbed me of the chance to talk to Witold after the funeral. It was quite possible that Witold would have wanted to speak to some soulmate at such a sad time, but wouldn't want to make contact with Vivian in front of all those relatives. He must surely have been looking for me. 'Thyra,' he would have said, 'come, dear faithful friend, let's go to your place and chat awhile!' Perhaps he might even have seen me going off with that repulsive Jürgen Faltermann.

I hid myself away in my bed and listened to the Brahms songs. Something about being 'beguiled by the kisses' fragrant power, Plucked from the bouquet of your lips at the midnight hour'. Witold was a good psychologist. He well knew how an old maid could cry her eyes out at words like these. Never in my whole life had I cried so much as now, at the pathetic age of fifty-two, when I had fallen in love, perhaps for the first and only time, but sadly too late.

Could I afford to wait patiently, to hold out until Vivian acquired a new love for herself? Every day made me irretrievably older and uglier. Perhaps something could still be salvaged in the short term – tinted hair, expensive make-up, vitamins and hormones – but the day was not all that far off when even these would achieve nothing.

Once, five years before, there was a man I ought to have throttled, and it would have been only right and proper. The memory of that experience was one I did not enjoy, the very thought of that creature was enough to make me blush with shame even now. My most recent holidays had been spent mainly in the company of some dogged package group.

'Elderly gentlefolk with a bit of spare cash, visiting ruins and bathing on the Turkish Riviera' – something like that would sum up my tedious undertakings.

Before that, though, I had liked going off on my own to foreign resorts and basically I had no objection to the odd sophisticated holiday fling. The young man on that occasion spoke German with hardly a trace of an accent, and had at first exuded such charm and wit that I had been all for him spending the nights in my hotel bedroom. After a couple of days, he had taken me to this expensive boutique, because he reckoned I should treat myself to an outfit with a touch of maritime flair. Bowled over by his expert taste, I followed his advice and bought myself a not exactly inexpensive sailor suit, dark blue with a broad white collar. Without his help, I would never have been able to decide on such a purchase. It suited me marvellously. Tall and slim as I am, I could carry off the style exceptionally well, and I was only surprised that I hadn't hit on such a brilliant idea myself.

The shop also carried men's clothing. After the purchase of the sailor suit had been concluded, my companion picked out an ecru-coloured silk suit for himself and tried it on. He cut every bit as elegant a figure in it as I had just done in my suit. I gave him an appreciative nod. At that, he discreetly showed me the price label and confessed that buying it would be well beyond his means and I would have to help him out. I immediately shook my head.

'If you can't afford this suit, then you'll just have to do without it,' I said, very matter-of-fact, but not rudely.

Whereupon my friend retorted at the top of his voice, 'In that case, you can't afford a young lover, either.'

The salesgirl couldn't suppress a grin. I paid for my suit, left it hanging in the wardrobe in the hotel, packed my things in confusion and left for home.

How happily I would have murdered that awesomely objectionable gigolo! For a long time afterwards, I pondered over how I might have gone about it. It wouldn't have been easy in the hotel, but a lover could be lured away to some secluded spot just as easily as one's best friend: I could have pushed him off some cliff-top.

Frau Römer phoned me at the office. Radiant with happiness, she told me her application for a pension had been approved, and she need never come in to the insurance office again.

'I'll look in tomorrow and clear my odd bits and pieces out of my desk; there's also an umbrella of mine in the cupboard.'

I offered to bring her things round in the next few days – after all, she didn't have a car, and her right arm was badly swollen.

So I started stuffing her belongings into a plastic carrier bag. There was not only her umbrella in the cupboard, but also a pair of slippers, a mauve knitted cardigan, decaffeinated instant coffee, a silvery cup from a department store and an opened tin of stale evaporated milk. In the drawers, there was an accumulation of packets of paper handkerchiefs, medicines, sweets, sewing things, brochures, safety-pins and a spare pair of spectacles.

I had a browse through the wide variety of medicines – a nasal spray, tablets for headaches and migraine, ointment for cuts and grazes and one full and one opened pack of some preparation based on digitalis. I knew she had been taking some medication or other made from this highly poisonous foxglove for her heart condition. My interest was aroused. I read the directions. Digitoxin was what the dangerous component in these intriguing pills was called. 'For myocardial insufficiency, recurrent supraventricular tachycardia, atrial fluttering and atrial palpitation resulting from cardiac insufficiency' – this was music to my ears. I decided not to hand over the unopened pack to Frau Römer, but to keep it for prophylactic purposes. You never knew what you might perhaps need such powerful poison for.

Back home, my curiosity increased. I decided to try out a little experiment: filling chocolates with poison. I would soon find a suitable customer for them, who knows, maybe even Vivian.

I left the flat again, albeit reluctantly, and took myself off

104

to the little shop round the corner. Now, washing powder, a wholemeal loaf, a wedge of cheese and some fruit were everyday requirements, but in addition I bought a box of chocolate truffles, filled with orange liqueur.

In the kitchen, I popped a tablet out of its protective silver foil. Would this awkward thing ever fit whole into a truffle? Carefully, I bored into a truffle with a kebab skewer. To my amazement, none of the liquid leaked out, the liqueur was bound into the soft, gooey chocolate mass. I managed to hollow out the truffle a bit, to press in the pill and to squeeze the praline closed again. All the same, it looked a bit misshapen, as if it had been lying in the sun.

Now I had to risk experimenting on myself and to put my concoction in my mouth. Rather fearfully, I read the directions a second time. If patients with a bad heart were supposed to swallow three such tablets daily, one couldn't hurt me. So, pluck up courage! I shoved the thing into my mouth. No, it really wouldn't work. My tongue had discovered the foreign body at once and ejected it, stained chocolate-brown. Too big, the pill.

I picked it up, wiped the chocolate off with a washing-up cloth and started to crush the tablet. All I achieved with a knife was crumbs, but a hammer produced the desired results. The second chocolate was pierced and filled with the powder; while this worked fine, it once again left me with a noticeably squishy truffle. I tried it: it tasted so awful that I spat the truffle straight into the sink. Ugh, yuck! Only someone whose taste buds had been anaesthetized would be able to get anything like that down. And even then they would have to put away, at a rough guess, at least a dozen of these truffles, one after another, before they keeled over.

No, I told myself, poisoning is not my thing. Even supposing I were to send my painstakingly and laboriously crafted truffles anonymously to Vivian or Faltermann, what then? Vivian would try one and junk the rest. Faltermann would probably not even try them (beer drinkers have other cravings), but would pass the gift on to his wife or some new conquest. It was absolutely pointless. In a bad mood, I polished off the rest of the truffles – quite contrary to my iron principles – and put the poison back among Frau Römer's other effects.

When, a few days later, I showed up at Frau Römer's and presented Dieskau with a big sausage and her with a copy of the Brahms cassette, she threw her arms round me for the first time, after all those years of a friendly enough relationship that had, however, never scaled such heights of familiarity as a pat on the shoulder.

'Frau Hirte, you're the only one in the office I'll miss. All that time, you looked after me and my dog with such kindness, so today I've got something for you, too.'

Making a bit of a mystery of it all, she led me into the bedroom and brought a jewellery case out of the wardrobe.

'Of course, everything I have to bequeath will go to my daughter. But there are certain reasons why I don't want her to have this particular piece. I'd like you to have it.' And, with great ceremony, she pinned a brooch on my blouse. It was an old heirloom, a profile of Hermes, cut in obsidian stone and framed in a fine gold border.

'You're very discreet, Frau Hirte, I've known that for many years. Nobody knows who the father of my daughter was, and I have no sort of contact with him any more. When it happened, he was seventeen and I was already in my late twenties. Naturally, I couldn't tell anyone I was carrying on with a schoolboy, and marriage was out of the question. I never told him anything about my pregnancy and I left my home town right away. This brooch came from him. He quite simply filched it from his mother. I've never dared to wear it, and I really wouldn't want my daughter to, either. I brought that child up and provided for her all on my own. If she were ever to wear this brooch, it would probably make me very unhappy.'

I didn't want to accept a piece of jewellery that was so steeped in memories.

'No, please,' said Frau Römer. 'My daughter doesn't like it. It would make me so very happy.'

With mixed feelings, then, I left the ornament dangling on my blouse, for the fine silk was having a hard time of it under the heavy weight of the stone. Did Frau Römer have an ulterior motive? After all, she couldn't very well take Dieskau with her on the planned trip to America.

7

I had been noticing something about myself lately: the over-whelming, youthful feeling of being in love was almost imper-ceptibly waning. It was hard to tell whether I felt a certain relief that my thoughts were now no longer so exclusively focused on Witold, or whether I was sad at the anticipation of the emptiness of old age. But strangely, something new came sliding insidiously into my subconscious, just as love seemed to be stealing away. The menacing vacuum of lost love was thus offset.

It isn't easy to describe the dawning of this realization in rational terms: at the cemetery, I experienced for the first time that extraordinary sensation of power. Later on, I suddenly became aware, in the middle of the street, of a sense of euphoria sweeping over me: no one would think, by looking at me, that I have two people on my conscience and could do away with others as well, if I so much as wanted to.

On the car radio I heard Lotte Lenya singing the Pirate Jenny song: 'Now you gents all see I've the glasses to wash, When a bed's to be made I make it . . .' Jenny had taken her revenge for all her humiliations. 'And they still have no idea who I am . . .' Lotte Lenya was singing with compelling insist-ence. It was the same with me, nobody had any idea who I was. The boss couldn't guess that he was fobbing off more and more unpleasant assignments, jobs that he was basically too lazy to do, on to a murderess. As I sat in my secluded little room in the office and, after the communal lunch in the canteen, let my guzzling and drivelling colleagues parade before my mind's eye, more than a few heads rolled, and, like Jenny, all I said each time was, 'Hoppla!'

Power over other people was almost better than love and was essentially the opposite of it. When you are in love, you are powerless, helpless and dependent. And yet I didn't want to write off my love just like that, not yet anyway. It had intruded into my life too deeply for that, given me youthfulness, energy and a sense of purpose, a new physical awareness and a different appreciation of myself. I wanted to go on fighting for it, I wanted to experience another blissful, carefree day like that one when we walked through the Odenwald.

I swore an oath, I even prayed, for all that my faith had been driven out of me at an early age by a mercilessly pious mother. 'If you do exist, God,' I said, 'then grant me for once in my life the happiness love brings, that happiness you so randomly and generously let fall into other people's laps. I've never asked you for anything. Now I'm in deadly earnest. If there is such a thing as God, then make Witold love me, let us have each other. But if you are unjust and hard-hearted and don't even take any notice of this prayer, then in future I shall pay not the slightest heed to your commandments.'

Rosie, you're trying to blackmail the Good Lord, I thought, and couldn't help laughing.

From Beate's children I heard not a word. Although I had previously given them hardly a second thought, I was bothered now about what was to become of them. Would Beate's flat have been sold? I decided one day to ring her number. The son answered, the one I knew least of all.

'Hello, Richard,' I said quietly. 'Actually I just wanted to ask whether Beate belonged to any society or charity that I could send a donation to.'

There was a pause, Richard was mulling it over.

'You could donate something to Greenpeace,' he suggested.

'Oh yes? I had no idea Beate was interested in that.'

'Well, not directly.' He was being evasive. 'But Greenpeace is a good cause, and my mother was OK.'

I asked how his sisters were getting on.

'Granddad was here recently. He reckoned he had to look

109

after us poor little kids, but of course it was the other way round. Lessi's still living here, I'm here only now and then. Vivian's back in Frankfurt. As for how we're feeling – rotten, naturally. You don't get over this sort of thing just like that.'

I asked whether Beate's flat was to be sold. Not for the time being, he said, all her things were still there and nothing had been settled yet.

'All of a sudden, our father's showing an interest in us, something he hasn't done in the last ten years,' Richard told me with a tinge of reproach in his voice. I said goodbye and promised a donation to Greenpeace.

All the same, I had found out that Vivian was back living in Frankfurt, now that it was term-time again. No doubt she would hardly be able to meet Witold every day, since an hour's drive each way was a bit much on a normal working day. Or didn't that matter to young folk? Vivian had never had a car of her own, but it was possible she was driving Beate's Polo now.

I phoned Witold. He sounded sorry for himself. He had just got over a heavy cold, he said, the Yugoslavian cleaning lady kept foisting fatty food on him, even though she wasn't supposed to cook at all, and he was absolutely up to his eyes in work at school. The autumn holiday was coming up soon, and originally he had intended going off for a few days with Vivian.

'What do you mean, "originally"?' I asked, more than a little intrigued.

'Sometimes I can't help thinking,' poor Witold sighed, 'I've aged. These young girls are so unreliable. We had worked out a lovely plan to go for a week's walking in Alsace. Now she suddenly rings to tell me she's going to Amsterdam with a girlfriend because there's a party on there! I ask you, Thyra, she's standing me up for some party! Well, I suppose "standing me up" is perhaps something of an exaggeration,' he corrected himself. 'As a matter of principle, I'm all for spontaneous decisions. But I had worked out these walks in the Vosges down to the last detail . . .' I was delighted at his disappointment, but politeness forced me to express my sym-

110

pathy. Nevertheless, here was the chance to offer him, as second best, an autumn day's walking with an older model, as I jokingly put it.

'What a pity you're not on holiday,' Witold gallantly regretted. 'As a matter of fact I'm wondering whether I might still go on this walking tour. It's all been carefully planned, and I could go with a group of friends and colleagues . . .' With great presence of mind I interrupted him and assured him I could take time off whenever I felt like it.

'Really?' he said slowly, almost in a drawl. 'Well, hold on for a while, Thyra, before you put in for leave. I've got a party of eight to ten people in mind, but I haven't asked any of them yet. I'll let you know as soon as I have any more details.'

He hadn't exactly been bowled over, but that was hardly to be expected when he was now merely going on the walking tour out of spite instead of on what was really meant to be a romantic trip with Vivian.

Vivian! In my imagination I carried on a conversation with her, in which, oddly, I was taking Beate's part.

'Quite right, Vivian,' I told her, 'off you go to Amsterdam! At your time of life it makes a lot more sense to have fun with people your own age than to go plodding through the Vosges with a teacher twice as old as you. Men! Always keep them dangling! Let them suffer! Who knows how much *you'll* end up having to suffer at *their* hands!'

I could see Vivian's fate clearly before me: she was not at all the motherly type, this freaked-out art student. She would probably never set her sights on some middle-class marriage, never have children. She would end up an old bag like me, albeit with a much more chequered past. All at once, Vivian struck me as no longer a threat, and I was amazed that I had ever toyed with the thought of doing away with her.

Without waiting for Witold to call me back, I presented my boss with my holiday demands: I wanted next week off to go walking with friends in Alsace.

'Can't be done, Frau Hirte,' he said firmly. 'That's the autumn holiday week, and Herr Müller and Frau Flori are off then. Anyway, you know perfectly well there are several

111

deadlines we just have to meet next week. In September I tried to persuade you to go off on holiday, but you wouldn't have it. Sorry!'

That, for him, was that; he turned back to his work and expected me to take my leave. Force of habit made me obey.

Back in my own office, I was consumed with rage. For years on end I had put in overtime, unpaid and whenever required, had never made any demands, had covered for the old man and backed him up with complete loyalty. On the one and only occasion I wanted something for myself, it was turned down. So what was the point of all his endless fawning patter? It was his way of ruthlessly exploiting me.

With relish, I pictured the boss biting into his mid-morning roll that he always kept ready in his bottom right-hand desk drawer. Rat poison! He would expire in agony. But in the event of his demise, I most certainly wouldn't get any leave, because all his mountains of pending files would be piled on to me to be dealt with.

I went to see him a second time.

'If you are going to take so little notice of my interests, when I have supported yours for many years now, then I shall have no option but to resign my position here,' I said, managing to speak coldly and distinctly, even though I was boiling over with the urge to kill him.

The boss was totally shocked.

'For heaven's sake, Frau Hirte! There must surely be a way – you've misunderstood me! I have always given generous consideration towards all members of staff where the holiday regulations are concerned!'

Yes, I thought, so long as you agreed to his plans, he would give you his bounteous blessing.

'Frau Hirte, you can't be serious about resigning! You've been through quite a lot recently; I heard about the death of your friend. You will get this leave, come what may, even if that means I have to take on a part of your workload personally!'

I had managed that, then, but would anything at all come out of the walking tour? What if Witold ended up going off

112

with his friends, but turned me down? But in that case, he wouldn't have needed to bring the subject up in the first place.

One further problem concerned me. These others – Witold's friends and colleagues – would they accept me? And finally, rambling itself gave me cause for worry; I was not the sporty type, I was out of condition, and would probably be the oldest in the whole crowd. If it was to turn out to be a group of ambitious, indefatigable athletes who thought nothing of a brisk route-march up hill and down dale for eight hours a day, maybe even with a heavy rucksack on their backs, would I be able to keep up with them? No way!

It was my fervent hope that Ernst Schröder would be among them; in the first place, because he was the only one of Witold's friends I knew, and in the second, because my memory of him was as a corpulent, easy-going and phlegmatic character, perhaps even older than myself. With this friendly fat man in the company, there would obviously be no question of it turning into survival training.

In my thoughts, I busied myself optimistically with my hiking outfit. I had the sneaking feeling that I had successfully blackmailed the Good Lord and I could look forward to a pleasant and happy time.

The bits of good news came thick and fast. Only two days later, Witold was on the phone. He had rounded up a group of interested ramblers, and they were planning to meet on the coming Sunday in the Schröders' weekend cottage in Bickelbach to discuss all further details. I knew, of course, where the cottage was, didn't I? and I was to be there at two in the afternoon, and if the weather was fine we'd all go for a walk for an hour or so. Witold was very nice and finished by saying, 'I'm glad you're going to be there. So, till the day after tomorrow, then!'

Well, if he was glad, I was practically beside myself! That same day, I bought hiking boots and began breaking them in by keeping them on while I watched television.

'Rosie,' I told myself out loud, 'even if your feet are absolutely killing you on this ramble, not a squeak! Just think of the Little Mermaid who put up with everything for the sake of her prince.'

In any case, at that moment I was much keener on being the charming mermaid than the bloodthirsty Pirate Jenny. In preparation for any eventuality, I got in a supply of sticking-plasters; I preferred to put off the purchase of a rucksack for the time being, because in such matters I had all the experience of a new-born babe.

At two o'clock on the dot, I arrived in Bickelbach. I was wearing my new, super-lightweight hiking boots, the first jeans I had had in my life and one of my dark-blue holiday sweaters. Witold's car was not there yet, the only one outside the house was obviously Ernst Schröder's. Since I already knew him and he could probably see me from inside the house, I walked up the well-worn steps as I had done that time in the summer. The door was thrown wide. A woman held out a welcoming hand.

'I'm Pamela Schröder, and you must have been summoned by Rainer.'

I introduced myself and went in. On a wooden corner seat, Ernst Schröder was lying fast asleep, swaddled around with an array of sofa-cushions. I tried to keep my voice down, but his wife only laughed. 'Nothing will disturb his rest, the louder it gets, the more contentedly he'll snore.'

She put water on to boil and started taking cups from a cupboard. She looked at me inquiringly.

'How many of us are there, anyway?'

I shrugged. Pamela Schröder had red hair and first impressions suggested she was the very opposite of her peacefully slumbering husband. She was vivacious, purposeful, a dominant type, of striking appearance. Even though she was wearing an ancient pair of slacks, much too large and liberally patched, she still sported stiletto heels and a purple brocade blouse. Her movements were agile, her red-varnished talons reached unerringly towards the crockery and cutlery, and all the while she chatted casually, a cigarette between her lips, while I rather awkwardly offered to help. Suddenly, Ernst yawned, opened his eyes and gazed, half mischievously, half guiltily, at the relentless preparations for the coffee session. At last, he heaved himself to his feet, greeted me and disappeared into the lavatory.

I heard a car pull up and looked out of the window. At last! Witold had arrived. Next to him sat a blonde-haired young woman.

They came in. I sized up his companion with profound mistrust. Witold explained straight away that three of those originally interested had called off, but the Mommsens would be along soon. Pamela counted up. 'Right, so there'll be seven of us,' she declared, and without a word of explanation she handed me the pile of plates. I started setting the table, at which the blonde sprang to my assistance. Witold introduced us.

'This is Frau Zoltan, a colleague of mine.'

My good mood evaporated. Probably he had brought this lady for himself. The Schröders were a couple, likewise the still-missing Mommsens; so I was cast once again in my usual role as wallflower.

Ernst emerged from the lavatory, the table was set and ready, Pamela fetched a plum cake from the car, Frau Zoltan whipped the cream. When the mysterious Mommsen couple had still not shown up half an hour later, we started on our coffee. Not a single word had yet been said about the expedition.

Ever the attentive host, Ernst proposed that all the future fellow ramblers should be on first-name terms. In fact, this concerned only me, since I hadn't come across the two women before. It was Pamela Schröder's idea that since everyone apart from her husband called her Scarlett, I should too. Frau Zoltan was called Kitty and would settle for that. Witold said, quite naturally, that I was called 'Thyra', and so there was no more talk of 'Rosemarie'. Everyone immediately got excited about the unusual name, and this gave Witold another good opportunity to quote 'Gorm Grimme', at which Kitty quietly recited the lines along with him, while the Schröders listened open-mouthed.

Kitty was smitten with Witold, it took me an hour at most to see that. Yet it didn't seem to be a blatant kind of affection, but rather a quiet devotion, which was obviously not reciprocated to the same extent.

Witold sparkled with charm and wit, for long periods he dominated the conversation and basked in his success. But in a certain way, Scarlett was a match for him, for she too was not backward in coming forward and enjoyed holding centre-stage. In the face of two such limelight-cases, the rest of us were reduced to the role of mere onlookers, but of course we lapped up their performances and applauded appreciatively.

The Mommsens failed to appear.

'There's rain forecast, so before it sets in, maybe we should stretch our legs a bit.' Witold's suggestion was as good as an order. The sky was clouding over. Two umbrellas were fetched from the cars, and there was another in the house. In addition, Witold had a waterproof jacket with him. So now we were fully equipped to face the rain, come what may, for Pamela didn't want to come for a walk but said she would wait for the Mommsens and do the washing-up.

Off we went, then. To my great disappointment, Witold was well out in front with his old friend in no time, and whenever Kitty and I quickened our pace and managed to get within reach of them, they seemed to go up a gear. Kitty laughed.

'The two of them must be talking about Oleg!'

So who was Oleg? Kitty explained to me that the Schröders had two children, fifteen-year-old Annette and Oleg, who was eighteen. The boy was intelligent, but a layabout, he had already had to repeat two classes at school, yet he was very mature for his years, which explained his scandalous love affairs. No doubt Ernst was wanting to pump Rainer Engstern about any staff-room complaints about his son. I asked Kitty if she taught him as well.

'Yes, I take him for history, and he has Rainer for French. Personally, I find his charms hard to resist, somehow he always manages to get off lightly with me.'

I liked Kitty, despite my fears about her designs on Witold. She was small and wiry, a real little girl scout, complete with healthy complexion; her looks were nothing out of the ordinary, her dress restrained. Her observations were acute, sometimes mocking, but never nasty. Occasionally she would pass some dry remark which struck everyone as very witty. I got the feeling that here was someone dependable, slightly introverted. My impression was that Kitty was unmarried, which I did find quite surprising.

Only once we had almost got back to the Holzweg in Bickelbach did the two men stop and wait for us. Now Kitty went on ahead with Ernst Schröder, to talk to him about Oleg. I deliberately dawdled, so as to have Witold all to myself for a few precious moments. I asked him about Kitty.

'A very dear colleague,' he said with some emphasis, 'highly regarded by everyone. We've run several class outings together in the past, and, in harness, we turned out to be a perfect team.'

The horsey metaphor fitted Kitty, even if she was no Clydesdale, more of a good-natured little pony.

'Is she married?'

'No, she's not, amazingly enough, she's never found the right one. But, you see, Kitty sets high standards, and rightly so,' he observed. Did she regard him as the right one, I wondered.

'And how did it go with Vivian?' I asked, rather indiscreetly, perhaps.

But Witold was not at all averse to airing intimate matters. His expression clouded with annoyance.

'Our last conversation was extremely unpleasant. I just don't know whether I should invest anything more in that relationship; the age difference is beginning to show, you see. It may well be that Vivian's interpretation of friendship is different from mine. Where it goes from here, I don't know – perhaps it's just not going to go anywhere.'

We both remained silent. We were now in sight of the house.

117

'Before we get back in there, Witold,' I said quietly and in a rush, 'for heaven's sake, tell me quickly, what's this Pamela really like?'

Witold loved questions like this and grinned at me.

'She's hot stuff, all right,' he said, and I blushed. 'Scarlett once wanted to be an actress or a singer, but nothing came of it. And now, there she is, mother of two and pharmacist's wife.'

After a brief pause for reflection, he went on, as if to himself, 'A few years back . . .' and said no more. I looked at him, intrigued.

'Oh, nothing,' he laughed, pensively, and I could feel goose flesh coming up all over my arms.

We could see the little house clearly now, and there was another car parked on the grass.

'Well, there are your friends now,' I said to Witold. 'Clever of you to have delayed the planning of the walking holiday.'

'That's not them,' Witold said. 'That's Scarlett's car. Maybe it's the children.'

We had caught up with Ernst and Kitty. Ernst grimaced and informed us that his son had passed his driving test a week before, but actually he hadn't had permission to tear around in his mother's car. Inside the house sat Pamela Schröder, the illustrious Oleg and his sister, in front of them the remains of the plum cake, which had noticeably diminished.

'What's up?' asked Ernst.

Annette moaned, 'Oh, Daddy, I've had such a ghastly sore throat since yesterday, and there's not a single throat lozenge in the whole house.'

'That's always the way with chemists,' Witold interjected.

The brats' mother was more than a little irritated. 'If it was that bad as long ago as yesterday morning, why has it taken you till now to think of asking for pills?'

'She didn't want to bother Papa on his day off,' Oleg said. 'But now it's got so bad I just had to bring her here.'

Witold gave him a wink.

Ernst sighed. 'All right then, come on, my poor sick trea-sure, your agony certainly didn't stop you getting stuck into the cake. I've probably got some medicine in the car.'

Pamela gave her son a hard look. 'Don't you really think your little game is a bit too obvious? All of a sudden you start playing the loving brother, just because you want to drive my car!'

Oleg protested. After all, he could have gone off for a spin to Frankfurt and not to Bickelbach, of all places, and then his parents would have been none the wiser.

Annette and her papa came back in, sat down next to each other in the corner seat, and the daughter snuggled up to her father. Ernst was beaming.

In the meantime, Oleg had struck up a cosy conversation with his history teacher, made Witold laugh with a string of jokes and wheedled permission out of his father to take a few bottles of wine with him for a party. Scarlett insisted on the children driving back while it was still light, since she was none too sure of Oleg's motoring prowess.

'If only you would finally get the telephone in here in Bickelbach, then we could phone you from home to let you know we've got back in one piece,' Oleg remarked, and his attempt at diplomacy was obviously a well-worn topic.

At last the brats left. I had been hoping that we'd get down to business at last. But the proud mother took advantage of the children's visit to go into their qualities in detail. Annette: well, she was still really a little girl, so clinging and loving, unlike her friends, still without a steady boyfriend and in that respect still charmingly childlike. I could feel rage welling up. But now it was boy-wonder's turn. He played the drums in a school band, and we were informed that there was a real artist in him. I felt like leaving. But then what I came here for was the chance to go on a ramble with Witold, so I had to put up with all this for the time being. We'd be in for a really jolly time and no mistake, if this woman was going to keep on about her spoilt offspring, whom she apparently left on their own without a second thought.

It was Witold who intervened.

119

'Since something's obviously turned up to prevent the Mommsens coming, I think we should start discussing the situation as it stands.'

Ernst grinned at me. 'Beware, teacher at work!' he whispered. From his briefcase, Witold took out maps and photocopied sheets and passed them round.

'I've made up a list for every participant of what he or she absolutely must bring, since not everybody has as much walking experience as the two of us,' and he turned towards Kitty. 'You all have a rucksack, I suppose?'

I shook my head. The others were reading their lists.

The silence was broken by Pamela's harsh voice. 'Rainer, this is absolute nonsense. If you lay any store whatsoever on my company, then there'll be no lugging of rucksacks!'

'What then?' inquired Witold.

'My God!' the redhead burst out, 'we're not a class of schoolkids! There must surely be some way of transporting our luggage by car. As far as I'm concerned, I reckon I'm too old to be playing Happy Wanderers. You'll be telling us next you're also planning on tents and building little camp fires, Scoutmaster Rainer, eh?'

A rather miffed Witold assured us that of course we'd be sleeping in hotels, perhaps once and once only in a youth hostel with family rooms. He spread the map out before us, with his proposed stages highlighted in fluorescent orange marker.

Now it was Ernst's turn to rebel.

'Listen, Rainer, this is all very well. But when I think of Alsace, the first thing that comes to mind is good food and a dry Riesling. Why on earth do we have to do so much tramping about?'

Witold groaned. 'I can't believe I'm hearing this! Here we are, planning a walking tour, and this blighter doesn't want to walk a step!'

Ernst Schröder was no spoilsport. He had to laugh. 'Rainer, of course I want to do a bit of walking, if only to work up an appetite. All the same, you've got to take my advancing years into account!'

120

'What do the rest of you say?' said Witold turning to Kitty and me for support.

'Oh, I'm easy,' Kitty replied. 'I can walk for ages, and I don't mind carrying a rucksack, too – as you well know. But I think it's also lovely sitting in these wonderful inns eating sauerkraut.'

'I'm certainly not in top condition for hiking,' I put in.

'Fine, all right, no rucksacks,' said Witold, looking hard at his friend, 'but that means we'll have to organize a complicated shuttle service with two cars: driving out every morning with the luggage in both cars to the next destination, leaving one car there and then back again in the other. Walking the distance and taking the car that's already there to go back and fetch the other. Clear?'

Ernst laughed. 'Rainer, you always plan everything far too expertly and precisely. I mean, we could just set off quite at random. On the first day we'll spend the night at Wissembourg and go for a walk about there, then we can go on a bit just as the fancy takes us.'

Everyone except Witold was nodding agreement. With a sigh, he capitulated and, looking slightly piqued, packed away his maps and itineraries.

'Don't sit there looking like the Mater Dolorosa,' said Scarlett.

Ernst tried to smooth the ruffled feathers. 'Take a look out of the window, it's raining like mad now. It could be exactly the same story next week, and you must admit it would be nice to have our luggage, the cars and a hotel all within easy reach. But now it's time to get down to the cosy bit of business. I hereby declare the fireside season open, and I'm going to set a nice little blaze going while Pamela throws something tasty in the oven and you, Rainer, can open the red wine.'

With that, the atmosphere became more relaxed as everyone got busy. The kitchen formed part of the living-room, which made up the whole of the ground floor. Scarlett allocated the jobs – Kitty was at the large dining-table chopping onions and tomatoes, I wrapped huge baking potatoes in

121

kitchen foil after I had scrubbed them clean, slit them across the middle and smeared them with salted garlic butter.

'What goodies have we got here, then?' Witold asked, licking his lips.

The red witch blew cigarette smoke in his face.

'I can't very well put together a banquet if I don't know in advance how many are coming and when, or even if anybody's coming at all. You're getting plain fare – potatoes, chicken legs and tomato salad.'

'But that's absolutely fantastic,' approved Witold, uncorking the red wine. Ernst was sitting pensively by the fireside, contriving to fill the whole room with smoke. Kitty had a coughing fit and rushed out into the fresh air. Pamela gave her husband a sound cursing for maltreating Kitty's sensitive lungs, whereupon he put the blame on her and Witold's chain-smoking.

On a wooden ledge over the fireplace there was an old iron trap door for ventilating the stove, and in front of it a sizeable collection of rusty metal dishes. Typical Scarlett.

In the oven, the chicken pieces and the potatoes were beginning to sizzle, all the work was done, the fire was now burning according to plan. Witold opened some windows and called Kitty back in. We all moved close to the fire and waited for the food, which smelled better by the minute.

'How's your rooster coming on?' inquired Ernst.

'A little while yet,' replied Scarlett.

Kitty started singing, 'The cock is dead, the cock is dead,' and Witold, with his mellow voice, joined in, in French: 'Le coq est mort'. Ernst droned out the third verse. I kept quiet, as I had only a sketchy memory of the old canon and anyway I was acutely embarrassed.

'Come on, Scarlett, you're the only one here who can really sing! Why is our nightingale silent?' Witold demanded.

'Rainer, I don't quite fit into your junior choir,' Pamela fired back.

Undeterred, Kitty sang the next song, and Witold lent his support. At last he tried again: 'So how, o fair Philomel, can we win your favour and participation?' and he bowed low before Pamela.

'Well, if you insist, but without your cats' chorus,' she retorted disparagingly. 'When it comes to "There is a Happy Land" round the old camp fire, you can count me out!'

Now it was Ernst's turn to have his say. 'She dearly loves a bit of coaxing. Ladies and gentlemen! I give you now the acclaimed Brecht interpreter with songs from the *Threepenny Opera*!'

All of a sudden I found my tongue too. 'Oh, please, sing the song of Pirate Jenny!'

Scarlett looked at me thoughtfully, then nodded. With a wave of the hand she commanded silence all round, picked up a plate and a kitchen cloth as props and nimbly jumped up on to the iron chest that stood by the stove.

Everyone was captivated by her performance. While Scarlett wasn't exactly possessed of a pleasant singing voice, she articulated the words crisply and with crystal clarity, and with an intensity that was spellbinding. The result was that our comfortably heated farmhouse parlour was transformed for a short time into a seedy hotel, and the housewife who had, a moment before, been busy cooking, into a Lotte Lenya. The applause was frenzied, however the prima donna declined to give an encore, but instead was now busy poking the potatoes and the meat with a skewer to test their tenderness. I was thrown into a confusion of contradictory emotions. Thanks to Witold I was getting to know people, the likes of whom would never have crossed my path in the insurance company offices! If only I had a wickedly smoky voice like this louche, exotic temptress, if only I could do something so well that everybody burst into spontaneous applause!

And yet, I thought, there is something I can do, only nobody knows about it; I have more power than all of them put together. But unfortunately they're not cheering me but the redhead. Even though she had sung my song for me, it was her triumph I couldn't forgive.

Then the meal was brought to the table. Witold laid a kitchen apron over his arm and served with due civility.

'Does Modom wish to partake of another leg? Would El Hakim deign to gargle a further modicum of this unassuming little red?'

The table had been set without a cloth, the lady of the house having merely cleared it of cigarette ash and onion skins with a somewhat suspect damp rag. My mind jumped to my refined, stilted dinner for Witold, and the very memory of it filled me with shame.

Our life-and-soul-of-the-party duo were in great form. After two glasses of wine, Kitty was cackling away like some boisterous schoolgirl, while Ernst was oozing bear-like charm. Suddenly Scarlett announced that red wine made you tired and lazy, so out with the bubbly! She fetched a bottle herself. 'Anybody join me?' Nobody spoke up. She took two glasses from the cupboard and gave me one.

'You're much too quiet, a touch of this is bound to do you good!'

I didn't dare contradict her, although I doubted whether a mixture of coffee, cake, red wine and sparkling, chicken and potatoes would make me exactly merry.

Scarlett raised her glass, took a hearty swallow, grabbed a chicken leg and stood on her chair as if winding herself up to entertain us with a further rendition.

I went as white as a sheet and let out a moan. Beate was standing up there before me, high on the parapet of the tower, champagne glass in one hand, chicken leg in the other.

'Good God, what's the matter with you?' came flying from all sides. I just managed to mumble something about not feeling too good and thinking I'd better get home.

'But at least wait a while, you can't get into your car in that state,' advised the concerned chemist and offered me something for my circulation. But I wouldn't be budged, said a hurried, 'Thanks very much,' and left the room.

As I was unlocking my car, Witold came running up. I slumped into the driving seat, and he hammered on the window of the passenger door, which I opened for him.

'Don't you think I should drive you home?' he asked, very

tenderly and solicitously. 'What came over you all of a sudden?'

Because he was being so sweet, I could no longer keep back the flood of tears. 'Champagne and chicken, that was Beate's last meal,' I sobbed. Witold put his arm round me.

'Thyra, I know exactly how you feel. Whenever I'm with the Schröders, there are some situations when Hilke keeps coming back to me. I can't count the times we all sat together in that house, drinking and enjoying ourselves. Then, from one moment to the next, there's just nothing to smile about any more.'

I nodded and snuggled into his shoulder a bit. The contact was so wonderful, I couldn't help giving his pullover a thorough soaking with my tears.

'There, there, then, it's all better now,' he soothed. 'You know, we're each mourning a very dear person and can't really let it all out. I've decided to start on a course of therapy; I can't get over the business with Hilke without expert help. Basically, it was crazy to try to take my mind off things by carrying on with a young girl.'

'Why can't you get over the business with your wife?' I sniffed, only to prolong the pleasure of leaning lovingly on his shoulder with his arm round me.

But already Witold was slackening his grip.

'I feel guilty. It's my fault she's dead. I don't blame you in any way.'

'But your relationship was already on the rocks, wasn't it . . . ?' I objected.

'That doesn't take anything away from my guilt, if anything it only makes it worse. Don't you see? The fact that Hilke started drinking, surely I'm in some way to blame for that.'

'But why?'

Now Witold let go of me altogether and, inconsiderately, lit up a cigarette.

'It all started very early on. Hilke came from a working-class family, only went to a secondary modern school. For years she suffered from my always trying to tell her what to do, to

125

educate her. It never occurred to me that way. And then –
well – I wasn't faithful to her, either.'

'Was she faithful to you, then?'

'Yes, for many years. When she finally did deceive me, it
was out of defiance. You might well be thinking now that I'm
suffering from a guilt complex, and that's probably right, but
one thing's sure, I did do a lot to hurt her, naturally without
meaning to most of the time.'

Abruptly, he kissed me on the forehead, said cheerio, he'd
phone me the next day. Not another word about him driving
me home.

Once again I lay sleepless in bed. Visions tortured me: Beate
on the tower, Scarlett on the chair, young Kitty next to Witold
in his car.

Besides, the aura around Witold was beginning to fade; it
was all rather sad. But after all, he was only human and not
without his faults and I was no swooning teenager, blindly
idealizing a man. I had enough experience in life to be able to
accept someone's lovable little foibles. Vain my hero certainly
was – that I had noticed very early on – and he craved admiration. When he was alone with me, he could be stuffy, yet
caring and considerate; it was only in company that he began
to sparkle. On top of that, I had noticed signs of a certain
moodiness and a latent hypochondria – well, all right, I could
live with that.

Towards his friend, Ernst Schröder, he had a matey, at
times competitive, relationship. The easy-going apothecary
was not one to be underestimated; while he cultivated the
impression that butter wouldn't melt in his mouth, he nevertheless seemed always to get his way. His wife didn't treat
him at all well, often poking fun at and making him look
downright ridiculous, but all the same she too seemed to
end up bending to his will. With Witold, too, she was forth-
right to the point of brazenness. The verbal skirmishes
of these two articulate men struck me as prickling with tension; there was an underlying spark that could easily burst
into a flame.

Scarlett and Vivian, two birds of paradise – was that Witold's taste in women? As for Kitty and me, we were undoubtedly the antithesis of this, the Cinderella type. In fairy stories, it's the downtrodden that come out on top. How does it work in real life, though?

Only towards morning did I fall asleep and into a very vivid dream. I was lying in my bed, which was desperately needing to be changed. My head was bristling with the most horrendous set of curlers, the kind I had used in my youth, and on my face was a herbal mud-pack. I was dressed in the most disgusting nightdress, one which I had got rid of long ago. The room was unaired, crockery encrusted with the remains of past meals lay about the floor, the mirror was speckled with fly-shit.

I, Rosemarie Hirte, was in the throes of decomposition, despite my efforts to fight decay with curlers and creams.

The door burst open; Witold, Ernst, Kitty, Scarlett, Hilke, Beate and Vivian came sashaying in, all done up in fashionable leisurewear, all tanned (except Vivian) and fit, cheerful and prosperous.

'We've brought something for you,' said Witold, the Good Samaritan, and crowned me with a garland of rosemary. That was too much, I murmured painfully, 'Hop . . .' and again, 'Hop . . .' but couldn't get as far as the magic word, 'Hoppla!' just as Ali Baba's brother never managed to get 'Open, Sesame!' out, and 'Mutabor' stuck in the throat of the Caliph who turned himself into a stork. But Kitty came to my rescue; she knelt beside me and whispered in my ear the liberating word, 'Hoppla!' I repeated it aloud, and with that, six heads rolled under my bed. Kitty, who was spared as a reward, gave the room a good airing, grabbed a brush and swept it clean.

The heads that she pushed along in front of her with the old-fashioned besom like so much rotting fruit had, in the wink of an eye, lost their tanned appearance and now displayed the appropriate deathly pallor; only Vivian's head, so sickly in life, now took on a blood-red bloom. The dew on my crown of rosemary, too, pearled into sticky beads of blood

127

on my forehead and ran in a fiery stream down my cream-smeared face.

With a horrible scream, I woke up.

8

In spite of this inauspicious omen – for that's the way I saw my dream – I went off on the collective outing. We started out with two cars and minus the unreliable Mommsens.

I had left my car in Ladenburg, outside Witold's house, and from there we drove to Schriesheim to pick up Kitty. Since the Schröders still hadn't been ready, we now had to go back to Ladenburg again, so as to leave in convoy with them. Witold was slightly irritated by this delay.

While I was doing my packing, I had had another close look at Witold's original list of contents for the rucksacks. Items like a water bottle, a sheath knife, felt-soled slipper-socks and tracksuit trousers didn't exactly feature in my bottom drawer, but anyway they were no longer required. For all eventualities, I had packed my jogging outfit as well as my silk pyjamas. I hadn't been able to pluck up the courage to inquire about the sleeping arrangements. But soon I discovered that they were very sensibly intending to book a double room for the Schröders, another for Kitty and me and a single for Witold, provided that was all right by me. I felt it tactless to suggest that I would have preferred a room to myself, because I didn't want to offend Kitty.

We set off around midday, and by late afternoon we reached Wissembourg. Then began the search for somewhere to stay. Naturally, Witold had a hotel guide with him, but the places he had ticked off were already fully booked. Then Ernst Schröder spoke up: he knew of a little hideaway, admittedly not in France, but right next to the border on the German side. We got in there without any trouble; Wissembourg was a quarter of an hour's walk away, so we could pay due homage to the French culinary arts there in the evening.

I unpacked my case. From the window I could look directly out on to vineyards. A light, fine rain had set in, but it was still remarkably warm for the time of year. Our first priority was to order coffee and fresh apple cake. In good spirits after that, we decided to ignore the rain and, suitably kitted out, to get our legs moving.

I took an umbrella with me, as did Scarlett. The others were wearing waterproof jackets.

Witold picked up walnuts and horse-chestnuts as he walked, and made a great show of presenting Kitty and me with some of them, even though there were plenty of them falling at our own feet. Scarlett spurned his gifts.

'Men always were, and always will be, infantile,' she announced. 'Because I've forbidden him to play the boy scout, no doubt he'll console himself this evening with building little men out of chestnuts and matches.'

'You're absolutely right,' Witold agreed with her, 'but then you are the wisest of them all.'

I held the smooth, firm chestnut in my hand inside my jacket pocket and resolved to keep it as a souvenir for ever.

Witold acted as our guide around the town; as a French teacher he had probably been here with many a class before. He knew his way around, pointed out picturesque angles for photographs along the River Lauter, talked about the town's history, leaving out not one of the disasters it had suffered, and ended the tour with a look round the church of St Peter and St Paul.

His programme could probably have gone on for hours if the Schröders hadn't insisted at the outset on sitting down to dinner by eight at the latest. Ernst Schröder said that this first evening was on him, reckoning he owed it to us, since his wife and he had put the damper on our anticipation of the joys of rambling.

Since we had no objections to his invitation, he now decided, as the host, on a standard choice for everyone: after the pâté de foie gras came pheasant on a bed of sauerkraut and finally freshly made *gugelhupf,* a ring-shaped poundcake; all the while, the waiter could scarcely replace the empty Riesling bottles fast enough.

Right at the start, Witold had asked the waiter for the menu in unbelievably elegant French, to which he received a response in the thick local Alemannic dialect.

The meal went on for hours. Both at our table and the neighbouring ones the conversation grew steadily louder and the laughter heartier. At the next table, where, at first, two doctors had done nothing but complain about the dwindling numbers of private patients while their wives made no secret of their boredom, great merriment had now erupted, so that we couldn't resist eavesdropping every now and again. One of the medicos was a dentist, and he delivered a highly comic description of how, in his young days, he had been given the job of working out the age of a corpse by its teeth. What he discovered was that the dead man had been wearing dentures. Nevertheless, he had been able to give a fairly precise estimate of the age by assessing the signs of wear and tear on the jaw.

'How can anyone ever make jokes about such a macabre subject?' Kitty demanded indignantly, her cheeks glowing. But Ernst and Scarlett could hardly contain their laughter, not because the story itself was all that funny, but because of the side-splitting way it was told.

Witold and I exchanged bitter glances. Corpses were not our favourite topic to accompany dessert. Witold suggested it was time to go. We still had a way to walk, and in the rain and darkness at that. Besides, we would be getting up early and going off for a ramble in the morning.

Scarlett said scornfully, 'Up the hill in the morning dew! You won't see hide nor hair of me before ten o'clock!'

Ernst suggested that, since breakfast was served until ten, it would be best if we all settled for an eleven o'clock start. Witold gave a sigh. 'Hakim, you are incorrigible,' he said, but he had to give in.

The room I was sharing with Kitty had its own toilet and shower. I let her have first use, since I go in for a thorough set of ablutions in the evenings and like to take my time. Kitty was finished in five minutes. She squatted on her bed in a pair of pink child's pyjamas, vigorously rubbing Nivea cream into her face. And all the while she chattered animatedly – the wine and the good food had made her quite chirpy. For my part, I disappeared into the bathroom, but decided against wasting my silk seductress's negligée on Kitty. When I finally climbed into bed, Kitty was still reading, but was already yawning widely. 'We're all getting on so well,' she said, 'I'm really looking forward to tomorrow.'

On the programme there was a walk to the ruined castle of Burg Fleckenstein. 'Just as a warm-up,' Witold had said. The rain had stopped, and we walked through autumnal woods and meadows without overtaxing ourselves. Now and again Witold asked Ernst for the name of some species of mushroom, but for the most part his friend's answer was merely a laconic 'toxic' or 'non-toxic'. Apart from that, there was no chance for little groups to form, as Witold was, like some sheepdog, tireless in making sure that his flock stayed together.

Scarlett was keen to know more about my job, and I was happy to tell her. Up till now, no one had ever shown any interest in what I did. But then she thoroughly got on my nerves by going on at length about her children's still half-baked career ambitions. The only mildly interesting thing was her complaint about the highly promising Oleg, that, where his sexual precocity was concerned, he took after his father, who in his young days had also been something of a tearaway. I found that hard to imagine.

Once, she also referred to Hilke Engstern, with whom she had been on quite friendly terms.

'What kind of a person *was* this Hilke?' I was curious.

'Rather reserved, compared with Prince Charming here,' Scarlett replied. 'Rainer just has to be always holding centre-stage. But she was very clever and had quite a personality, though maybe a bit too thin-skinned. You always had to be on your guard – at the drop of a hat you might offend her, without having the faintest idea why.'

132

Well now, I could certainly imagine Pamela Schröder offending more than a few folk, because she was never slow in letting fly with an opinion.

'Rainer and I . . .' she began again, pulled herself up abruptly, then said only, 'Now, I've lost the thread.'

I hated her.

Up on Fleckenstein Castle, there was a guided tour, done in a very traditional, schoolmasterly manner by a German-speaking veteran; he spared no statistical particulars, and all these details of length, breadth and height soon became tedious. Witold would certainly have done it better.

That first day went off harmoniously, the pleasant autumn weather doing its bit. Our walk took four hours, and I found it bearable. In the afternoon we had a short siesta, followed by a second stroll through the little town and a good meal to round it off. This time there was *Coq au Riesling*, preceded by a quiche lorraine and followed by a sorbet, all washed down with a great deal of wine. I had helped myself more generously than the evening before, for all this unaccustomed time in the fresh air had given me an appetite. Besides, since I had fallen for Witold, I had been getting thinner and thinner, so I decided to force myself to eat more.

But there was one thing I hadn't reckoned with. In the middle of the night, I felt ill, more than that, I felt like death. I didn't dare sneak into the hotel kitchen to make a cup of tea for myself. In the end, I was forced, in a bout of excruciating retching, to part with my delicious dinner, and after that I felt somewhat better. For all that, I still couldn't get to sleep. For one thing, I was not used to hearing a stranger breathing next to me. Not that Kitty was in any way a restless sleeper. Like a little tin soldier, she lay stretched out stiff and straight, without so much as twitching in her dreams or rustling her duvet. It was around four o'clock before I dropped off.

But shortly after seven there was a quiet knock at our door. I was wide awake at once, and Kitty, too, reacted immediately. Witold popped his head in – it was only by his whisper that I recognized him. 'I'm going for a little early-morning stroll, anybody coming? We'll be back long before ten o'clock breakfast.'

No way, I thought, not at seven in the morning! After all, I'm on holiday and I've had a rotten night! I shook my head. However much I loved him, that was going too far. But Kitty brightly agreed.

'Wait for me downstairs. Five minutes, I'll just brush my teeth and throw on my things!' In no time at all, she was ready and, quickly and quietly, gone.

How is anyone to get back to sleep after such a disturbance? It still wasn't even properly light outside. From the window I could see the two of them striding out across the dew-covered lawn towards the country road.

I yawned a few times, switched on the bedside lamp and picked up my business magazine. But for the first time in my life I found it numbingly tedious. What was the point of all these dead statistics when you were dealing with living people? – And with dead ones.

What was Kitty reading? A bestseller in English. I was impressed. Yet again, I felt old, uncultured, philistine and boring.

I went to clean my teeth. Kitty's cosmetics kit was sparse, none of your make-up or painting accoutrements for her. A jar of almond-meal paste, a bar of honey soap and a sea-salt toothpaste. How old might she be? I opened her bedside drawer; her purse and her identity card lay spread out before me – typical of the trusting Kitty. Thirty-five, I read in amazement – well, well, as much as that. I looked round for her luggage. Kitty was able to make do with a remarkably small holdall. Underwear, two white blouses, a second pair of jeans, a spare sweater, socks – that was the lot. I had brought easily four times as much.

Now I was wide awake. I took a shower and dressed. Still only half past eight. I went out into the corridor. Witold's room was next to ours, the key was in the lock. Not a soul about. I tiptoed in to have a look around here too. What kind of toothpaste did Witold use?

But the first thing that caught my eye was an overflowing

ashtray by the bed. Pah! I thought, are you really the right one for me! You smoke the place out at night, and during the day you come the child of nature bit. On the bed lay crumpled dark-blue pyjamas. He might at least have opened the window, I thought. Beside the washbasin lay a frayed tooth-brush, shaving things and a cheap aftershave. Here, too, I opened the bedside drawer, but as I did so, I sensed a thrill of apprehension, which was increasing by the minute. I had had this feeling earlier, when I had watched Witold from his darkened garden. An addictive urge, all longing, fear and strength.

A photograph in his wallet: it seemed to be of Hilke with their sons, no doubt taken a few years ago. Hilke was laugh-ing, her black hair shining, and she looked very different from that time when her green blouse was darkening with her oozing blood. One of the sons – presumably the elder – bore a striking resemblance to her. I had never seen Witold's chil-dren, so I stared at them, eagerly but without any affection.

A letter from Vivian, four weeks old, though. Her handwrit-ing was virtually illegible, the contents an outpouring of allu-sions and disjointed references I could make no sense of. Only the ending was obvious: LOVE, YOURS EVER, VIVIAN. In the end, I did also manage to decipher the opening form of address: 'Beloved Pharisee'!

Never in my life have I been able to write letters like that, I couldn't read books in English, couldn't sing Brecht songs, and I was well past ever having children.

I gazed again at the ashtray, the stale bed and the sweaty socks on the carpet. How oddly had Nature fixed things, that people should be capable of overlooking such nauseating details and should even be obsessed with the desire to share such a bed. 'Do you really fancy creeping in between those sheets, Rosie?' I asked myself. I was having severe doubts. For one thing, they centred on my sensitivity to smells and my aversion to undressing in front of anyone, and for another, my fears about not living up to a man's expectations. Did I really love Witold?

I went back to my room, lay down fully dressed on my bed

and took up my magazine again. But instead of reading, I lay staring at the ceiling.

The door burst open. Kitty wafted in, fresh-faced and sparkly-eyed. 'It was so-o-o lovely,' she enthused, 'you simply must come with us tomorrow!' And with that she thrust a bent purple aster and a late pink rose into my hand. ''Tis the last ro-hose of summer,' she warbled as she threw one item of clothing after another on to the bed. 'I haven't even had a shower yet,' she said, already stark naked. All relaxed and uninhibited, she stood by my bed: 'Everything's at its most beautiful in the mornings, there's mist rising from the fields, the meadow saffron's blooming, in the village they're taking the milk to the collecting point. And the dahlias in these gorgeous farm gardens, so-o-o big . . .' And she used both hands to demonstrate.

I had to force myself to look at her, for I have such inhibitions about nakedness, and I had to admit that Kitty, unobtrusive little Kitty, looked wonderful out of her clothes. Her body was strong, yet slim at the same time, radiating a natural *joie de vivre*. Singing, she hopped into the shower. What had she to be so happy about?

I made my mind up – no tears. After all, Kitty was thirty-five and still single; was I supposed to envy her, to hate her? That would be a waste of energy. You don't do anything to hurt a companion in misfortune. I had another kind of woman to hate – mothers.

As we all sat at breakfast, Witold let us into the secret that today was Kitty's birthday. So the reason behind her high spirits wasn't a declaration of love by Witold after all – I kicked myself for having paid attention only to her year of birth when I was checking her ID card. Witold had garlanded Kitty's coffee-cup with ivy and red rose-hips. She was to decide the course of the day's activities.

'Terrific!' Shy little Kitty was beaming. 'In that case, I'd like us to drive on a bit farther, find a new hotel and explore another part of Alsace.'

'Town and culture, or country and nature?' inquired Ernst.

'Nature!' Kitty demanded. 'Some villages with gardens, and above all, good food.'

'Well, it's not been very different from that so far,' retorted Scarlett. 'We've not exactly been starving up till now!'

So off we went, and Kitty, sitting up in front next to Witold, had the privilege of giving orders like a driving instructor: 'Right,' 'Left here,' 'Stop!' She picked out the tiniest side roads, enthused about farmhouses, spotted a stork and, after a couple of hours, stopped us in a tiny village and ordered a search for an auberge. Here, and nowhere else, was where she wanted to stay. The inn on the main street had only one vacant room, but they directed us on to a former manor house that had been converted into a hotel. It took some finding, but it was heavenly.

'If we get in here,' Kitty said with childish fervour, 'then I'll have a whole year of good luck!'

They had two double rooms free, but they could squeeze an extra bed into one of them.

'Done!' exclaimed Kitty.

'Yes, great,' said Ernst Schröder, 'then we'll have a boys' dorm and a girls' dorm.'

The house was ancient, with very thick walls and a broad outside staircase. The green folding shutters were gradually crumbling, where they were not missing altogether; our rooms lay on the first floor, and there was a second one above that. At meal times, you had to cross a cobbled courtyard, the little restaurant being housed in the former servants' quarters.

We three 'girls' had the larger of the rooms. I sat down on the windowsill, with a view over the small restaurant building. Five cats had gathered at the door. The moment it was opened from outside, they flitted in like phantoms. A few minutes later, the door was opened from the inside, a cook appeared on the step and threw the whole lot of them down the stairs. That didn't deter them in the least from regrouping and slipping in again with the next delivery of meat or green-groceries.

Once we had had enough of admiring the beautiful autumn colours, we tackled the day's expedition. The vineyard garden was full of sunflowers. Dogs and calves, children and vineyard workers scurried around. Kitty was as happy as a sandboy.

The chef came running after us. Did we want to try *baecka-offa* this evening?

'Oh yes!' said Kitty.

Timidly, I asked what it was, for my stomach was still in an extremely delicate state after its bad night. The chef went on about pigs' tails, shoulder of mutton and brisket of beef, which he would cook for hours in a hot oven with potatoes, generously laced with onions and garlic, herbs and lavish quantities of white Pinot, all in an earthenware tureen. My fellow hikers fell into raptures at the very sound of it. They could have their pigs' tails to their hearts' content, I would be ordering a plate of gruel.

Nor was that day's trek much fun. I was having stomach cramps. At breakfast, I had had only a cup of tea, and I would have happily stayed behind in the hotel in that comfy big rustic bed, opened the window wide and dozed off now and then in between listening to the strange human and animal noises outside. But was I going to let them think of me as an ailing old sourpuss, a killjoy? I gritted my teeth and walked and walked . . .

In the end, I felt like one of Napoleon's foot soldiers, tramping through the endless Russian steppes and marshes, with certain death staring me in the face.

Nobody noticed anything. But once I had said nothing except 'yes' and 'no' for three solid hours, the ever-solicitous Witold latched on to the fact that Trooper Thyra was a bit under the weather. I admitted that the previous evening's meal hadn't agreed with me. Witold whipped a hip flask out of his anorak pocket.

'Have a sip of this, it'll help.'

Because it was he who was holding the pungent liquid under my nose, I obeyed. It was some gruesome herbal liqueur, but it did in fact do me good.

'Well now?' he asked eagerly, expecting a reassuring reaction. I nodded weakly.

'Tell you what,' he said, 'we're heading towards a road at

138

the moment. When we get there, I'll wave down a car, and you can get a lift back to the hotel.'

Contrary to my expectation, it worked. A van loaded with paint-pails and decorator's tools stopped at once. This also gave Witold a chance to exercise his perfect French to explain that Madame had suddenly felt extremely queasy.

'I'll come with you, then,' said Scarlett out of the blue. 'If it's going to take another three hours to trail all the way back, then that's more than I can take, too!'

By means of gestures, she convinced the driver that she was going to look after me, the desperate invalid, then she climbed into the back and perched on a paint-splattered ladder. She gave the others a regal wave, while I slumped into the passenger seat in boundless relief.

Scarlett chatted with the driver in execrable French backed up by violent gesticulations, while he was able to maintain eye-contact with her through his rear-view mirror. Although I could spot her many mistakes, I would certainly never have been capable of carrying on a conversation in the language. When we finally arrived and had thanked the driver, Scarlett said, 'You go straight in and lie down, I'm just off for a coffee,' and with that she disappeared into the restaurant.

That was just fine by me. Shivering, I stripped off my hiking gear, got into my mouse-grey jogging suit and pulled the duvet up over my ears. Ten minutes later, there was a knock. A little girl of about ten, looking very self-important, strode over to my bed, presented me with a hot-water bottle in a little basket and explained that her mother had sent it. She gave an earnest nod and left; of course it could only have been Scarlett who had organized all that. I would never have expected it of that hard-nosed vamp.

Some time later, she herself came in, bearing a tray with tea and biscuits.

'You must get something in your stomach, otherwise you're not going to survive our party this evening,' she stated with maternal sternness. She eyed me intently.

'You don't seem to be a great fan of Shanks's pony, not like

139

Kitty. Probably you've only come along because of him and his blue eyes!'

I drank the tea, nibbled at the biscuits and, shortly after, fell fast asleep.

Around seven, I was wakened by whispering, which penetrated my subconscious far more sharply than conversation at normal volume would have done. Scarlett was painting her claws.

Kitty asked, 'Did we wake you? How are you feeling now?'

I was much better, in fact. I suppose I do have a pretty tough constitution. I sat up and asked when the party was to start.

'First, we have to doll ourselves up, gels!' said Scarlett, putting on her best old-time games-mistress's voice. Her red hair was freshly washed and curled.

Kitty was rummaging in her holdall and then she pulled out one of her cute white cotton blouses. Scarlett let out a whistle of disapproval.

'Haven't you anything else? Here you are, thirty-five today. You've got to wear something grown-up, just for once!'

Nothing could faze Kitty.

'I don't possess anything fit for a diva, here or at home!'

Scarlett scrutinized the contents of her own case and pulled out a golden-brown heavy velvet top.

'Try that on. The colour suits my red hair, but it might go even better with blonde. None of your cheap rubbish, that!'

Kitty pulled on the expensive item, and looked ravishing.

Scarlett was delighted, with not a trace of jealousy. 'You can have it as a birthday present from me,' she said generously.

I was impressed by this extravagant gesture, the kind of thing that was very foreign to my nature. Nevertheless, because of her remark about Witold's blue eyes, I was still absolutely furious with Scarlett.

Kitty accepted the pricey blouse without so much as a token, 'Oh, I couldn't . . .' She hugged and kissed Scarlett and posed in front of the mirror for a while. In the end, I caught the bug from the two of them, because Scarlett was now trying on one thing after another and bossily shoving Kitty away from the mirror. So I got out of the comfortable bed and my warm jogging suit and started doing myself up. When we finally joined the men, Kitty was glowing in her dark gold, Scarlett in emerald green and I in pale blue; to go with it, I had put on Frau Römer's brooch.

In the restaurant, Ernst Schröder was sitting opposite me. As if hypnotized, he stared at my brooch, while Kitty and Witold went on about how the rest of the walk had gone without us weaklings.

'Where did you get that brooch?' he asked, giving me a cold look. I didn't want to give away Frau Römer's whole story.

'Bought it,' I said shortly.

'Where?'

'At an antiques fair,' I lied.

Ernst stretched out a hand. 'Can I have a closer look at it?' I fumbled the heavy thing loose and gave it to him.

He gave the brooch a thorough examination.

'Strange,' he said.

'What's so strange about it?' I asked, as associations began to form dimly in my mind.

'Oh, nothing,' he murmured. 'My mother had a brooch exactly the same, that black profile of Hermes.'

Witold shoved his oar in, taking the brooch in his hand to have a good look at it for himself.

'Late nineteenth century,' was his estimate. 'Probably from our grandparents' generation. So who inherited your mother's brooch?'

'It was stolen, and my mother was inconsolable. She had intended bequeathing it to her first granddaughter, since I don't have a sister, as you know. Well, that would have been my daughter. But my mother died before Annette was born, and by that time the brooch was long since gone.'

The *baeckaoffa* was brought to the table, giving off a spicy aroma. They all helped themselves with gusto. Witold decreed that I should mash up a few of the potatoes, without the delicious, thick wine-stock. I managed to get down a few

141

mouthfuls and made a great effort not to notice Kitty and Ernst dividing up the disgusting pig's tail.

The feasting and drinking matched the gorging and gargling of the two previous evenings, and the mood became extremely merry. Ernst Schröder had an incredible liquid capacity. Although he had fallen on the *baeckaoffa* like a hungry horse, after a couple of hours he was visibly inebriated and extremely talkative.

'When I look at the youth of today – particularly my brilliant son – I can't help going green with envy. The number of women he's got through already, at eighteen – I couldn't catch up with him in the rest of my lifetime!'

Scarlett was looking daggers at him.

'At seventeen, I had my first erotic adventure, but then, for long after that – nix! Mind you, in those days, that was an exceptionally early start,' he boasted. 'When I look at Thyra's brooch, it all comes back to me!'

'Tell all!' Witold cheerfully egged him on.

Scarlett hissed, 'You're getting out of order, Ernst!'

'Well, that was really something,' Ernst carried on undeterred. 'I was pretty inhibited as a schoolboy, as we all were in the fifties. One day, on my way home from school, a young woman spoke to me, because she was looking for a particular street. As chance would have it, it was the one I lived in. By an even greater coincidence, she wanted to get to the people who lived in the basement of our block of flats. But there was nobody in. My parents were away for three days. I invited the strange young lady in, so that she could write a note to leave for our neighbours.'

We were all hanging on his words.

'A true-life novel,' Witold sighed with gentle mockery.

'Go on,' pleaded Kitty.

Scarlett had given up trying to kick her husband under the table.

Ernst, the great Don Juan, was basking in our attention.

'You can believe it if you like, but on that very first encounter, I, the totally inexperienced schoolboy, seduced that even more inexperienced young woman!'

142

'I am lost for words!' said Witold. 'Hakim, if you're not lying in your teeth, you are an incredible philanderer!'

At that, Scarlett pinched Witold's forearm.

'You're a fine one to be complimenting him!'

'Where did it go from there?' Kitty wanted to know.

'My lover was at least eight years older than me. In those days, a woman over twenty-five and still single probably was beginning to develop complexes and a fear of being left on the shelf.' Ernst beamed a charming smile at Kitty, as if to apologize for having come out with this less than tactful remark.

'Yes, well, to cut a long story short: we made passionate love at every available opportunity. Greenhorn that I was, of course I wanted to marry her. But to come back to the brooch – I pinched it from my mother and gave it to her as a pledge of my undying love.'

'And what became of the woman?' Kitty asked.

Ernst gave the brooch a faraway look.

'I don't know. She left the area suddenly, wrote me a fare-well note and left no address. I was only a young pup, and never managed to find out where she had gone.'

'So, are you saying this is your mother's brooch?' asked Witold.

'There's no way of being absolutely certain, although, with such an unusual piece, it's hard to believe there would be many of its kind in existence.'

Witold picked up the brooch again. All of a sudden, he gave Scarlett a mischievous look.

'What would you reckon a real lad has in his trouser pocket?'

She turned up her nose. 'Ugh, yuck! Any moment now and you'll be pulling out worms and lizards!'

Witold laughed. 'A rotten guess! Naturally, a Swiss army knife!'

He already had the shiny red object in his hand.

'Thyra, may I take the back off the brooch with the smallest and thinnest blade? I'll be very careful. Maybe, between the gold cover and the stone, there's a lock of hair, or a jeweller's hallmark, or an inscription.'

I nodded, and he began, very gingerly, to prise up the numerous gold claws. And there, invisible from the outside, engraved in the back casing, was a monogram, ES. Ernst became quite agitated, insisting it must be the name of his grandmother on his father's side, Elise Schröder.

'That means,' he said, 'that my first love is either dead and her legacy was sold by whoever inherited it, or she fell on terribly hard times and had to part with it.'

Scarlett was scornful. 'You're looking at the whole thing through rose-coloured spectacles! Maybe she didn't particularly fancy your brooch, and maybe the memory wasn't anything like as sacred to her as you'd like to think.'

They went on eating; the *baeckaoffa* stayed hot for a long time.

'How much did you pay for it?' asked Ernst, still preoccupied by the subject.

I gave a shrug. 'I can't remember exactly, but it certainly was expensive.'

Witold was interested in antiques. 'Things like that have a special value as collectors' pieces; I could imagine it costing at least three thousand marks in an antique dealer's in Heidelberg.'

In a very quiet voice, Ernst said to me, 'I'd love to buy the brooch from you, but, please, don't feel under any pressure. Think it over in your own time. I'd pay any price you ask, or I could replace it with any piece of jewellery you choose.'

So Ernst Schröder was the father of Frau Römer's daughter! How weird! Did she look like him? I had seen the woman, who was older than Kitty, only once. She was Oleg and Annette's half-sister!

I stared at Ernst Schröder with a sense of some disgust. He was the one who had messed up Frau Römer's life. Then I recalled Scarlett's selfless gesture, when she gave away her golden velvet blouse.

'I'm not going to do any deals with you, Ernst,' I said with icy arrogance. 'I'll give you the brooch, as a present for your daughter.'

He couldn't accept that. He got more and more worked-up, but always keeping a covetous eye on the heirloom.

'Thyra,' he said, 'I could never, under any circumstances, accept such a gift. Before Christmas, we'll go to one of the big antique fairs, and you'll pick out something wonderful for yourself. But you do understand, don't you, that this piece has a very special significance for me?'

The others had only half heard our haggling. They were already working out the next day's itinerary. Kitty wanted to go again for as long a walk as possible through the woods and across the fields, but this time it was Witold who had something else in mind.

'Either Colmar or Strasbourg,' he proposed. 'Come on now, boys and girls, we can't spend a whole week going round Alsace and completely neglect any kind of art and culture.'

'Well, all right, Strasbourg then,' said Scarlett. 'Years ago, I bought some dead classy shoes there, and I bet I can find that shop again.'

'Philistine,' scoffed Witold.

The birthday girl was admiring the brown-glazed ceramic tureen, decorated with little white flowers and green leaves. 'I'm going to buy one like that in Strasbourg, and I'm going to write down the exact recipe for *baeckaoffa*, and precisely one year from today, I'll invite you all to a commemorative dinner.'

'Why, that's marvellous,' Ernst said graciously.

Muttering half out loud to himself, Witold was planning visits to the cathedral, the Alsace Museum and the 'Petite France' quarter.

A degree of lethargy was taking over after the enormous meal. Kitty in particular was yawning heartily and without inhibition. After all, Witold and she had been out for a walk at the crack of dawn.

'So when should we make a start tomorrow?' Witold asked.

'Oh, Rainer,' Scarlett moaned, 'we're on our holidays.

Surely we don't have to fix that now. It'll all sort itself out after breakfast.'

Kitty, yawning incessantly, asked, 'Will you come and get me for our early walk?'

'Sure thing,' said Witold. 'I'll give a knock on the door again. Maybe Thyra will come with us this time.'

'Maybe,' I replied.

Kitty wanted to get to bed, and with that everybody rose to go. In less than no time, she was ensconced in the big double bed that it was my turn to share with her tonight, since Scarlett had bagged the additional single one for herself. Kitty stretched, sighed, 'Good night', and immediately sank into the eager rambler's sleep of the righteous.

9

Pamela Schröder pulled on a tracksuit borrowed from her son. 'My nightwear isn't suitable for this mass camping lark,' she said. I didn't quite catch her drift.

She grinned. 'Usually I sleep in the nude,' she explained, trying to shock.

No sooner was I lying next to Kitty than she started to snore.

Scarlett cursed.

'That's bloody awful. Does she always do that?'

I assured her that, during the two previous nights, Kitty had been perfectly behaved in her sleep, with never a sound.

'Turn her over,' ordered Scarlett. 'That usually stops it.'

I tried. But Kitty rolled doggedly back into her accustomed position, flat on her back, and carried on snoring.

Scarlett was standing at the window. Abruptly, she put on her anorak, grabbed her cigarettes and lighter and said she was going for one last smoke.

I looked out of the window into the darkened garden. There was already one cigarette glowing down there. Scarlett had strode outside, and now two little glowworms could be seen, heading towards a secluded garden seat.

That could only be Witold she was meeting. Did the two of them merely want to puff away in peace, without being nagged at by their non-smoking room-mates, or was there something going on between them? If only I could hear what they were saying.

Five minutes, and my patience was at breaking point. Up here, Kitty was snoring with unwavering regularity; down there, on a bench, sat Witold and the Red Witch. I pulled my jacket over my jogging suit, socks and slippers on my bare feet, and wrapped a scarf round my neck. While the autumn night air was not exactly icy, it was damp and fresh.

Kitty didn't notice me leaving the room either. The stairs down to the ground floor were broad. I felt my way down without putting a light on, and slipped through the open door into the garden. I was overcome by a feeling of elation. Once again, I was about to share in Witold's private life, to hear words intended only for one particular person. Of course, it was also possible that their conversation would be completely superficial.

I really didn't know my way around in this garden with its gravel paths and flower beds. It took me quite a while, along a roundabout route and stopping a number of times, to creep close to the garden seat in question – without the glow from the cigarettes, I could only guess at its position. In the circumstances it would have been mortally embarrassing if they had discovered me. Now I could hear them talking, but very quietly and confidentially, so that I had to get much nearer if I was to make out what they were saying. Like some hunter, I crawled along on all fours, because the shrubs were no more than waist-high and didn't give me enough cover.

Scarlett was complaining about her husband.

'I can't stand his showing off. Once he gets wound up, you can usually bet he'll trot out another dozen of his sexploits.'

'I must say, that one tonight was a real revelation for me,' Witold said. 'He's never told me that story before.'

'If there's so much as a grain of truth in it,' snorted Scarlett. 'It really does hurt me terribly when he goes on about his past amorous delights in front of me, and what I find downright horrible is his lamenting that they're all a thing of the past.'

'You'll have to get your own back,' Witold suggested. 'Do you still think back a lot to Portugal, too?'

Both of them were quiet.

In the end, Pamela Schröder suddenly asked, 'By the way, where on earth did you dig up that old boot?'

'Who do you mean?'

'Come on, that Thyra, as she so pretentiously calls herself.'

'When you talk like that, you're betraying sheer jealousy because you're no longer the queen of the exotic names in this company. I met her in Weinheim, at the fair.'

'Rainer, you're lying. Starchy old sticks like that don't let themselves be chatted up at the fair.'

'Oh, she wasn't there on her own. Didn't Ernst tell you about it? When you were in America, Ernst and I went along to the fair, and quite by chance we got talking to Thyra and her friend.'

'Ah, yes. Her friend – that's the one that was toppled from the tower, isn't it?'

'That's right. Beate was her name, a really nice woman. What actually happened at the tower is something even our super-cops can't get to the bottom of.'

'Rainer, you've set it up quite cleverly, getting all your fans swarming around you on this Alsace trip . . .'

'Would you by any chance be one of them?'

Scarlett laughed and asked for a light for her second cigarette. 'I heard something rustling about just then,' she said, to my dismay.

'Mice, cats, lions and tigers. And the jealous Ernst as well, with a hunting knife,' joked Witold.

'Oh, if only he *would* feel jealous! I've got the feeling it wouldn't interest him a bit whatever I got up to.'

'Should we put him to the test again?' Witold suggested.

'That's the best offer I've had in a long time,' retorted Scarlett. 'And for a start, you could warm me up a bit. It's getting quite nippy out here.'

Witold appeared to have put an arm round her; the two cigarettes were now very close together. I had the urge to lynch the two of them on the spot.

'But to come back to your admirer,' Scarlett started up again. 'Haven't you noticed she would do anything to win your favour?'

'So, wouldn't any woman?' Witold inquired cockily.

Scarlett must have retaliated forcefully, because he yelped, rather too loudly, 'Ouch! Have you gone crazy?'

149

'And you've got dear little Kitty under your spell as well. Tell me, have you been to bed with her?'

'My God, Scarlett, you must be madly in love with me to come up with so much jealousy!'

'You're a bit of a bastard for a grieving widower! You've got a woman somewhere, I can tell. Or was it that Beate, by any chance?'

'Not a bad guess. But Scarlett, my dear, it must surely have dawned even on you that I have a preference for under-thirties!'

Right in the middle of all this niggling, she started to sob. The bitch was cunning, for, right away, this brought out the comforter, the friend-in-need in Witold, and he started whispering to her and seemed to be fondling her.

It was like a dagger piercing my heart. This woman had a nice husband and two children, she had beauty and vitality, money and friends. Why was she trying to snatch this man for herself, when she must know that Kitty and I needed him?

Very quietly and softly, she said, 'It's a bit warmer in the car.'

At that, the two of them stole away, just as I had crept up on them earlier. Shortly after, I heard Witold's car starting up. Apparently they had at least had the decency not to have it away right there in the car park.

There was no need for me to creep about any more. Trembling, I went back into the house and lay down next to the unsuspecting Kitty.

I waited. Two hours passed, Kitty's snoring had become less thunderous, and I kept dropping off for a few seconds, but then immediately waking up again with a sense of dismay that I had lost my struggle for Rainer Witold Engstern. Not to Vivian, my young rival, nor to Kitty, to whom I had come within a hair's-breadth of conceding, but to a she-devil. In the Middle Ages, they would have burned her at the stake.

I must have slept rather longer than I thought. Suddenly, it seemed I had been roused by a noise. Kitty was breathing quietly; was Scarlett back and already in bed? I switched on the bedside lamp. It was half past three, the extra bed was empty. And so was my stomach: it was rumbling and I had a scorching thirst. I put out the light again and groped my way the four paces to the bathroom door for a drink of water.

The bathrooms in that old house had been built as an afterthought. One corner of what had been a generous-sized room had been carved off and transformed into a mini-bathroom. The architect had ingeniously managed to fit in a bidet on a swivel, a small bath, toilet and washbasin, thus complying with regulations.

The bathroom light was on, but the door wasn't locked. Scarlett was lying in the bath. I gaped at her as if she were a ghost. She was slightly embarrassed.

'Come along in,' she said. 'I never lock the door. I was chilled to the bone, and the only thing for that is a hot bath.'

I picked up the toothbrush glass and filled it with water.

'You've not been to bed?' I asked.

Her reaction was irritable and aggressive. 'If you already know, why ask?'

My anger boiled up. 'You obviously think an old boot, a starchy old stick is bound to be stupid as well. I know who you were out there with.'

Scarlett was ready for a fight. 'You were snooping on us,' she snapped, 'and it's because you want him yourself. Christ Almighty, that makes me want to throw up!'

'Scarlett, as you so pretentiously call yourself, I suppose what you have just done is, of course, noble and decent,' I countered.

'I've done absolutely nothing wrong,' she said, 'but when prudish and frustrated old maids go around sniffing sin behind everyone and everything and eavesdropping on people, then that, for me, is a perfect example of an inferiority complex.'

I was snorting with hate and struggling for the right words to get back at her.

Scarlett raised her pretty little foot with its red-varnished nails and gazed at it smugly.

'What was the story about Beate?' she asked.

That took my breath away. 'What about her?'

'There was a thing going on between her and Rainer.' The bitch was letting her imagination run. 'And you shoved her off the tower in a fit of jealousy.'

I grabbed the electric curling tongs that Scarlett had used to do herself up earlier in the evening. They were still switched on at the wall socket. In a flash, I swept them into the bath water.

The short-circuit cut the mirror light, but fortunately the one in the ceiling stayed on. Scarlett had passed out. Or was she dead?

With surprising presence of mind, I locked the door. Had Kitty been wakened by our conversation – although it hadn't been all that loud? What was I to do now?

I pulled the plug out of the wall, and the curling tongs out of the bath. I took a look at the naked body and felt for a pulse, but I couldn't be sure whether there was a faint beat or not. Somehow, I had a feeling she was alive. She would soon come round, start yelling and give me away – not only that I had tried to murder her, but also the business with Beate.

I had to avoid getting my sleeves wet. I rolled them right up, perched on the edge of the bath and slowly pushed her head under, until it was completely submerged, which made her legs stick up out of the short tub. I looked at my watch and held her head in this position for a full quarter of an hour. Scarlett didn't move. Her eyes stared out at me greenly through the red seaweed strands of her hair, her freckled body seemed limp and spongy. She was dead.

I dried my arms thoroughly, wrapped Scarlett's curling tongs in a hotel towel and listened at the keyhole in case there was any sound to be heard from Kitty. Not a thing. Carefully, I turned the key and opened the door, slowly, noiselessly. Kitty was fast asleep, as she had been for hours. With the curlers in the towel, I slipped out of the bathroom, closed the door, groped my way back to my case and hid the damp bundle under my clothes. Then I tried to slide into bed without causing the slightest movement. Kitty stirred slightly and murmured, 'Rainer.'

I lay there, and I knew that I was going to be ill again. This time, a corpse would be found in my immediate surroundings. One towel was wet, but Scarlett was lying in the bath and hadn't used it; the second towel was missing altogether – was that not extremely suspicious? Had anyone perhaps seen me in the garden in the night? Maybe Ernst had been spying on his wife? Could you tell by looking at a body that it had had an electric shock, did it leave traces? In the case of injuries from high-tension cables, I knew, the result was severe burns. I hadn't noticed anything superficial on Scarlett, but then I was neither a doctor nor a detective. On no account must I be the first to get up and discover the body. Witold would be coming to give Kitty her early call again. She would then flit into the bathroom, and I would have to let myself be wakened by her terrible shrieks.

I lay there as it gradually got light, waiting for Witold's knock and Kitty's scream, but it was now eight o'clock and no one had stirred.

As the minutes slipped by, I reflected yet again on whether I still really wanted Witold at all. I had made such sacrifices for him, put my freedom, my social standing and all my previous way of life on the line. If – and it was a very big if – he were suddenly to love me, to want to share a roof and a bed, money, holidays, friends and day-to-day routines with me, was that actually worth all the effort? Everything seemed hedged in by doubts; when you came down to it, he was so terribly distant towards me. I was overwhelmed by despair; why had I killed three women? The first more or less by accident, I hadn't much to reproach myself with there. The murder of Beate, that was a nasty business, totally unnecessary. I preferred not to think of it. But today's deed, the drowning of a witch, filled me with a certain satisfaction. In contrast to the others, this woman had hurt me to the quick.

Kitty stirred. I had to pretend to be fast asleep. From the movements of the mattress, I could tell she was sitting up, swinging her legs off the bed, probably looking at the clock. I knew it was half past eight. She let out a tiny squeak of amazement, had a good stretch and trotted off barefoot to the bathroom.

The expected scream didn't come, but in its place a resolute teacher's tone she hadn't adopted until now. 'Thyra, come at once!'

The command was so urgent that I had to obey. Whey-faced and with stomach churning, I approached the scene of my crime. The bathroom windows were completely misted over. Kitty was holding Scarlett's head above water.

'Grab hold!' she ordered. 'Get her under her right arm, we'll lay her over the edge of the bath so that the water can run out of her lungs.'

With our combined strength, the slack torso was draped over the rim, while lukewarm water formed large puddles on the floor.

'Get the men in here right away! I'll keep her in this position,' was Kitty's next command.

I rushed into the next room, throwing the door open without knocking. Witold was standing at the washbasin, shaving. Ernst was still asleep.

'Come quick, there's been a terrible accident!' I yelled; it wasn't Kitty, but I, who was having hysterics. Witold dropped his shaving-brush, wiped off the lather with a towel and rushed, stripped to the waist, into our room, with me at his heels. Ernst Schröder was awake by now all right, but not yet able to react so quickly.

Kitty was in complete command of the bathroom. 'Get Ernst to help me carry her over to the bed, so that I can start mouth-to-mouth resuscitation right away. Rainer, phone for a doctor and an ambulance!'

At this point, Ernst reeled sleepily into the room and got such a shock that he staggered and fell. Nevertheless, Kitty chased Witold off to phone, because he was the only one who could speak good French. I had to help Kitty take hold of the body and lift it over to the bed; Ernst hauled himself to his feet and gave a hand.

Kitty threw a blanket over the naked corpse and began purposefully with the resuscitation. Ernst had taken Scarlett's hand and was repeating over and over, 'She's not dead.'

As a matter of fact, the bath water wasn't yet cold, and so the body hadn't gone rigid and hadn't chilled either.

At some point, Witold dashed back up the stairs and took over from Kitty. Scarlett was a terrible sight, but fortunately I didn't have to look at her. I knew that their frenzied efforts were in vain.

After a remarkably short time, we heard the wailing of the siren. Two paramedics and a doctor hurried in with a stretcher, breathing apparatus, a drip-feed and a doctor's bag. It was not long, however, before the doctor ordered the body to be taken down to the ambulance. She was laid on the stretcher, strapped in in no time and, again at incredible speed, put in the ambulance. The doors were closed and the doctor began his attempts at resuscitation.

We stood around in silence, unable to see what was going on inside the vehicle, but anticipating that it was about to speed off, with its siren howling, at any moment. Only I knew that, because of the impossibility of any revival, it would not do so. At the same time, every bone in my body was shaking with fear at the thought of the consequences of a successful resurrection.

A quarter of an hour later, the doctor stepped out of the vehicle, looking very grave, and it was obvious from his face what he was about to say. He asked in French who he might talk to.

Witold explained that Ernst Schröder was the casualty's husband, but that unfortunately he spoke almost no French. All the same, the doctor looked towards Ernst and said, in laboured German, 'I'm sorry, sir, but there's nothing we can do.'

Turning to Witold, he said he still had some questions.

None of us was dressed. I was in my jogging suit, Kitty in her pyjamas, Witold in only pyjama trousers and Ernst in a dressing gown. We went into the house. Kitty ran upstairs to get a pullover for Witold. After she had left again, I went into our room, pulled the wet hotel towel out of my case and threw it into a corner of the bathroom, rolled up the electric

155

tongs in dirty washing and buried them carefully again at the bottom of the case. Then I dressed quickly and went back down to join the others. In the corridor, I came across the fuse-box. With a handkerchief, I opened it and pressed the telltale blown fuse back in.

The doctor wanted to know whether Pamela had suffered from a heart condition or any other chronic illness, and also whether she had been taking any regular medication. To my surprise, Ernst said his wife had had a congenital cardiac defect, although she had never required any treatment. She had certainly avoided any strenuous physical activity – like arduous hikes, for example. But basically she had hardly ever been ill, apart from the usual minor ailments.

The doctor wrote everything down, with Witold acting as interpreter now and again. Finally, the medical man reckoned he could not definitely establish the actual cause of death, since the deceased had not been known to him as a patient. He could not issue a death certificate, but, in a case like this, would have to order a postmortem and, as a matter of routine, call in the police.

At last he took his leave, but not before asking whether Ernst would like a sedative injection. Witold explained that Monsieur was himself a pharmacist by profession and was well kitted out with all kinds of drugs.

At the word 'pharmacist', the French doctor's eyebrows went up a notch and he gave Ernst a long, searching look. By the time he left, it was almost ten. The body had been taken back out of the ambulance by the first-aid men, who were not allowed to transport corpses in their vehicle, and placed in a small anteroom on the ground floor. Ernst went to be with the deceased, who was to be collected very soon. He sat down near her and virtually turned to stone.

While the landlady, too, was practically beside herself, she was still all sympathy and kindness. By a stroke of luck, the other guests had set off very early on an outing, and so the great calamity could perhaps be kept from them. With motherly concern, she instructed us all first to put on some clothes, and then to drink some strong coffee. The police had already phoned to request that nothing in the bathroom should be touched.

Kitty and I showered in another room. Witold was ready by this time. He took a cup of coffee from the breakfast table through to his friend. Kitty and I also had coffee, and even managed a dry croissant with it.

Witold looked the personification of a stricken conscience. Of course, he hadn't the slightest idea who among us knew anything of his nocturnal escapade. To camouflage his obvious nervousness, he worked up an exaggerated bustling activity. He scuttled incessantly from the breakfast room, where we women were sitting, to the kitchen to see the landlady, and then into the quiet room where Ernst sat by his dead wife and didn't want to be disturbed.

'I can't help blaming myself,' Kitty said to Witold and me. 'Last night of all nights I slept like a log; anyone could have carried me off, and I wouldn't have wakened. Thyra or I ought really to have heard when Scarlett ran a bath so late at night, and maybe we could have done something to help.'

'She probably had a heart attack, lost consciousness and drowned,' was Witold's theory. 'That could have happened without so much as a sound. Kitty, you mustn't feel guilty. Failure to provide assistance is really not your style at all, and anyway, you responded magnificently, doing everything right as if by instinct . . .'

That bucked Kitty up. In her turn she now praised us, too, for having reacted so fantastically quickly. How dreadful that it had all been in vain!

'Poor Ernst,' she sighed. 'How is he now?'

Witold reckoned he would soon have to persuade him to leave that room.

Where Kitty was concerned, Witold seemed relieved, but of course he still had no idea whether Ernst or I knew anything about his rendezvous. I set his mind at rest by telling Kitty, in his presence, that after the previous night's stomach upsets, I too had enjoyed a deep and dreamless sleep.

A police officer was ushered into our bedroom and the bathroom by the landlady. He sealed off the bathroom door and, after taking out a thermometer and testing the bath water, which was still there, he asked Kitty who had slept in which bed. The young man didn't speak in the Alsace dialect, so Kitty was able to reply in fluent French, although she fell silent when Witold appeared, leaving the rest of the conversation to him. The officer said we would all have to remain there until one of his colleagues had questioned us, and it would be at least another two hours before he could be there. He also went to have a look at the deceased, but first he asked Ernst Schröder to leave the room.

Ernst joined us. All at once, he was racked by an uncontrollable fit of crying. Barely intelligible, he reproached himself bitterly. He had, he said, hurt Pamela deeply with the rubbish he had talked during the meal, because for years now she couldn't bear to hear such subjects discussed. In all probability, she had quite literally died of a broken heart. Kitty stroked him like a child, put her arms round him and tried to comfort him. The policeman came back in and said he would wait until his boss came. Then he went into the kitchen, where the kindly landlady warmed up some *baeckaoffa* for him. We sat there anxiously. Witold was just itching to know whether Ernst had heard him come back in during the night. No doubt he must still have been awake when Witold left the room with his cigarette. But we learned from Ernst himself that he had taken a sleeping pill, because very often, after overdoing the drink, he would get too worked-up to be able to get to sleep properly.

The landlady brought us each a bowl of hot onion soup. And then at last the vehicle showed up to take the body away, but the driver had been instructed to wait for the inspector before taking it to the pathology lab.

It was a good three hours before the inspector appeared. He too spent some time with the landlady in the kitchen first, where the two attendants and the other policeman were sitting. At last, armed with his photographic equipment and a mysterious little case, he went through to the deceased, who was then driven away. Kitty, who had discovered the body, had to give him an exact description up in the bathroom of when and how that had happened. He did in fact inquire as to why the towel had been lying, wet, in the corner, since dead bodies didn't usually dry themselves off, did they? Kitty replied that probably she had taken hold of Scarlett with it. Scarlett's luggage was taken down into the police car. I was half dead with fear that my case might be searched. But that didn't happen.

Finally, we were each interrogated in turn. Apparently one of the other guests, who lived below us, had heard water running at quarter past three. This had annoyed him, so he noted the time. Kitty and I stated that we had been absolutely unaware that Scarlett had taken a bath so late. Nor did Ernst say anything about Witold's late cigarette, since he had presumably forgotten all about it, or didn't think it important. The landlady had heard a car drawing up late at night, but couldn't say when that was. The interviews with the German-speaking inspector dragged on and on. It was late afternoon before he was finished with us. We were to call in at his office the next day to sign the statements.

After his flood of tears and the interrogation, Ernst had pulled himself together somewhat. His main concern now was for his children. He wanted to break the news to them himself, but under no circumstances over the telephone. Against that, though, he would have to wait here, whatever happened, until all the formalities had been cleared up and arrangements for transporting the body back to Germany had been settled.

Witold suggested, 'When we're finished at the police station tomorrow, I think you, Kitty, should take my car and drive home with Thyra. After all, there's nothing more you can do for Ernst here. I'll stay with him, translate all the official stuff, and then I'll drive him home in his car. But Annette and Oleg will really have to be told right away.'

Kitty asked Ernst for someone he could trust, and who was also on good terms with the children. Now Ernst himself hit upon the idea of phoning his long-serving assistant in the pharmacy and a couple who were close friends, and they assured him they would look after the children and break the terrible news as gently as possible.

That was when it struck me that I had already rendered seven children – although no little ones among them – motherless.

Nobody felt like eating that evening, but the landlady brought us, unbidden, a snack up to our room, since she wanted to shield us from the merriment of the other guests. Afterwards, we went for a short walk outside. Kitty took Ernst's arm, let him talk, blame himself, have a cry and work off his feelings. Witold walked behind with me. He, too, was at the end of his tether. Once or twice he started, as if to say something, but he couldn't manage to get it out.

'Thyra . . .' he began again, very quietly. 'Oh, nothing.'

I didn't possess Kitty's knack of just slipping her hand into his, and neither did I feel the urge any more. This man, it was becoming clearer and clearer to me, might, if I was very lucky, have a little flutter with me some time. But I harboured no illusions that he would remain with me, faithful and true. Beate had once hinted at something like that: A relationship with such a man could only bring grief. Scarlett, too, had referred to him as 'Prince Charming', beside whom his wife, Hilke, had always had to stand in the shade. No, no holding hands.

But suddenly he found the words, and nothing would stop him. 'Thyra, three women are dead. One of them was my wife – you never got to know her, but you were there when she died. We both share the blame in that case. The next one was Beate, your friend, whom I got to know through you and whose daughter became my lover. Pure coincidence, you might say. In the case of the third one, who was my friend's wife, we were both barely a few metres away while she was dying. Is that a coincidence too?' Nervously, he snatched at a falling leaf.

'If I were superstitious,' he went on, 'I would think that you and I, when we're together, exert some kind of mysterious and fateful power. But I don't believe in the supernatural. All the same, these three deaths give me the creeps. I know the first one was my fault. But the two others – they have something in common: they were women who were neither ailing nor old, and they met an unnatural end. What do you think?'

I considered for a moment. 'I'm not superstitious either. It's inconceivable that the two of us could be bringers of disaster, like some angels of death. How's that supposed to work?'

Witold whispered, barely audible, 'Murder.'

'On one occasion it was unpremeditated manslaughter, twice it was an accident,' I replied coolly. 'The accident up on the tower was a spectacular one, I'll grant you that. But the one in the bath – looked at in statistical terms – not at all. Most accidents, and this I know better than you through my work in insurance, don't happen on the roads or at work, but in the home environment.'

Witold seemed content with that, or at least he pretended to be.

10

The next day, after a night of harrowing dreams, we drove to the police station. The statements had been drawn up in French, neatly typed, and were ready for signing. Witold translated for us, and we added our signatures. After that, we went back to the hotel, where Kitty and I got down to our packing.

'I seem to remember Scarlett having curling tongs lying about somewhere,' Kitty said.

'So?' I asked.

She looked around, then shrugged. 'Oh well, maybe she had already packed them. Anyway, the police have her case. They're very likely looking for drugs or something like that, with her being a pharmacist's wife.'

We took our leave of the men. I really did feel sorry for Witold then, pasty-faced and unshaven, pouring his eighth cup of black coffee; he was now faced with the arduous job of helping the grieving Ernst through at least one more day.

Kitty drove smoothly yet at a fair speed. She had little to say, which was fine by me. Each of us was lost in our thoughts.

'Are you fond of Rainer?' Her question was sudden and blunt.

'I suppose so,' I replied cautiously.

She gave a light laugh.

'We all fall for him. Why should it be any different for you than for me? He's a dear friend, if that's all you want. And if I can give you a piece of good advice, try to let that be enough.'

I would have loved to tell Kitty the whole story, the way I used to enjoy confiding in Beate. But I couldn't talk about my love, since it was after all the motive behind my crimes. Although I was not altogether clear about that myself.

'Ah, Kitty . . .' I began, but I was making heavy weather of it, just like Witold the previous evening.

'Kitty, I'm past running after men. What attracted me about this walking holiday was the mixed company. I had never tried anything like that before.'

'Yes, I can understand. I was just talking without thinking – don't take it the wrong way. I didn't mean any offence.'

'That's all right, Kitty. Besides, I'm enjoying driving with you, you seem to be so completely in control.'

'It's just as well I'm not having to drive our chemist's great gas-guzzler. I wouldn't be at all sure of myself then.'

Kitty dropped me outside Witold's house, where my car was parked. She shook hands and said how sorry she was that the trip to Alsace had ended so tragically.

I put my case in the car and drove off towards Mannheim, frantically racking my brains as to how I could get rid of the curling tongs right away. I stopped on the banks of the Neckar river, took the *corpus delicti* out of my case and stuffed it in my handbag. Then I walked along a rough track and, at a secluded spot, threw the thing into the water.

I had been home about two hours when Witold rang. He reckoned that he and Ernst would be allowed to drive home next day. The body was to be brought over from France to Ladenburg. The police had one more question, though: in Scarlett's luggage they had found the box for a set of electric curling tongs, but there was nothing in it. Had we, Kitty and myself, packed this item by mistake? I said no, but I did add that Kitty had thought she had seen them somewhere.

'So, did she actually bring the damn things with her?' Witold wondered. 'You see, I had the idea that Scarlett might have brought the empty box, out of carelessness. Well, I haven't a clue what a thing like that looks like, never mind why the police are interested in it.'

He rang off with a promise to get in touch again soon.

Afterwards, I was annoyed with myself. Maybe the right thing would have been to claim I had packed the tongs in my case by mistake. It would have been easy to buy another set. On the other hand, I had no idea about the make and age of Scarlett's tongs. It would certainly have looked much more suspicious if the appliance hadn't matched the original box. All the same, I was worried and edgy. Fortunately, I still had two more days off; I wanted to devote them entirely to my physical and emotional recovery.

Next day, Frau Römer phoned. Could she pop round to see me that afternoon? When she arrived, Dieskau nestled in my arms and I was very touched. Frau Römer gently steered the conversation round to her planned trip to America. I assured her that the dog was more than welcome at any time, and she was delighted. If that really was so, then she would book a flight first thing and go and spend three weeks with her daughter in the States. I encouraged her to go ahead and stay twice as long, since, once she was there . . . I took the opportunity to ask her whether her daughter knew who her father was. No, she believed her father to be dead.

I hadn't handed Frau Römer's brooch over to Ernst Schröder yet, planning to send it to him after the funeral. In fact, I was wearing it that afternoon in honour of Frau Römer, who was delighted to see I had pinned it on.

She chatted about her old dog, whose sight and sense of smell were apparently deteriorating rapidly.

'In his young days, Dieskau was a great one for chasing cats. In fact, he would be off after anything that moved, even birds. At least he gave that up as he got older and wiser.' She laughed to herself.

'Once, when he was very young and stupid, I took him with me to an aerodrome where they had gliders and small sports planes. From a distance, we watched one of these giant birds approaching the grass airstrip and landing smoothly. Dieskau was off his lead, and he shot off to catch this prey – with me right behind him, of course, because he had slipped through under the barrier. It took me a great deal of calling and yelling before I got him to come back to heel. Well now, my little lad, I said, and what would you have done with that big bird if you had managed to catch it?'

Dutifully, I gave a sympathetic laugh.

Frau Römer went on. 'Later, that scene often came back to me, like a symbol. I, too, or all of us, if you like, we all go rushing after some great prize, want absolutely everything, and yet we have as little realization as that small dog that what we are chasing is out of our class and we wouldn't have the first idea what to do with it.'

She gave me a long look, and said, 'By the way, to change the subject altogether, you ought to go and see the doctor, Frau Hirte, I don't like the look of you lately.'

I spent most of that free day in bed. On the Sunday evening, Witold got in touch, although there had been not a word from Kitty. Ernst and he were back home. The chemist's shop was closed. Ernst was totally preoccupied with his children.

I asked about the funeral arrangements.

'This Wednesday,' Witold replied. 'Incidentally, the post-mortem showed that Scarlett died of drowning. As we thought, she had a heart attack, lost consciousness and drowned.'

'Witold, how are you?' I asked.

'Much as you'd expect, in the circumstances,' was all he said.

I plucked up my resolve and came straight out with it.

'You had a smoke with Scarlett that night,' I began. 'However, since that's obviously of no material importance to the case, I didn't mention it to the police.'

Witold let out a sound like a wounded animal.

'Thyra, for once and for all, you don't need to protect me. I can look after myself.'

'So why didn't you say anything about it?'

'Out of respect for the deceased, and of course for Ernst. It was bad enough for him as it was. Is he now supposed to start wondering whether his wife was cheating on him with his best friend, on top of all that?'

'But she was,' I pushed the point home.

I heard the click of a lighter, then Witold inhaling and exhaling deeply.

165

'Absolute rubbish,' he said angrily. 'We sat outside chatting for quite a while, but that was all.'

'So why did you get into the car after that?' I demanded.

Witold was getting agitated.

'If this is supposed to be some kind of third degree, then if I were you I'd put my own house in order first. We drove into the village to get cigarettes. Goodbye!' and he crashed the receiver down.

Ten minutes later, he rang back.

'Thyra, don't get me wrong, it's just that I feel as though I'm cracking up. Of course it was good of you not to have given anything away about our late meeting, and I'm grateful for it. So, did you hear Scarlett coming back in?'

Aha, so the long time they were in the car wasn't just for a trip to the cigarette vending machine. Witold was obviously afraid that I had a pretty good idea that there had been more than just smoking going on in the car.

'Of course I didn't hear her,' I assured him. 'I fell into a deep sleep, probably around twelve.'

That seemed to reassure him; he went off on another tack altogether and finally asked whether I would be coming to the funeral.

'What time is it to be, then?' I inquired.

'The service is at two in the chapel at the Ladenburg cemetery, as far as I know.'

'I won't be able to make it. I can't take time off again so soon,' I explained, for I had no desire to attend a second funeral ceremony in such a short space of time. Then, after exchanging a few more platitudes, we rang off.

I had to go back into the office, although it was not at all easy. None of my work had been delegated to colleagues, far less taken over by my boss; everything that I would have had to get through in that week was piled up on my desk. They wouldn't have got away with that if I had in fact been off for the full three weeks! I would be putting in overtime for a fair while to come. Mounds of tedious files would take up all my office and leisure hours. Any thoughts of being in love, of good food and country walks were far away, but then again, memories of dead women, danger and jangling nerves were also pushed well out of my mind by my professional activities. In the past, it had never bothered me much, if now and again I had to spend my evenings working through some vital case. No doubt I was now going through a phase in the ageing process, or the final onset of the menopause, but I was finding it extremely difficult to get up early, to concentrate fully on my work throughout the day and still have laundry to hang up and my cup to wash late in the evening. I almost forgot to think my daily thought of Witold, to whom only recently my first inward good morning and my last good night had been directed.

About five days later, days that had been packed with grinding toil, he phoned. Witold was in a state. He barely managed to get out his usual chatty introduction, with which he always opened our conversations, and which was always devoted to my state of health.

'Thyra, do you remember how people always used to talk of "Inspector Chance"? Today, that most successful of all policemen has been replaced by "Inspector Computer". At any rate, there are now a lot of young detectives tirelessly and mercilessly feeding data, facts, people and atrocities into their computers, and that way they occasionally come up with connections they would otherwise have missed.'

I was hanging on his every word. 'Well, so what?' was all I could whisper.

'Well, so I was summoned once again to the Ladenburg police station. Just after Hilke's death, I was there a lot, but lately there's been not so much as a squeak from them.

'But I'll not keep you on tenterhooks. The police in Alsace have concluded their investigations into the case of Pamela Schröder and have passed it on to their colleagues in Ladenburg. And in Ladenburg, there's one who's a computer freak. Even without any technological aids, it had already struck him that the wives of two close friends had died within a short space of time and in fairly dubious circumstances. But this is where it gets interesting. He knows a colleague down

167

the Bergstrasse who has been working on Beate's case, and who happens to be computer mad, too. The two of them reckoned that all these incidents took place in close proximity to each other, and that all three women were neither elderly nor in poor health.

'Thyra, I said exactly the same thing to you recently – and I'm no detective inspector!'

'I can't for the life of me see what you're getting at with the computer bit,' I said.

'I'm just coming to that. Right, the two detectives feed into their computers all the people who had anything to do with the three dead women. Naturally, they followed lots of other trails, all leading nowhere. Well, anyway, they established that I had known all three, two of them very well. Incidentally, the fact that I was friendly with Vivian was something else they knew; they must have been watching me now and then.'

'Yes, but what conclusions have they drawn from all that?'

'Well, of course, Thyra, they didn't come straight out and tell me to my face they regarded me as a devious killer who preys on women. But maybe that's the line they're thinking along. At any rate, I'm under surveillance again, I spotted that quite clearly today.'

'Have they said anything about me?'

'They said that Ernst Schröder, for one, knew these three women as well – he's in the same boat as me. Without doubt, they'll be taking a close interest in him. Presumably I'm under even greater suspicion, because the sequence began with my wife.'

'And what about me?' I asked again.

'They didn't mention you by name. The fact is, you didn't know Hilke. A lot of people in my circle knew Scarlett as well as Hilke, although not Beate. They're presumably concentrating for a start on those people who had some connection with all three dead women, and that, in all probability, boils down to Ernst and myself.'

'Do you think they'll want to talk to me, too?'

Witold thought this over, briefly; at that moment he was thinking first and foremost of himself.

'I couldn't say. Maybe amongst the "also rans". But they'd never find a motive for you.'

'Witold, for God's sake, where are you calling from?'

'From a phone-box. I'm not completely crazy. In my case, there is, in theory, a motive for me killing my wife – I couldn't stand her hitting the bottle any longer. But the two others? Beate had no objection to my seeing Vivian, and nobody could believe I'd have had to get rid of her in order to get the girl. And, should anyone accuse me of angling after Scarlett, then it would have made much more sense for me to murder her husband.'

'Are they treating it as murder in each case?' I asked, by now thoroughly confused.

'They didn't say so in as many words. They must feel there are too many loose ends. How would you act, if you were in my shoes? My conscience isn't exactly clear, neither with Hilke nor with Scarlett.'

'Make sure you don't let that show, whatever you do,' I advised.

Wasn't he thinking of me at all? Wasn't he even the slightest bit suspicious? A short time before, he had in fact come very close to the truth. He's so self-centred, I thought, he's not particularly concerned even about Ernst. I promised to think it all over, to say nothing of his (and my) part in Hilke's death, nor anything about his rendezvous with Scarlett shortly before her demise.

I had to be on my guard. So, they believed all three women could have been murdered, and possibly all by the same killer. I had to work out what I would say in the event of my being questioned. And it was not at all unthinkable that my phone might be bugged and I was being shadowed.

Wednesday evening. Scarlett's funeral must be over by now. Witold and Kitty would surely be back home again. I didn't want to phone, but drove straight from the office out to Ladenburg. Outside Witold's house stood Beate's car. My heart skipped several beats, till I realized it must be Vivian.

169

No, no, I certainly didn't want to surprise her in the middle of a tête-à-tête with him. I drove straight on. I didn't want to head for home, so I decided to call in on Kitty.

Although I had already driven out to Kitty's with Witold, I had some difficulty in finding her place in Schriesheim, and had to stop twice to ask the way. It was a house divided into several flats in a residential area. I rang the bell. The door swung open at once. Kitty was standing there in the hall with a child. She didn't seem surprised by my visit, but said goodbye to her private pupil and fixed the next date with her before we both went into the living-room.

Kitty's flat was all Nordic lightness, a guitar hung on the wall, there were blue patchwork carpets on the floor and sheepskins draped over the sail-cloth armchairs. Along the walls, rough wooden bookcases full of books, and, on the desk, a cat, squatting watchfully.

In an attempt to get over the first moments of awkwardness, I went over to the cat and tried to stroke it, but the animal took fright and jumped away and hid. Kitty offered me a seat and disappeared into the kitchen to put the kettle on for tea. Witold's book was lying on the desk. A picture of the two of them, in a very dainty frame, hung half hidden in the window recess. I could feel a jealous rage welling up in me, for I didn't possess any such photos.

When Kitty returned with two wide tea-cups in unglazed earthenware, brown sugar and some ginger biscuits, I asked whether she'd had her snaps of the walking tour in Alsace back yet. She gave me a look of horror.

'My God, after that terrible shock, and you're thinking of photos! The film's only half exposed, and no doubt I'll keep the other half for months before I feel like using the camera again.'

Then I asked how the funeral had been. Kitty trotted back to the kitchen to pour the boiling water into the teapot.

'Well, of course it was awful,' she began. 'At least the minister spoke well, neither sentimental nor banal. We were all very moved. Ernst and the two children – that was almost

170

unbearable! Such grief, I just can't describe it to you!' Tears welled up in Kitty's eyes.

'Were there a lot of people there?'

'The whole of Ladenburg, or so it seemed to me. As well as half the school staff, Oleg and Annette's classmates, various clubs. The Schröders are very popular . . . Oh, it's such a tragedy, the death of a mother of two children.'

Once again, it gave me satisfaction to listen to the story of the big funeral. All my own work. Now I was really quite sorry not to have been there.

'Why didn't you come?' Kitty wanted to know.

I explained how I had had considerable difficulty even getting the time off work for the walking holiday; it had simply not been possible to get an afternoon off again so soon afterwards.

'What do you think, should I just parcel up the brooch and send it to Ernst Schröder?' I asked.

Kitty thought this over as she stroked the cat.

'I'd wait a while yet. I'm sure he has very different things on his mind at the moment. Anyway, that brooch would remind him of their last evening together. I'm afraid he thinks he hurt his wife deeply with that story about the brooch. No. Wait at least until these difficult times are over. Then Rainer can make discreet inquiries as to whether he still wants the brooch at all.'

Sensible advice, but I had an almost irrepressible desire to give Frau Römer's brooch away, to be rid of the thing. Maybe it was a way of trying to make amends for something . . .

'How's Witold?' I couldn't help it; I just had to come out with the question.

Kitty gazed at me. She was tired. In her old jeans and an even older Norwegian sweater, she sat slumped in the sheepskin and much of her fresh, outdoor glow was gone, replaced by a strained schoolteachery friendliness.

'Rainer was very fond of Scarlett, I think. Her death has upset him a lot,' and here she hesitated, 'but I suppose his young lady friend will bring him some consolation.'

There was a tinge of provocation in these last words. Kitty

171

wanted me to learn of Vivian's existence; obviously she, too, had been let into the secret as the 'sole confidante', the same as I had. I decided not to lie.

'I know of his friendship with Vivian,' I said. 'He told me about it, of course.'

That seemed to come as no great surprise to Kitty, merely to confirm her suspicion that both of us were fulfilling the function of mother confessors for this Lothario. And who could blame him? Obviously, he was not going around making any false promises and declarations of love, but simply making the most of having as many irons in the fire as possible.

Kitty sighed. Similar thoughts seemed to be running through her mind. All the same, I didn't dare ask about their relationship.

It was already getting dark early at this time of year. I decided to drive home via Ladenburg. By force of habit, I parked some way away and walked past Witold's house, staring at Beate's car. I crept in among the apple trees, although they were now shedding their leaves and were already bare in some places.

In the living-room sat Vivian, all alone and in tears. Actually, I had anticipated something altogether different, like a seduction scene. From the kitchen, enter a young man, presumably the eldest son, who placed a tray with bread, butter and cold meats on the table. Witold called from the kitchen, and the son fetched a heavy corkscrew from a drawer and exited again. Vivian blew her nose. Her eyes were smudged with mascara, her nose reddened. Now came Witold, who ruffled her black hair in passing and placed a bottle of red wine and glasses on the table.

The three of them sat down and ate. They seemed rather subdued, nevertheless, this whole scene of a shared meal under a drop-light exuded a magical aura of warm security that aroused me more than any erotic performance could ever have done. A deep yearning for human company and for a sense of belonging came over me. My exclusion from any kind of family life would not end until my own death,

172

that much was obvious. And once again my thoughts turned to the revolver that was still lying hidden in my bathroom. It was in an old sponge bag I no longer used, right up on the top of the bathroom cabinet. Maybe I should put it to my own poor head before much longer.

The French windows were tightly shut, so that I could hardly make out anything that was said. The son picked up a newspaper and seemed to be looking up something they had been talking about. I didn't dare creep any closer. It was cold. I was lonely.

At last, the son left the house with Vivian, and they drove off together in Beate's car. Witold carried the dishes back to the kitchen. His movements were lethargic, and his face betrayed a trace of resignation. I decided to head for home.

Quite abruptly, Witold opened the French windows and stepped out on to the terrace. He took some deep breaths, and suddenly he spotted me. Apparently he could only make out a shadowy figure, for he called out, somewhat fearfully, 'Who's there?'

It was horrendous. Not even a hole in the ground I could crawl into. Should I run away? Then he would be sure to catch me quite easily, like some intruder, up to no good. I was mortified, but I stepped into the light and said, 'It's me.'

Witold stared at me, utterly baffled.

I stammered, 'Actually, I wanted to come and see you to ask how the funeral had gone. But when I saw the car at the door and realized you had visitors, I didn't want to intrude.'

Witold was struggling for words.

'Let me get this straight – are you spying on me?'

'No, for heaven's sake, no! I'd never do that! But something drew me here into the garden, to the spot where I was standing that night when it all happened with your wife.'

'You mean, the criminal returning to the scene of the crime?'

Witold seized me roughly by the wrist and dragged me inside. He closed the door.

'How often have you been standing out there?' He was so angry that I became really afraid of him.

'Today's the second time. It all just sort of came over me,'
I stammered.

'I can't believe a word you say any more.' Witold lit up a
cigarette and fixed me with a look of undisguised hostility.

'If I ever happen to catch you again in my garden, I shall
call the police and show them your big feet!'

That was unfair. I dissolved into tears. Not so much because
of the big feet as because of his sheer spitefulness. But I knew
full well that floods of tears were sure to soften him up, and
that despite his outrage he was still the born comforter of
damsels in distress. And I was right: after a few puffs at the
cigarette from him, and a few sniffs from me, he yielded.

'Thyra, you're a very lonely person. No, don't try to contradict me; since Beate died, you don't seem capable of unbur-
dening yourself to anyone. Maybe you should join one
of these women's encounter groups, or try psychiatric
counselling . . .'

'You think I've a screw loose, don't you?' I sobbed.

He put his arm round me.

'But we all have. I'm sure I'm every bit as neurotic as you.
Only interesting and sensitive people need a psychiatrist.
I'm due to go and see one myself soon, I've fixed an
appointment.'

'Nobody can help me,' I bawled, 'the best thing would be
if I were dead!'

Witold was stroking my back, which was extremely agree-
able. So that he didn't stop, as much as anything else, I carried
on blubbing.

'Come, come, now. Here's a handkerchief. If, in future,
you're ever standing at my door, then you just ring the bell,
it doesn't matter if I have visitors. It's as simple as that.'

I calmed down and finally managed to ask Witold about
the funeral. His face darkened at once.

'I've no sooner gone through the whole palaver with my
wife than now I have to endure it all again with Ernst! My
poor friend was as helpless as a child. You've just no idea
what you have to listen to when the undertaker gets going.
''Providing a fitting conclusion to a life'' for them means lay-

ing out as much money as possible on a coffin. In the past, Ernst would have turned down flat any idea like that, and he would have donated the cash to a children's home instead, but he was so bewildered and unhappy that he was ready to order only the very best for his dead wife.'

I had never given that side of the whole business so much as a thought. How much money must people have spent altogether on these three funerals?

We sat next to each other in silence, Witold smoking and I kneading his damp handkerchief between my hands.

'The children have gone off to the cinema,' he said, apropos of nothing. 'I was too tired, and anyway, I didn't fancy it.'

'The children?' I asked.

'Well, I mean,' he explained, 'as far as age is concerned, Vivian belongs to my children's generation, not to mine. And besides, she seems to look on me more as a Daddy than a Sugar-daddy. My God, she has thousands of problems she can't come to terms with.'

I would have loved to know whether she was now his steady girlfriend or not. The way we sat there hunched so sadly, side by side, I thought, we could be some married couple, lapsing into silence again after a visit from their children. Witold seemed to sense my curiosity regarding Vivian.

'I'm too old for that girl,' he muttered. 'After all, I do have my job, and then there's the house to run and the garden. I can't take the late nights any more, and I don't want to – I need my sleep.'

My head was whirling with thoughts. Should I profess my love for him, should I at least make a move in that direction? And supposing, in a fit of loneliness and emotion, he wanted to go to bed with me? I thought hard whether that was what I really wanted. On the other hand, nothing ventured, nothing gained, as they say. I leaned lightly against him, tentatively sounding him out. The pressure was not reciprocated. He simply let it happen, so as not to appear impolite, but, after a few minutes had elapsed, he made an effort to disentangle himself by fidgeting about in search of another cigarette.

What was I doing wasting my time brooding about possible moves, when they were doomed to failure before they even started! He didn't want me; it was only my platonic worship that made him feel good, and in order to maintain that, he was even prepared, as the occasion demanded, to put an effort into being comforting and caring. I got to my feet. He followed suit immediately, without so much as the slightest gesture to encourage me to prolong my stay. We went to the door.

'Right, now remember in future, I'm always here for you. But I don't like anyone lurking about in my garden keeping a secret watch on me. The very thought could be enough to send me over the edge!' But he was smiling slightly, as if to take the sting out of his words, and then, light as a feather, his lips brushed my cheek. I left.

Frau Römer went off to America. I got her dog again, and his presence was something of a consolation. I talked to him a lot, the way lonely people usually do; I also talked to the dead, to Beate, my mother, even Scarlett, and tried to explain to them all about the torments I had endured and the troubled emotional state I was in.

One evening, Witold phoned; I had neither seen nor spoken to him since the time when he had caught me in his garden. In retrospect, the embarrassment of that situation had become even more painful for me, and all of a sudden I found myself wishing I'd never see him again.

He came straight to the point, without the usual preliminaries.

'The Computer-Cop has just been here again. I thought I'd ring to warn you. It could well be that he'll turn up on your doorstep.'

'Has anything new come up? Is there anything special I have to be careful about?' I demanded.

'Well, we've been through that already, haven't we? You promised you would say nothing about my rendezvous with Scarlett that night, and nothing about both of us being involved in Hilke's death. Can I still depend on that?'

'Of course you can. In Hilke's case, the whole thing is a question of mutual interest.'

Half an hour after we talked, the Ladenburg detective was at my door. I shut the growling dog in the bedroom. The man was polite but cool. He had a few questions, he said, because there were still some loose ends in the three murder investigations, and perhaps I might be able to think of something that could help.

First, he quizzed me in depth about my relationship with Beate, although that case wasn't exactly within his sphere of responsibility. Anyway, I was to tell him precisely what I knew about the accident.

'I can only tell you what was in all the papers,' I said.

'Well, maybe a little more than that. I can imagine your friend might have phoned you and told you about a picnic she was planning. It's not inconceivable, Frau Hirte, that you are trying to cover up for someone or other, Herr Engstern, for instance. After all, you were the only one who knew that your friend was in love with him; it seems that she never said a word to anybody else about that.'

'Yes, she did confide in me about it. But Beate made it quite clear that, up till then, the attraction had been a one-sided thing. If she had had a date with Herr Engstern, she would probably have told me. But she did not!'

The detective was watching me very closely, he still seemed to be having some doubts.

'Your friend's shopping list was in her purse, and the basket with her weekend shopping was in the car. Of course, she could have taken the champagne with her from home, but the food wasn't hers; somebody else must have brought that. You see, the butcher she bought her meat from does not in fact sell ready-roasted chickens. By the way, how did you know that Beate Sperber had been eating roast chicken?'

'Did I say that?' I asked.

'That's what you told Herr Engstern,' he insisted. 'In fact, he talked about that last meal as if he had been there. Beate Sperber is supposed to have been standing on the parapet of the tower, holding a champagne glass and a chicken leg, when

177

she fell off. We didn't make any information public about the contents of the dead woman's stomach. All that got into the papers was the thing about the empty champagne bottle. Herr Engstern insisted at first he had read about the roast chicken in the papers, but after some considerable discussion he believed you had said something about it.'

I shrugged. In my mind's eye, I could see the scene in Bickelbach: Scarlett, with the bubbly and the chicken. That had been something of a jolt to my memory of Beate, and probably I had mentioned it to Witold.

'I can't remember,' I said, trying to act naturally. 'If I did in fact say such a thing, then I must have read it somewhere or heard it from somebody. Beate certainly told me nothing about any picnic.'

The policeman went over to the display cabinet where I kept my glasses. Unerringly, he homed in on my five crystal champagne glasses.

'A crystal glass just like this was used by your friend for her champagne. Where is your sixth glass?'

'Oh, come on now,' I retorted indignantly, 'glasses are always getting broken. Who on earth has a full set of all their glasses?'

'You, Frau Hirte,' came his laconic reply. 'I can see here, for example, six sherry glasses, six wineglasses and six water tumblers. Everything looks almost as new – and extremely tidy indeed.'

That was a barefaced trick, and I got angry.

'So what? I have no family and few visitors, so it follows that my crockery and glasses don't get much use. But I do drink champagne, even when I'm on my own, because I suffer from low blood pressure. One of my glasses cracked ages ago. Are you going to use one missing champagne glass against me?'

He didn't reply, but was looking at my feet.

'What size shoe do you take?'

'Thirty-nine,' I lied. Let him measure them if he wanted.

'I'll take one of your glasses with me, and your photo albums, if you don't mind. And I'd also like to have a look at your shoe cupboard. Do you own a pair of training shoes?'

I shook my head. I wondered whether I should demand to see a search warrant and call my lawyer.

He got to his feet.

'Oh, yes, and I'd like to have a glance round your bathroom.'

I went with him. First, he went to my shoe cupboard, which he found, without asking, in the bedroom. The dog gave him an angry growl. He examined several pairs and said accusingly, 'Size forty-one. In thirty-nines, your feet would be killing you.'

He wasted little time on the wardrobe, but made for the bathroom. I followed. He pulled open the white Formica drawers of the little bathroom chest and checked to see if my hair-drier was working.

'Open up the medicine cabinet,' he ordered like some customs officer. I was standing closer to it anyway. His eyes flitted over my stocks of pills and cosmetics.

'And what's in that?' He pointed to the sponge bag lying on the top.

'Hair-curlers I don't use any more,' I said.

With a jerk of his head, he commanded, 'Bring it down, open it up,' as he dropped to his knees to open the trap door under the washbasin, behind which stood a bucket, some scouring powder and a cloth. I whipped the revolver out of the sponge bag and, from close range, shot him straight in the left temple. He hadn't even had time to look round.

There he lay, with a hole in his head, blood was running over the bath-mat and the detonation was still hammering in my ears. It was clear he had been looking for Scarlett's electric tongs, he had confiscated my champagne glass, and he would certainly have succeeded in rooting out the fact that I had bought the roast chicken from my own butcher.

I sat dazed and distraught on the edge of the bath (not for the first time), staring at the blood. The couple downstairs, being hard of hearing, would probably not have noticed the shot, but my next-door neighbour surely must have done. I rushed out on to the landing and listened, but there was no sound from her radio, which was usually switched on all the time, and there was no light to be seen through the milky glass panel in her door.

11

So what was I to do now? First, I retrieved the glass, then I wiped up some of the blood, distracting myself with all the stooping and strenuous effort that involved.

All of a sudden, I had to throw up. I missed the toilet bowl, and the sight and smell of blood, death and acrid stomach contents brought me to my knees. I staggered out of my normally spotless little bathroom and subsided on the sofa in the living-room. There was a thumping in my temples, my heart was beating like a pneumatic hammer, while an icy sweat broke out on my forehead. I was on the verge of total collapse, I knew. Mercifully, nature provides her own instant remedy for moments of crisis, and now she switched off my battered brain in a faint. But I could have been out for only a matter of seconds. Soon, dread and realization returned with a vengeance. All that lot in the bathroom has got to disappear! they screamed at me.

A few minutes later, I dialled Witold's number, my fingers trembling so much that I got it wrong twice. He answered immediately and could tell right away from the flatness in my voice that some disaster had occurred.

'What is it? Tell me!' he practically yelled.

'Come at once,' was all I was able to manage before hanging up. Then I sank back on the sofa and sensed I was in for an acute bout of diarrhoea at any moment. Going back into that bathroom was sheer torture, but there was nothing else for it.

Not long after that, I was opening the door for Witold, who stared at me with horrified foreboding. I'm sure I must have been looking like a corpse myself. From the bedroom came the dog's wolf-like howling.

He shook me by the shoulders.

'Well, say something!' he shouted in his panic.

'I had to kill him!' I blurted out.

'Who?'

'The policeman.'

Witold didn't believe me.

'Why? Where is he? Now don't crack up on me.' And he pushed me back down on to the sofa. At once, he noticed blood on my grey sweater. He lit up a cigarette.

'Calm down, now, Thyra,' he said, fast becoming a bundle of nerves himself. 'Calm down and tell me, slowly and rationally, what happened.'

'I've murdered him.' I could barely get it out, my teeth were chattering so.

'But where?' Witold was getting dreadfully worked-up.

'In the bathroom.'

He rushed out, firmly convinced that he would be able to rid me of the monstrous inventions of a hysterical imagination. After what seemed an eternity, he came back. He drew on his cigarette and went over to the phone.

'Witold, he was going to arrest you,' I said. 'I had to do it.'

'Arrest me? Why?' Witold stood hovering over the phone.

'He knew that you and Scarlett had been together, because a waitress thought she had seen you both in the garden.'

Witold stared at me, open-mouthed.

'That would hardly be grounds for an arrest,' he reckoned.

'And besides, he wormed it out of me that you fired the first shot at Hilke. I'm just so bad at lying,' I lied.

Witold was obviously debating whether he should call a psychiatrist or the police.

'Why, oh why do you have this manic delusion of having to save me from the guillotine?' he demanded sternly, yet in a way his heart seemed touched by the fact that I had committed the murder of a policeman for his sake.

'I've loved you from the first moment I saw you,' I whispered.

Witold was visibly taken aback. Now he was faced with the terrible duty of handing me over, me who loved him and wanted to protect him, to the law or to a mental institution.

'What am I to do?' he was asking me and himself. 'What did you shoot him with, anyway? Not with the same revolver as Hilke . . . ?'

I nodded. Then, in explanation, I murmured, 'I suppose I kept it so that I could do myself in with it. Life has no more meaning for me, because you'll never love me.'

Witold couldn't fight his own nature. He took my hand. 'Thyra, don't say things like that! You know I'm very fond of you and I want to help you.'

He eyed the telephone again, weighing things up.

'That dog's driving me crazy,' he cursed, as once again a long, drawn-out howl came from the bedroom. I went through and let Dieskau out. Excitedly, he rushed to greet Witold before making a move towards the bathroom. I held him back.

'Did the policeman come by car?' Witold asked. 'They probably know at the station that he's here, and they'll soon report him missing.'

He glanced at the clock.

'Strange that the fellow should be on the road so late – it's nearly nine. He left my place around half past seven.'

He paced up and down, undecided.

'I'll have a look in his pockets to see if he has car keys with him.'

Witold had to force himself to go back into the bathroom. He came back with a wallet, keys, a handkerchief and a notepad.

'I remember now. He came to my place by car, too. He must have parked it outside. I'll have a look-see,' he said, and set off downstairs. I was worried that he might go to a call-box and dial the emergency number, but Witold returned quickly, with an almost boyishly conspiratorial expression on his face.

'I parked his car a bit farther down, but it isn't a police car,' he said breathlessly. 'And now we're going to work out what's to be done next.'

By this time I had read the dead man's notes, at least insofar as his abbreviations and scraps of words could be interpreted. After his visit to Witold's, he had written: 'Call on R. Hirte. Suspicion re. Engstern's statement – chicken leg.' I tore up the page and flushed the scraps down the toilet, so that Witold wouldn't be able to read it. 'We'll have to get rid of the body,' I said.

'No bother,' said Witold, 'nothing easier! We just take the body out and lay it in the street.'

He blew smoke into the beam from the lamp.

'And just how do you mean to go about that? You can count me out! I can recommend a good lawyer, I can lend you money, but disposing of a body – that I can't do.'

I couldn't come up with anything myself. After all, I lived in the middle of Mannheim, in a block of flats in a busy street. But the dead man had to go, that was priority number one.

Witold, too, was thinking.

'All right, he's not married, but he's probably got a girlfriend who'll be waiting for him. Maybe she'll ring the station if he's not home on time.'

'But maybe,' I argued, 'she's used to him coming home late, or maybe, even, he lives alone. Anything's possible.'

'I'm going to phone them now.' Witold reached his decision. 'Thyra, we're not a pair of criminals. The wrong that's been done just gets worse the longer we wait.' And he got to his feet again.

'I only did it for you,' I warned him. 'If they question me, I'll have to tell them everything about you.'

'It'll all come out anyway. I made a big mistake in trying to get out of Hilke's death the way I did. Thyra, it's no good.'

I burst into tears, but this time it didn't seem to produce the desired effect. All the same, he still hadn't touched the phone.

'We could take the body down into the cellar,' it suddenly occurred to me. 'We can park his car in an entry they used to use for delivering the coal. Then we could load him into his car without anyone noticing and drive him away.'

'Thyra, the body will be examined, whatever happens, and

then of course they'll discover that he was killed with the same gun as my wife.'

Witold stopped short. He realized with a shock that now suspicion would most likely fall on him again.

'If only you had thrown away that gun!' he yelled at me.

Now it was my turn to be calm.

'Once he's in the car, you can drive him to a quarry, let the car fall over the edge and burst into flames. I'll come along behind in my car and bring you back.'

'Tell me, just how many murder stories . . . ?' But then he seemed to be having second thoughts about my suggestion after all.

'It wouldn't work. We could be spotted right here, on the stairs.'

'If we wait till around midnight, there's no problem at all. The woman next door goes to bed early, the old folk down below even earlier, and the young couple are away on holiday, anyway . . .'

'I'm starving,' Witold said out of the blue. I took that as a positive sign.

'What can I make for you? A cheese sandwich, eggs?'

'Yes, a sandwich. Bread, with a fried egg on top, if you like.'

I went into the kitchen and heated butter in the frying pan. The smell turned my stomach over. But I'm nothing if not tenacious, and five minutes later I was serving up his order and asking what he wanted to drink. He wasn't listening, but seemed deep in thought, eating mechanically.

Now I plucked up courage and went back into the bathroom. Again, I wiped everything thoroughly and took a good look at the dead man. The head wound hadn't bled too much, and only the small terry-towelling bath-mat was blood-soaked. Nor had his brains or any other slimy stuff leaked out.

The first man I had murdered! I took a long, close look at him; he was fairly short, wiry and athletic. If he hadn't been so sure he was in no danger from me, I'd never have stood a chance of overpowering him. Now I felt a tinge of pride and

185

relief, even though fear and the imminent threat of physical collapse were still uppermost in my mind.

By now, Witold had finished eating. He had managed, even in such a short space of time, to pollute my little living-room with cigarette smoke. However, I wasted no words on that, since he seemed to be giving serious consideration as to how we might dispose of the body.

'The idea of the quarry isn't such a bad one,' he said. 'If we can get the body into the car without being seen, the rest shouldn't be any real problem.'

'We'll have to fold him over a bit,' I suggested. 'I mean, I don't know how quickly he'll stiffen up.'

Witold found my uncompromising choice of words revolting, but he did take the point. He stood up, and I followed him into the bathroom.

'Have you a large bin-bag?' he asked.

The only bags I had were fairly small, suitable for my kitchen bin, since I naturally had no garden rubbish. I wrapped the bloody bath-mat round the dead man's head and pulled the biggest available plastic bag over it.

'I could get a duvet cover, if you like,' I suggested. 'Then, if anyone did see us on the stairs, it would look like a big bag of laundry.'

All Witold had to say was, 'Let's give it a try.'

I fetched my shabbiest cover from the cupboard. Together, we got the dead man into a huddled position, which in fact he had half assumed already when he had been crouching, and pushed him into the duvet cover. He made a most unwieldy bundle. Witold tried lifting it; he would be able to carry it all right, but it didn't look at all like a bagful of laundry.

'We'll have to wait a while,' I said. 'It's only eleven now, and there are still too many people out and about in the street, and maybe even going up and down the stairs.'

Dieskau suddenly came darting out of the living-room and started on a thorough sniff around our parcel of laundry. I shut him in the bedroom again; in a strange way, I felt ashamed in front of the dog.

We sat down together to work things out.

'We could use either the quarry in Dossenheim or the one in Weinheim,' Witold reflected. I had a feeling that he was beginning to regard finding the perfect solution to this problem as some kind of sporting challenge. Boy scout dreams, singing round the camp fire, whittling sticks with a penknife, covering up tracks, playing cops and robbers – instead of withering away inside him, such childish desires had just been lying dormant, waiting until some opportunity arose to translate them into actions. On top of that, there was his marked inclination to play the big brother who treats all women as little sisters, takes them by the hand, and, comforting them and showing them how to cope, earns their adoring respect. He was the perfect accomplice. That aside, though, his morale and his resolution rested on pretty wobbly foundations; where the ability to come quickly to pragmatic decisions was concerned, I was streets ahead of him.

'I'll bring the car back here around twelve. For now, you could show me where the driveway leading to the cellar door is.'

I took Witold downstairs, and he inspected the place where he was to park. He was happy with that.

'We'll lay the body on the back seat, not in the boot. At night, we certainly shouldn't be stopped on the way to Weinheim. But just in case, bring an old blanket and we'll spread it over him. Do you have a spare canister of petrol in your car?'

No, of course I hadn't. And that reminded me that my tank was practically empty.

'Then take my car,' decided Witold. 'The joke would really be on us if we got stuck on the way home because we had run out of fuel.'

I don't like driving unfamiliar cars, but nodded obediently. Witold was going to help me, so now was not the moment for being awkward. The time crawled past so slowly. The dead man was lying neatly parcelled up in the bathroom and the door was shut. The dog was wailing quietly. All the lights were out except for one small lamp in the living-room. If the doorbell were to ring, I wasn't going to answer it. An old blanket lay ready. Witold was again polluting my whole place with smoke and talking a lot of meaningless rubbish.

Shortly before midnight, he went to get the car. I was alone, and anxiety welled up in me again. When Witold returned, the first thing he did was to light up another cigarette. Then, with almost too much bravado, he said, 'Right, let's get on with it!' I tiptoed into the hallway. Not a sound. I beckoned to Witold, who shouldered his bundle while I switched off the hall light. He moved quietly and slowly; his load was a heavy one; twice he had to put it down.

On the stairs, I noticed the hall light coming on in the old couple's flat. We froze. They might just happen to look through the spy-hole; were we in their field of vision? But everything remained quiet, and Witold started on the second flight of stairs. When at last we were halfway down the cellar steps we heard the front door opening and stiffened again.

At long last, we reached the bottom, and I opened the cellar door. There in front of me, in the shadows, stood the stranger's car. Witold put down the body and handed me the keys. I opened up, he deposited the bundle on the back seat, and I covered it with the rug. We both took a deep breath.

'Do you know where the Weinheim quarry is?' asked Witold. 'The thing is, you're going to have to go first, and if there's anything at all out of the ordinary – an accident, a patrol car or the like – give a warning signal.'

I didn't know the way to the quarry. 'Then you'll have to drive this car. It's quite simple,' said Witold, almost relieved, or so it seemed to me. Was he going to leave me in the lurch?

'I'll go on ahead in mine,' he ordered, 'and you follow, keeping me in sight. If there's anything at all wrong, I'll give a quick flash of the hazard lights. Then you stop and wait.'

I nodded in mute apprehension and got into the strange car, complete with a murdered detective inspector on the back seat. This whole thing was like some bad dream. Rose-marie Hirte sits working in an office, she's not the sort to go chauffeuring corpses to rock quarries at dead of night.

Witold drove up and looked round to see whether I was

managing the unfamiliar car. Gingerly, I set it in motion; basically, the layout of the gears was no different from my own, and Witold had already switched on the lights for me. We drove in convoy down the motorway leading to the Bergstrasse. There was little traffic about at that hour, and I found that having to concentrate so hard on my driving helped to distract me from my fear of discovery. No, Witold was not going to pull a fast one, he held back as soon as the distance between us became too great, for which I was immensely grateful.

We drove at a steady speed and as unobtrusively as possible towards Weinheim. Witold knew the way and swung off on to a road that led up a steep slope. At the top of the hill, he pulled up in a car park, and I stopped the policeman's car next to his. Everything was dark and deserted. Off to the left, the road led on up to one of the two old castles.

'We'd better leave my car here and drive the other one up to the quarry. As far as I remember, it's along an unmade track.'

Delighted at not having to drive any further myself, I scrambled across into the passenger seat. Without a word, Witold took the petrol canister out of his car and stowed it next to the body. Quite unexpectedly, he gave me a brotherly kiss. 'No going back now,' he said sadly and drove slowly on sidelights along the bumpy track.

We had gone barely a hundred metres, however, when a barrier loomed up ahead. Witold couldn't remember it being there. We got out, and in the beam of the headlights and a torch we examined the massive padlock on it.

'It's no good, I'll never get that open,' Witold reckoned. 'We'll have to turn back and try Dossenheim.'

The prospect was appalling, but we would have needed a sledgehammer at least if we were to break that lock.

'You wouldn't have a hairgrip, would you?' asked Witold, and I could only shake my head guiltily. He went back to the car.

I shone the torch on the barrier again. I let out a muted cry of triumph, and Witold stopped.

'Look,' I called, 'the pins on the mountings are rusted through!'

We made another inspection of the whole works and discovered that, with a bit of effort, the barrier could simply be lifted up; that would leave the padlock intact and thus still a deterrent for any other vehicles. Witold raised the barrier, I drove the car through, and then we changed places again and drove on.

It seemed to take us an eternity to go jolting along between chestnut, oak and beech trees, until at last the track ended at a head-high wire fence.

'Damn it, that wasn't there the last time!' cursed Witold. We got out again. Witold turned off the lights and took the torch. Together, we walked along the fence for a bit on both sides; it was solid, and beyond it, there were rolls of barbed wire.

Witold opened the boot of the car and, while I held the torch for him, investigated the contents of the tool-kit. It was well equipped, right down to a hefty pair of pliers.

'Great,' Witold applauded the dead man. 'I wouldn't have had anything like this in *my* car. But then again, he doesn't have a flashlamp.'

He made a fairly clumsy attempt at cracking open the fence. In the end, he succeeded, but it required a lot of effort. Despite our taking turns at the work, it took us over half an hour before we had snipped one section of the wire netting from top to bottom. But the anchoring at the base of the fence gave us more trouble and we had to clip off a stretch some two metres wide.

When we were finished at last, we took the dead man from the back seat, removed the plastic bag and the bath-mat and sat him behind the wheel. Witold doused the body, the seats and the mat with petrol and released the handbrake.

'Right, now let's give it a good shove!' he ordered. Together, we heaved, but couldn't get past a large stone block lying awkwardly in the way. Witold pushed the dead man farther towards the middle and squeezed in beside him.

'I'll reverse a little to get up enough speed to clear that

stone,' he explained. 'You stand at the edge with the torch.'

I clambered over the roll of barbed wire, switched on the torch and waited. Even using the power of the engine, it didn't work first go.

'That was stupid of us,' Witold said. 'We should have cut the hole a few metres farther to the right and we'd have had no problem. We'll probably have to get to work with the wire-cutters again now.'

He got back out of the car. We were both exhausted.

'I'll give it one more try,' he decided and squeezed back in beside the corpse. I took up position at the edge of the abyss and signalled with the torch.

Witold reversed again. I couldn't help thinking we had created a great deal of noise, but at this time of year it was extremely unlikely that some courting couple, or anyone else, would be roaming around here in the middle of the night.

Witold got up to a good speed and, surging forward, managed to clear the stone block. But obviously he didn't manage to come to a halt at the right place – the car flew on beyond the bright circle of my torch beam and crashed down into the depths.

Had Witold been unable to stop, or had it been some new ploy of his to jump clear at the last moment?

From the distant depths came the sounds of explosions, and then flames. I stood petrified, like some statue, staring downwards. Other than the brightness of the blaze and the flashes of some small explosions, I could make out absolutely nothing in the dark, gaping chasm.

So now Witold was dead, too. 'Jump after him, Rosemarie!' my mother's voice was calling to me. I stepped to the very edge of the abyss and decided to hang about no longer. In the distance, I heard the siren of a fire engine, and that brought me back to the reality of the situation. I had to get out of here.

Torch in hand, I ran along the dark woodland path. Despite all my efforts, I wasn't making much headway. As I ran, I kept thinking I could hear human voices in front of me, behind me, and on both sides. Witold's car was standing on its own in the car park. The keys were in the tailgate lock; Witold had clean forgotten them when he took out the petrol can. Where had the canister got to? It was probably still lying in the wood as an unmistakable pointer to the fact that this was murder: a hole punched in the fence and a corpse doused in petrol. Even if everything had been burnt beyond recognition, no one would be in any doubt that this was no accident.

Mechanically, I took the car keys, opened up, sat myself in Witold's driving seat and set off. It would have been much too far to walk home.

Home? On no account must I park Witold's car outside my flat in Mannheim. Now that he was dead, then let them assume he was the culprit, that couldn't hurt him any more. So I would have to park it outside his house in Ladenburg. It would have to look as if he had shot the policeman and then got rid of the body, possibly even committed suicide at the same time.

But if it was a question of killing himself, would he not have taken the gun and shot himself at home, rather than going through all the toil and trouble at the quarry first?

So I drove to Ladenburg. In Weinheim, I heard all sorts of sirens blaring and howling, but strangely enough, I met none of the vehicles belonging to them. Not knowing my way about, I couldn't duck around back roads, but had to head straight through the centre of town. Apparently they were trying to reach the burning vehicle from below and, luckily for me, no one had thought of approaching the quarry from the top end.

In Ladenburg, I got out of the car at Witold's place and left the keys in the ignition. First, though, I wiped them, the steering wheel and gearstick thoroughly clean.

Now I stood there in the street, wondering how I should make my way home. Train, taxi or tram seemed much too conspicuous, and I certainly was not going to stop someone and hitch a lift. There was nothing else for it but to set off on the long trek through the cool autumn night. How far? I had no idea. What was a short hop by car would take for ever on foot. Of course, I could hide somewhere along the way and

192

take an early-morning tram. That was when it occurred to me that, in all the excitement, I had brought no money with me, and all I had in my coat pocket was my identity papers and the keys to my house.

I strode out on my way. It was a clear, starry night. I stuck to the shadows as much as possible, dodged along side-streets and avoided making any noise.

'Mur-der-ess!' My pulse was hammering the message out. I marched along quite briskly to this rhythm. Why had I always had such luck in the commission of my crimes? Why had I never been suspected, far less convicted?

Once again, luck was on my side. I discovered a man's bicycle, black, ancient, dilapidated, but unlocked. I didn't hesitate a moment before commandeering it. Anyway, it was leaning against a refuse container and was obviously waiting for the bulky refuse collection. As I was still struggling to mount the thing, the lid of the garbage skip was jerked open. In my terror, I fell off the bike. Like a cuckoo in a clock, a vagrant poked his head out and yelled, 'Stop, thief, murderer!'

It would be hard to describe my sheer horror, but at the same time, my instinctive urge to escape came to the fore again – get the hell out of here, get the hell away from this monster, who no doubt took all ten of the Commandments even less seriously than I did.

Before he could clamber out of his bedchamber, I had managed to gather myself together, perch on the saddle and, summoning up all my strength and practically standing on the pedals, to race off. A few minutes later, I had to stop to get my breath back, but I was gripped by euphoria: I had got away!

Out of cycling practice as I was, I didn't find it at all easy to make my way home by that means, especially since the bike had no lights. All the same, I did still have some reasonable hope of not having to spend the whole night on my feet.

It was still pitch dark when I reached Mannheim. Lights were going on all around, as workers on the early shift were getting under their showers and cars were setting out towards the town. I left the bike in a car park and walked the last few

193

minutes. When, at long last, I had climbed the stairs and reached my flat, I resolved never to leave it again. Into bed, never more to rise from it. Best of all, to fall asleep and never again wake up.

Cold, musty smoke confronted me, a sudden attack of cramp shot through my right calf; an overflowing ashtray and a sandy-coloured sweater that had slipped off a chair were reminders of Witold, who, only a few hours before, had been sitting here, hale and hearty.

I opened the window, staggered into the bedroom and threw myself, fully clothed, on the bed. A black shadow shot out and threw itself on me. It was a very scared Dieskau; I hadn't even taken him for his walk the evening before. It was hardly worthwhile going to bed. I would have to get up again soon and go to the office. Nevertheless, I stayed there, lying on the bed, stroking the dog's ears, no longer capable of any clear decisions, never mind actions.

I wanted to be ill, I wanted to be lying in a sterile, white hospital bed, seeing only total strangers and having to talk to no one. No more duties, no more responsibilities. My one desire was to doze off into a vegetable state.

But after half an hour of this, I got up and showered. I made myself office-presentable, cleaned the place up, drank some tea and led Dieskau briefly out on to the grass verge. Morning paper in hand, I came back upstairs, but I knew from experience that the previous night's events were never published the next morning, unless, that is, they were of worldwide significance.

Punctually as ever, I left my now tidy flat with the dog and drove to the office. Getting through this day was certainly going to be especially difficult.

Shortly before the lunch break, I received a phone call from the police requesting that I make myself available for a brief chat in my office. This time there were two of them, looking very serious indeed. Had a colleague of theirs, an Inspector Wernicke, phoned me or perhaps even called in on me yesterday?

I denied that. Where had I been? After the office closed, I

had gone home, although I did stop off on the way to do a little shopping. Back home, I had, after a short breather, taken the dog for a walk in the evening. I gestured towards Dieskau under my desk, as if he could testify as a witness.

Had Herr Engstern phoned or visited me?

Again I said no, and told them the last time I had seen him had been some ten days ago. In the end, I demanded, with as much force as I could still muster, to know what all these questions were about.

One of the policemen, young and wiry like his late colleague, heaved a deep sigh. When he spoke, it was in clipped tones.

'You'll read about it in tomorrow's papers anyway. Last night, my friend Hermann Wernicke was burned to death in his car.'

'How did that happen?' I asked.

'If we had a clear idea about that, we wouldn't be here,' the second officer explained, rather more pleasantly. 'But one thing's sure, we're talking murder here. Wernicke was well on the way to solving those particularly difficult cases of the three murdered women. It's probable that Engstern was guilty of them all, even though a number of things are still a bit confused. We know that Wernicke intended going to see Engstern, because he had come across some new circumstances that seemed suspicious. After that, he was never seen again, and last night he was pulled out of his crushed car, burnt almost to a cinder.'

About Witold's body, not a word. Should I ask after him?

I didn't dare. 'So, where did this happen?' sounded much more noncommittal.

'The car crashed down into a quarry near Weinheim, but, before that, someone had drenched my unconscious, or maybe even already dead, friend in petrol,' the younger of the two said accusingly.

My face was pale and miserable, I knew, but, in view of what they had just described, that was obviously only to be expected.

Once again, they urged me to think back carefully over

195

everything Witold had said to me lately, and to get in touch the moment anything occurred to me that didn't seem to add up.

'And what does he have to say, himself?' I asked innocently.

They exchanged glances.

'He can't say anything,' said one of them.

'Why not?' I asked. 'Has he disappeared?'

'He's lying at death's door,' came the reply. 'Today will probably see the end of him, without him having regained consciousness. The doctors don't hold out any hope for him. He was also sitting in the car that went over the top, but he was thrown clear. He was probably trying to jump out, and didn't manage to time it right.'

I stared at them, horrified.

'So where is he now?' I asked.

'In the St John's Hospital, but visiting him is out of the question. He's still being kept on a respirator, but I wouldn't build up any false hopes if I were you.'

The policemen took their leave politely. As soon as they had gone, my boss came in, curiosity written all over his face.

I told him, briefly and succinctly, that there had been another death in my circle of acquaintances.

'Frau Hirte, it's you I'm most worried about!' he exclaimed in consternation. 'Take a look in the mirror, will you? You're the very picture of misery. You must get yourself off to the doctor this very minute, and that's an official order! And after that, I don't wish to see you back here. You'll be a good girl and go home to bed and do everything the nice doctor tells you. I'm beginning to think you've been overdoing things with your iron sense of duty. After so much human suffering, even a superwoman should be flat on her back!'

I thanked him and packed my sandwiches away again, took my dog and my coat and disappeared. I really did call in at the doctor's, where, however, I discovered that consulting hours didn't begin until four.

So I could go and have a lie-down in the meantime.

Before that, though, the bathroom had to be disinfected. I

196

had bought a jumbo-sized bottle of Sagrotan disinfectant at my local drugstore, where I had casually remarked that my dog had had the runs during the night. I spent two hours scrubbing out the bathroom, and then went on to do the whole flat.

My so-called family doctor, who had set eyes on me only very sporadically for many years past, didn't like the look of my conspicuous weight loss and my deathly pallor. My whole abdomen was tense and sensitive to pressure, and he arranged for further appointments for tests, the first of them for the next morning, when I was to give a blood sample for further exploratory lab testing.

Back home, I went straight to bed, with the dog in mourning beside me and the tape playing the harrowing Brahms music. Next to me lay the revolver and Witold's sweater. The rest of the day was swathed in black and purple, my life passed before me in a sequence of sombre images, my head was no longer capable of thought.

The next day, the newspaper carried an extensive report of the murder of the policeman. The suspected perpetrator, who was also being investigated in connection with three other crimes, was reported to be in intensive care, suffering from critical injuries, any one of which could on its own prove fatal.

I drove to the doctor's and gave some blood samples. I was told to come back again the next day and written off work for two weeks. Totally exhausted, I went straight back to bed. Never again would I be able to lead a normal life.

Once – I don't know when it was – Kitty rang me. She was crying and barely comprehensible.

'Is he dead?' I asked.

'Worse than that, much worse,' Kitty sobbed. 'He's still alive, and if he goes on living it will be the most dreadful fate imaginable. Paralysed from the waist down and brain-damaged.'

'Is he conscious?'

'He was for a short time.'

That almost terrified the life out of me.

'Did he say anything?'

'No. Mercifully, he's back in an induced coma. If he does pull through, he won't have the power of speech, and he'll probably have lost his memory and his reason and will just vegetate in a wheelchair for the rest of his days. I just can't get over it.'

'What do you think of all the things he's supposed to have done?' I asked Kitty.

'I don't care what he's supposed to have done,' she retorted proudly. 'I would still love him even if he were an infamous killer, which he isn't. At the moment, I'm in the crazy situation of actually wishing him dead as an alternative to all this.'

Her words shattered me, and now I was crying too. Kitty was a good person, and I was a bad one, but then what meaning did such concepts have?

A few days later, the next blow fell. I learned that I had a carcinoma and an operation was essential as soon as possible.

What to do with the dog, that was now my most pressing problem.

I sent the brooch by express post to Ernst Schröder. In a short letter, I hinted at the truth about it, namely that I hadn't bought the thing, but had got it as a present from its owner. At the same time, I inquired whether he might ask his children to look after a strange dog for a fortnight. Ernst rang me right away, thanked me very much and promised to come and collect the dog that very evening. He came with Annette, who immediately fell on Dieskau's neck and accepted responsibility for him with delight.

Once Annette had gone back down to the car, I said quietly, 'Your daughter has a sister you knew nothing about. You can think it over at your leisure, whether you want to pay any heed to what I've said, or whether you'd prefer to remain in ignorance.'

Ernst took both my hands in his, but was unable to speak.

I was absolutely terrified at the thought of the anaesthetic and the operation. In the past, I had never been able to understand it when my acquaintances dodged out of visits to the doctor or got into a panic at the prospect of a necessary operation. I had even expressly insisted, 'For the doctors, it's a purely routine thing: day in and day out, they do their cutting and stitching as if on a conveyor-belt – there's absolutely nothing at all can go wrong.'

Now, where I was personally involved, the assembly-line work looked very different. Time and again you read of patients who never came out of the anaesthetic, but, thanks to dehumanized technology, occupied a bed as living corpses. Would that be a way out for me, just never to wake up again?

In the hospital, I was shown into a room with two beds; all the previous tests were repeated yet again. In the bed next to me lay a taciturn woman in her middle years, who busied herself crocheting a shocking-pink cosy for a toilet-roll holder and, only after I had asked her for a second time, informed me she was to be discharged the next day.

The evening before my operation, a Greek anaesthetist turned up to check my blood pressure and to study the results of my lab tests, ECG and chest X-rays, and to quiz me on any ailments I or anyone in my family had had and if I had any allergies.

'Are you afraid?' he asked.

I nodded.

'A lot of people are afraid of the anaesthetic, because they imagine themselves waking up and finding themselves dead,' he joked (I didn't find it at all amusing), 'but I could let you have an epidural, which would anaesthetize only your bottom half.'

'For God's sake! Then I'd be able to see the surgeons' ugly faces and listen to them talking about football and sharpening their knives!'

'You'd be sedated into a state of sleep and have your eyes shut. And there are headsets for your ears. I have a cassette of marvellous Sirtaki music.'

I was sorely tempted to tell him where he could stick his Sirtaki. But I remained polite and asked him just to slip me a decent, common-or-garden anaesthetic, so that I wouldn't know the first thing about the whole proceedings.

Next, a surgeon explained the methods and risks involved in the operation. I nodded knowledgeably, although afterwards I had the feeling that, in my state of high apprehension, I hadn't understood a single word.

That night, I slept unusually well, lulled by a sleeping pill. The woman next to me was collected early by a sour-faced man, who deemed it altogether unnecessary to wish me so much as good morning.

Even before they wheeled me into the operating theatre, the neighbouring bed had been changed and occupied again. A white-haired old bird shook my hand in a painful grip.

'I'm your new room-mate!'

My new neighbour pulled on a set of lilac terry-towelling pyjamas and began her stay in hospital with somersaults, shoulder-stands and back-bends on the narrow bed. I was treated to the information that, in her youth, she had been a gymnastics champion on the giant Rhön-wheel. Just as she was launching into reading out recipes for macrobiotic dishes from a cereal diet book, I was wheeled away.

I came to some hours later, with a drip-feed in my arm and a nurse by my side. I was still in the land of the living.

At some time or other, the pains started up, slowly I emerged from my drugged sleep and dreams and realized that something awful had been done to me. On the wall facing me hung Dürer's praying hands and van Gogh's drawbridge, put up as harbingers of hope by some zealous senior nurse.

My room-mate was operated on the next day. When we were both feeling better and she insisted on giving me a reading from the diary of some Bavarian woman water-diviner, I was praying for a new neighbour.

That was one of the few prayers that were answered, and that was only because I was confined to the hospital for a particularly long time.

The newcomer was badger-haired and dressed, like some little girl, all in the one colour: green her socks, green her skirt and sweater; shoes and scarf, all green. When the green lady had finally stretched out in a moss-coloured nightdress, her husband, who had been waiting out in the corridor, came in. Once again, after all these years, the familiar Berlin twang filled my ears.

'I brung yer a pitcher o' the little 'un,' he said tenderly and stood a photo in a silver frame on the bedside locker. Once he had gone, I squinted over at it. It was a picture of an Alsatian bitch.

In time, the doggy's mummy turned out to be a pleasant next-door neighbour. Now and again she would take a swig from a bottle of schnapps she had had smuggled in, and always generously invited me to partake, but not before giving the mouth of it a good wipe with her sleeve.

'Gutted me like a Christmas goose, they 'ave,' she complained.

Whenever she had cold feet, she would sit at the foot of my bed and quite happily stick her icebergs under my blanket. With anyone else, I would have protested strongly at such pushiness, but with this Berlin woman it all seemed completely natural, and I was ashamed at my starchiness. She had this great urge for physical contact, and liked to touch me as she talked. Maybe she felt she had earned this right, because she had once quite spontaneously taken me in her arms. She must have been wakened in the night by my quiet crying. All of a sudden, she was cradling me and rocking me like a mother and telling me with great conviction, ''S OK, 's gonna be awright.'

But nothing was all right any more. Nobody came to visit me. From the office, I got a pre-printed card, 'With best wishes for a speedy recovery', and the signatures of my colleagues underneath. The boss did send an expensive bunch of flowers and a handwritten card promising a visit. But he never did come.

Two days before I was discharged, Frau Römer came to see me, fresh from her return from America.

'The things you get up to!' she exclaimed. 'I just got back from the airport, read your letter and came straight here. I haven't unpacked a thing. And where, for heaven's sake, is Dieskau?'

I put her in the picture about my sudden, or rather, long-suppressed, illness.

'I've passed Dieskau on to friends. I'll give them a ring, so that they can get him back to you.'

Frau Römer protested that she could collect Dieskau herself, but I gave her neither Ernst Schröder's name and address, nor any clue as to his identity. I didn't want to get mixed up in that business. I listened at length to Frau Römer's story of her travels.

'Would you believe it, I've got used to drinking iced water with my meals! And what do you think of my new hairdo?'

Frau Römer, whose dull, mousy hair had long since been infiltrated by numerous white strands, had put herself in the hands of some American master coiffeur, who had banished the beige and underlaid her new snow-white glory with a bluish tinge.

'Would suit you, too,' said Frau Römer.

She stayed for a long time, and that did me an enormous amount of good.

Once she had gone, I phoned Ernst Schröder. He apologized at once – thoroughly ashamed of himself – for not having visited me. Fortunately, he didn't try to come up with any excuses.

He talked about Witold, who was still lying in the clinic, in a bad way and unable to speak. He also told me about problems with the children, who had turned extremely difficult in the aftermath of their mother's death. Only the dog seemed to be getting on fine.

Then I was able to tell him that I would soon be getting out and that Frau Römer was back in the country and desperately wanting her dog back.

Ernst Schröder drew a deep sigh.

'I'll take him back this evening and have a talk with her. By the way, what does she look like? All I have in my memory is a delicate, doe-eyed creature.'

'She's had a breast amputated and has blue hair,' I said.

'Has she?' Ernst was silent for a while. Then he confessed, 'Well, look at me, almost completely bald and with a beer-belly.'

Later, Frau Römer told me he had rung her doorbell that very evening. Neither recognized the other. She had been happy to see her dog, and had hardly looked at the stranger. When he mentioned his name, she had looked up at him, disconcerted. Then, by turns, she had gone pale, red, blotchy and patchy, and then white again. At last, she had invited him in and they talked things over for a long time. But no new love was born.

Finally, I too was allowed home, but as a result of the operation my life was drastically altered. They had fitted me up with an artificial outlet from the bowel, and, despite the constant improvements in the hygienic technology for coping with this, I still felt like a leper, to be shunned by human society. Like Frau Römer, I also got a fixed-term pension, but I had little hope of ever being able to work in my office again. I lived as a recluse, leaving my flat only to go shopping for absolute necessities and to drive to the clinic for my after-care radiotherapy sessions and regular check-ups. Now and again I'd pick up the phone and talk to Frau Römer, and once I gave Kitty a call.

From her, still grieving deeply for Witold, I learned that the police had closed the Engstern case. Although there were still many question marks, Witold was deemed to be the sole guilty party. Kitty had contemplated having the whole case thoroughly reinvestigated by a private detective, but she had finally rejected the idea.

'There's nothing more to be gained, even if he were cleared,' she said. 'His sons? Oh, they've sold up the house, and left Heidelberg; one of them is studying in Paris, the other's travelling around South America. Well, it's up to them to take care of everything themselves now . . . I don't even know how I'll get in touch with them when Rainer dies.'

But Witold didn't die. For a long while, they had kept him hooked up to tubes and machines, a living corpse: but any hope that a scrap of his former personality might be restored, or that he might be able to lead more than a vegetable-like existence was virtually nil. After consultation with his sons, who, despite what Kitty had claimed, did turn up to visit their father from time to time, the respirator was finally turned off after several months. Contrary to all expectations, he started to breathe naturally, and Witold was transferred to a rehabilitation centre and finally to a nursing home.

The first time I drove out to see him, I thought hard, as I had that summer I fell in love, about what to put on. Would he remember my blue floral summer dress? But I was no longer in the mood for feminine daintiness. I dressed very discreetly, very respectably. I was an ageing woman, and looked it; maybe I really should give serious thought to Frau Römer's matronly blue rinse after all.

I now visit Witold twice a week and take him out in his wheelchair for walks. He stares fixedly at me, but no one can possibly tell whether there is pleasure, recognition or profound hatred lying behind that gaze. How much can he remember? No doctor can say. The nurses always insist that he is delighted by my visits. Every Tuesday and Saturday, they tell him, 'Rainer, Rosie's coming today! Today's your day for walkies!'

He understands every word, so they say. His own nurse always tells me, full of admiration, 'Really, Frau Hirte, it's so kind of you to take such care of the poor soul! You have a heart of gold!'

They pull on his windcheater, a strong nurse heaves him into his wheelchair. I kneel before him and pull up his zip-fastener. Then I wheel him away. Sometimes I tell him how, once upon a time, I loved him so very much.